The Preacher's Boy

The Preacher's Boy

a n o v e l b y Terry Pringle

Algonquin Books of Chapel Hill *1 9 8 8*

Published by
Algonquin Books of Chapel Hill
Post Office Box 2225
Chapel Hill, North Carolina 27515-2225

in association with
Taylor Publishing Company
1550 West Mockingbird Lane
Dallas, Texas 75235

Design by Molly Renda.

Library of Congress Cataloging-in-Publication Data
Pringle, Terry, 1947–
   The preacher's boy: a novel / by Terry Pringle.
   p.   cm.
[1. Conduct of life—Fiction.   2. Fathers and
sons—Fiction.   3. Christian life—Fiction.]
I. Title.
PS3566.R576P7   1988
813'.54—dc19
[Fic]   CIP 87-28948   AC
ISBN 0-912697-77-6

First Edition

To Nancy Nicholas. For her brown eyes.

Author's Note

Fifteen years ago I began writing about the little town of Ashworth and the larger town of Stanton before I knew there was a Stanton in west Texas. The Stanton of this book and the university there are found only in my mind, as are all the places and people of this book.

The Preacher's Boy

I

Prologue

Michael Page stands at the window of the parsonage, watching his father. Dressed in a dark blue suit, the father is looking for beans in a garden that occupies what was once the backyard. It's quite a garden—okra plants as big as trees, several rows of corn that run the length of the yard, peas, squash, tomatoes, peppers, and plants that he cannot identify. The father has given up every kind of food bought in a store and now eats only what God allows him to grow. This is a demonstration of faith. The father hasn't revealed this to the son; the mother has. All the father says about his garden is, "It's coming along pretty well." And it is.

What mystifies him is that his father is picking beans in his suit. Here it is July and the sun seems to fill the sky. But then, Brother Page, the father and pastor of First Baptist Church in Ashworth, Texas, is a man of faith, and the suit seems to be his uniform. He is so used to seeing the man in a dark suit that when he spots his father at night walking from the bathroom dressed only in underwear, he feels as though he's broken a commandment.

Brother Page is the only man of faith he has known. He considers this to be a common mistake—assuming every preacher is a man of faith. Men of faith do not appear on television to beg for bucks or build empires. They are not among those who, as W. C. Brann once said, mistake chronic laziness for a call to preach. A man of faith, by his definition, is one who not only believes that Abraham did indeed set off on a journey to Moriah for the purpose of sacrificing his son, Isaac, because God directed him to do so, but who believes that story contains the most impressive demonstration of faith in the history of man.

He has always had a problem with that story. He understands how Isaac must have felt. There the poor kid was, son of Abraham and gift from God to his mother, sitting around wondering why he couldn't take advantage of his special status, when he heard his father just outside the tent talking to—to whom? No one else was around. But Abraham was talking to someone about a trip to Moriah. And the next thing Isaac knew, Abraham was gathering wood and had stuck a dagger in his belt and was saying, "Let's see, it's a three-day trip. . . ."

There was never any question in his mind—his father had chosen roles for them. Abraham and Isaac. What Brother Page didn't understand was that if *he'd* had the liberty of choosing a biblical role, he would have taken David. A king. A king who watched Bathsheba wash herself and then sent out for her like a hamburger. Gimme one broad with aloes and cinnamon, cut the husband.

Still, Brother Page was hopeful. Abraham and Isaac would play in 1979, wouldn't it? If only Isaac would cooperate. But when Abraham had saddled his ass and was ready to set off to Moriah for the ultimate demonstration of his faith, Isaac had wandered off after an Egyptian girl. What was the Egyptian girl doing on the set?

She had a voice sweeter than a sackbut. (A sackbut is a musical instrument mentioned in the Bible, and every member of First Baptist Church knew this, especially the kids, because Michael Page had taught them. By the age of twelve, he'd won over a hundred dollars in other kids' Sunday school offerings betting on the presence of a sackbut in the Bible.) The girl liked Isaac because he talked a lot of trash, but she couldn't be playing gigs in Memphis and Thebes if she was busy getting biblically acquainted with a gift from God in a nomad's tent. So after a brief dalliance, she hiked off toward the pyramids, unable to understand why she kept looking back.

Isaac had a choice. He could stay with his cousins Huz and Buz in the desert and take his chances at Moriah, or he could follow the singer's sweet scent that still hung in the air, turn his back on Abraham, and cross into the land of Cheops and mummies.

The growing logic behind his choice seemed, in the end, to bear no relation whatever to his reasons in the beginning.

I

A mistake. He could feel one coming.

In his father's spot on the podium, he squirmed. This was Sunday morning, and he was scheduled to preach in place of his father. Youth Day, the church called it, that one Sunday of the year when all the positions of leadership were filled by kids. He had a fairly smooth thirty minutes' worth of sermon ready to deliver unto three hundred folks sitting before him.

The auditorium was a big cubicle in a building eighty years old. Lamps hung from the ceiling on long chains, and every window was stained glass. He knew all those people sitting in front of him, all the farmers and merchants and teachers and housewives. And he knew one face much better than the others, that of his father, the man with the dark hair and dark eyes sitting in the front pew. Brother Page looked perfectly comfortable, maybe even proud; he wasn't getting the same signal Michael was—*Error Ahead*. At the age of eighteen, he was more adept at receiving signs of impending doom than his father was.

His sermon was on Peter. What a great Baptist Peter would have made, in his opinion, this man of great ambitions and picayune faith. Peter was always talking when he was supposed to be listening, sleeping when he needed to be awake, demonstrating weakness when he should have shown strength. Peter wanted to walk on water. He saw Jesus doing it, and he wanted to emulate the master. Poor Peter had just enough faith to get him in trouble, just enough faith to get him out of the boat, just enough faith to demonstrate his stupidity.

Oh, Lord, he thought, looking into his father's black eyes. He hoped he didn't say, "just enough faith to demonstrate his stupidity." That line had been delivered only for the benefit of a very nonjudgmental mirror during rehearsal. The old man wouldn't tolerate such a statement. He's a serious sort. If the church were a hospital, the father would have wanted all the members in ICU, even though his son, all things considered, would have settled for outpatient status in the VD clinic.

The special music was coming to an end, and his time was at hand. Amy, his girlfriend, was singing, and her voice was something. It lived within her and when released seemed to exist on its own, carrying its own personality into the air and leaving memories behind. Her voice was so sweet he almost cried.

But she stepped down from the podium, and, giddy or not, he had to fill the pulpit.

"Faith," he said. "I don't know about you, but I have some trouble with it. I always think about the man who decided to

4

try out his faith on the pecan tree that grew outside his bedroom window. It was a huge pecan tree and had been there probably fifty years, shading his house, but the man wanted to test his faith. He knew that Jesus said if you had faith as a grain of mustard seed, you could move a mountain, and he had at least that much faith, and a tree wasn't nearly as big as a mountain. So the man prayed.

"'Lord, you know that pecan tree right outside my window? Well, I'm praying tonight that you'll remove that tree from the face of the earth. I'm praying that when I wake up in the morning, that tree will be gone. I mean, *gone*. I want it to have disappeared, I don't want to see a leaf. I'm claiming the promise of Matthew seventeen-twenty. I have complete and total faith. Praise your holy name, I know that when I wake up in the morning, that entire tree will be gone.'"

It was a good opening. No one was moving or shuffling hymnals or correcting children. And he was glad to be there because they were all one big family gathered together to consider the elusive matter called faith. He was feeling emotionally unbalanced though, as if he might weep over their problems. He loved each and every one of those members. He wanted to hug and comfort them all. He had forgotten even his reason for accepting the invitation to preach on Youth Day—that of seeing how persuasive he could be. After all, he was going to be a lawyer.

"Well, the man went to sleep and when he woke up the next morning, he remembered his prayer. Before he even opened his eyes, he remembered asking God to remove the tree. And when he turned over and looked outside, there stood that pecan tree, just like it had for fifty years. It hadn't moved an inch, hadn't lost a leaf. It was untouched by human or divine hands.

"The man turned back over and said, 'Just as I thought—it's still there.'"

Suddenly—he didn't know why—that story seemed funnier than any he'd ever heard, even though in all his rehearsals he hadn't even cracked more than a small Bob Hope smile. But now it was insanely hilarious. He tried to keep from laughing by holding his breath, but a few in the congregation were already snickering, and he had a bomb in his gut. He stood behind the pulpit without breathing but a growing spasm was racking his body. He knew that one word, one move, and he was going to explode in laughter.

A farmer broke into a loud guffaw. "Har har har har har."

He couldn't hold it back. He began to laugh in earnest.

He tried to hide behind the pulpit because his first wish—to disappear for ten years—wasn't going to come true. And as he sank behind the pulpit, he saw in the opening at the bottom a box of d-CON mouse poison. He thought, "If the church has mice, why do we use poison? Why don't we ask God to get rid of them? If only we had faith the size of a d-CON granule."

It was a painful laugh. He knew his father wanted to come grab his collar and evict him from the house of the Lord. His stomach hurt as if he'd strained a muscle. He couldn't stop laughing so he couldn't apologize to the congregation. He walked to the door that led to the hall, holding his aching stomach, and followed the hall into the educational building. There he found a classroom and laughed until he couldn't stand up anymore, wondering what on earth was so funny.

He sat in his bedroom, listening to his mother set the table for lunch, and couldn't figure out a way to approach the meal. The best he could come up with was Rodney Dangerfield. Twitch, twitch. Hey, what happened? I can't believe it, you know, I don't even know what happened. Twitch, twitch. Talk about strange. I blacked out right after I stood up to preach and just now woke up in my bedroom. Hey, what happened?

He didn't think his father would react; he'd overreact. The man had caught him once trying to break the record from the city limits sign to L.C.'s, a bootlegger's house on the river. The record was seventeen minutes, twenty seconds. He was in his mother's car, outbound, when he had passed his inbound father returning from a visit to an elderly couple in the country. Michael was carrying, as custom required, two sober witnesses, and they had blown by the preacher at one hundred fifteen miles per hour. Brother Page had been so irate when his son got home that he could barely talk and had grounded him forever. Until Jesus came again. He would never sit behind the steering wheel of a car. "*Ever. In your *entire life*.*" Mrs. Page had subsequently arbitrated a one-month grounding and a defensive driving course.

The old man had probably misread the name of the church when he'd joined years ago, thinking it was the First Fascist instead of the First Baptist. Benito Page.

As he walked to the table, which was set with the normal Sunday fare of roast and potatoes, he found encouragement in his father's face. The man's eyebrows had all but met and disappeared in the furrows of his brow, and he knew his father hadn't yet come up with any suitable punishment.

Brother Page hadn't yet assimilated the damage. He had been sitting on the front row watching Amy Hardin sing, Michael waiting to preach, and he had entertained a vision—Michael and Amy as an evangelistic team, going forth into all the world to lead the lost to Christ. "This week at the Civic Center—The Pages!!!" It had been a vision of stained-glass beauty, illuminated by a warming sun, something that had made Brother Page's heart swell with hope.

And then Michael had stepped up to the pulpit, as much as stuck his thumbs in his ears, and wagged his hands. Nyeh, nyeh, nyeh.

What folly. The father had traded in his understanding for an absurd hope. Why expect a sermon any different from a boy who had obtained a mail-order sermon from the University of Hell? Did a chicken lay a strip of bacon?

Michael ate, watching his father stare at his empty plate. Mrs. Page followed the lead of her son and lifted her fork, although she had little appetite. She hadn't quite expected the debacle she'd witnessed, but then she wouldn't have hired Donald Duck as a speech therapist, either. One of these days, she thought, one of these days, *surely*, the men on either side of her would grasp the personality of the other. They were both intelligent; they had to possess some understanding.

Brother Page didn't look up until the phone rang. Mrs. Page answered it and then handed the receiver to her husband.

Suddenly he saw his exit, the doorway to an afternoon with Amy. But timing was everything. He speared a big chunk of roast as though he were going to continue eating and so his father wouldn't feel compelled to order him to remain in attendance during the phone call. And then, when he heard his father say, "No, at the last deacons' meeting . . ." he left the table and walked out of the house.

2

He knew a surefire way of finding Ashworth on the map. "Look for the blemish." The town had distinguished itself among other small towns that had the same slow-death appearance by "remodeling." A city council member with vision got the idea a few years ago that the downtown area could be beautified by repainting all the storefronts. So now the town had a green grocery store, an orange pharmacy, and a hot pink bank.

The streets of the town were in terrible shape, rising and falling and patched so many times they seemed to have been constructed piecemeal with different grades of paving material. The street signs were new, however, because the post office had made everyone start using their addresses. Before that decree, if one person had asked another where Snakebite Sanders lived, the answer wouldn't have been 603 Church Street. It would have been, "Oh, it's next to Witherspoon's rent house where that Clayton boy lived after he got all his hair burnt off." Then the other person could ask, "He was kin to Rabbit Clayton, wasn't he?" and for an hour, two citizens could have occupied themselves.

"No, he wasn't kin to Rabbit. He was John Earl's youngest son."

"John Earl. That old rascal. I never will forget the time his wife caught him in bed with his sister-in-law and shot him in the family jewels with a .22 Hornet."

"Yeah, that was a hard year on Sissy. When was that? 1974? It was the same year her brother stole that dump truck with Jaybird Morton and the highway patrol got after them and they ran off the river bridge."

"That was Jaybird's last ride. He got his head sliced off slicker than a nickel at the fair. I came up on that wreck bringing the wife home from her mother's, and there was Jaybird's head hanging by a thread, just kinda rolling around on the hood."

"Yeah, it was 1974 because that was the last four-yard dump truck the county had. They started buying six-yard back when old what's-his-name. . . ."

People talked about anything but mostly about the weather because Ashworth was a farming town and the livelihood of its residents depended on the weather. But they also talked about their neighbors. And their nonneighbors. When Lottie Swenson noticed the president of the bank passing her house every Tuesday and Thursday promptly at three o'clock, she watched as long as she could without investigating, and then she acted. She rounded up three of her friends, packed them into her 1958 Imperial, and followed the banker to the cemetery, right outside town, to witness his meeting with his own vice-president's wife. Michael had heard that when the trysting lovers lay down on one of the graves in the Nelson section and Lottie refused to share her binoculars, an old-fashioned hair pulling had developed in the Imperial.

The school in town was an old red brick building, and its appearance was a good indication of the emphasis placed on education. The mortar was cracked, weeds grew unmolested, and the trim needed painting. The school wasn't viewed as an educational institution; it existed because the football team needed a sponsor. He had always found the teachers likable but not inspiring. This year, when the regular English teacher had quit at midterm, they'd got a teacher from some nursing home with lax security. Miss Montgomery, the escapee, was older than dirt and looked like an emaciated fortune-teller. She sent a sheet around at the beginning of each class and required that everyone sign it to verify his or her attendance, and she used the sheet for the selection of a name when she needed to call on someone since she wasn't familiar with the students.

"What is the conflict in *Romeo and Juliet*, Miss—" She'd look at her sheet, searching for a name. "Miss Borden, can you tell us?"

Silence from the class.

"Miss Borden? Where is Miss Borden? Isn't Lizzie Borden here?"

At other times, she had called on Alfie Capone, Frankie Roosevelt, and Atilla Hunsucker. Kids who had hated English all their lives suddenly loved it, until the day Miss Montgomery was returned to her bed in the nursing home and was replaced by a human tank from the plains of Nebraska. She rolled into the class and fired this opening barrage: "Shut up, sit up, and listen up."

Her first assignment was to reread *Romeo and Juliet,* and Michael and Amy had planned to read the play after church, so he drove in his mother's car, a 1976 white Chevrolet, after receiving his temporary reprieve provided by the phone call.

Amy. She enrolled in school last year and created the biggest single stir he had seen since the Spanish Club got the teacher drunk on a trip to Mexico City and persuaded her to first remove her girdle, then to fling it from the hotel window. The female part of the student body studied Amy's brown hair and brown eyes, tried to find something wrong with her, couldn't, and started recruiting her into their cliques. The boys fell immediately in love. The simple beauty of the girl promised the quick release of those mysterious emotions that they themselves couldn't draw forth from their hearts.

He was about to ask her out when another guy did. She refused. No excuse, no "some other time," just no. Within an hour, every guy in school was flying around looking for an expert with whom to confer. What had she meant? Who'd ever heard of such a thing? Was the world coming to an end?

They got together when she and her father began attending church. They were socialite Baptists, not very serious and in attendance only on Sunday morning. Her father didn't tithe but usually dropped a five into the offering plate. They never rededicated their lives, didn't come to revivals, and didn't cry when they prayed. He started sitting with her in church and thought at the time—he was wrong but had never known a thing anyway—that it was nice getting to know her that way. They were together and he didn't have to worry about whether he'd make strange noises when he kissed her.

Before coming to Ashworth, she'd experienced a rather riotous life, and all he knew about her had come as the result of arduous digging. She was something of a book with the pages glued together.

Mrs. Hardin wasn't stable. Over the years, she'd gone off searching for rainbows, the first time when Amy had been five. Once she'd gone off to Florida to study marine biology; another time she'd set off searching for fame as a model, returning three months later with a one-sheet portfolio—a glossy photo of her wearing camouflage fatigues, standing beside a huge rubber raft, an advertisement for an army surplus store. "My mother really did wear combat boots," Amy said. Mrs. Hardin had told Amy she wasn't cut out for motherhood. "Call me by my first name. You need friends more than a mother." Thereafter, Amy's friend had wanted to drag Amy along on her visits to a therapist, then adjourn to a coffee shop or sidewalk café to discuss the hour. "The doctor thinks I'm probably a genius. I've been limited all my life."

Amy's reaction to all this hadn't been that of a friend. At the age of eleven, she'd learned to stomp her foot, and she spent the next five or six years perfecting the technique. If her mother told her to wash the dishes, she stomped her foot. If she was told to clean up her room, she stomped her foot. When her parents confined her to her room, she went on a hunger strike.

She dated a string of losers, the greatest of which was Jesus, a Mexican dope dealer in junior high who sported homemade tattoos—daggers—on both hands. As far as most people knew, Jesus had a three-word vocabulary. "Good chit, man." Amy had been picked up by the police along with Jesus, who was arrested for possession of dangerous drugs, an illegal knife, an automatic weapon, and a Dallas Cowboys playbook. Mr. Hardin had intended to leave his sales job and take up ranching full-time, and the arrest accelerated his decision.

They moved to Ashworth, where Mr. Hardin already owned

a ranch, and he told Amy if she ever saw Jesus again, or any of her old friends, or any new friends who even vaguely resembled her old friends, he was sending her to a special home in Corpus Christi run by a preacher. Amy did some research, decided she didn't want to wear plain clothes with no makeup and sing in a traveling choir, so she changed her ways.

When he finally decided to ask her for a date, he almost got an ulcer. And when Amy said yes, he couldn't figure out how to shift gears. He'd been sitting with her so long in church that when they went to a drive-in movie, he kept expecting to see an usher hand him the offering plate or his father to appear on screen, preaching. He looked at the beautiful girl beside him, the changing lights on the screen casting different levels of illumination over her face, and he couldn't bring himself to make a move. If his father didn't catch him as he tried to kiss her, Amy would stomp her foot.

She finally kissed him.

The Hardins lived in a big two-story house that had once been owned by two unmarried sisters who now resided in the very same room of the nursing home in which Michael's grandfather had died. He occasionally wondered if there was some connection among all those people, then decided only a Baptist would wonder about such a thing. Mr. Hardin had remodeled the house, painted it gray with red trim, and had resodded the entire yard. It no longer looked like the home of old maids.

Today Amy was home alone and she met him at the door eating a jello square. The entire family had a lousy diet because no one ever cooked. Amy glanced at his book, offered him a bite of her jello square (which he took, only because her lips had touched it), and said, "Let's go for a ride. We're not going to read, and I hate sitting around with a book staring at us."

They drove out of town in Mrs. Page's car, past the cotton gin, a well-dented sheet-metal building that sat on a block of weeds and blowing trash, and moved into the country toward Halton, the county seat and Amy's former home. In that direction lay mostly farmland that rolled and gently sloped into occasional creeks and woods.

"What got you so tickled this morning?" she asked she asked.

"I wish I knew. God's jokes, I guess."

He waited for her to ask about which of God's jokes he was talking about, but she didn't. Instead she sat very quietly in her blue shorts and T-shirt. At times she could sit for hours without speaking, as still and silent as a vase of flowers. He always grew nervous when she fell into an untalkative mood, fearing she didn't find him worth talking to.

"Did I sound all right this morning?" she asked.

"You were great, as always. Absolutely great."

She sighed. She wanted substantive answers to questions about the quality of her singing but had limited him in his responses. Once he'd told her she'd put the congregation into a trance, and she'd said, "You know, I wish you'd quit saying that. I get up and sing and I wait for everyone to go into a trance and nobody ever does. So don't tell me that, okay? I looked up 'trance' in the dictionary and it's a state where you don't function. The only people I've ever sung to who were in a trance were in the nursing home."

They were near his grandfather's farm, so he turned down the long dirt drive and parked in the pecan trees behind the house. His grandfather, his mother's father, had tenant-farmed the place, so it had never belonged to the grandfather, and the house had been unoccupied for several years. None of the windows was broken, but the house was suffering without an occupant. The wood was weathered, the paint long worn away, and the green shingles of the roof looked like dead scales flaking off.

"Your father get upset?" Amy asked, turning toward him once

they'd stopped. She smiled because they'd spent hours talking about wars with parents.

"Now, *he* went into a trance. We ate an entire meal and he never even noticed there was food on the table."

"Hmm," she said. "That's bad."

"It will be, once he gets it all straight. This may be the last time we ever see each other."

He waited for her to swear vengeance on anyone who tried to come between them, to pull a .357 magnum from her purse and say, "We'll be the last couple he ever separates," but of course she didn't. People rarely said what he wanted them to say.

He was experiencing a powerful urge to kiss her, but she turned facing the windshield. She didn't shave her legs from mid-thigh up, and all those tiny hairs were shining golden in the sun. She had a little white scar on one knee. He pulled her toward him, and she came with a clouded look, not protesting but neither was she desirous of rape. He kissed her and moved his hand beneath her T-shirt, his palm flat on her stomach, his thumb at the bottom edge of her bra. When they broke the kiss, she looked away. Touching her always did something wonderful to him because she was soft and strange, foreign to his fingertips, as new and exciting as another person's warm flesh always was.

He rested his head on his arm, which lay across the seat behind her, and stared at her neck and the profile of her face. The wind blew through the trees, the shadows of the branches bouncing across the windshield. He found that his thumb, as if it had ideas of its own, was stroking the satin-smooth cup of her bra.

"Maybe . . ." she said, looking off to the right.

He waited for her to finish, but she didn't. He was sorely afraid she was going to say, "Maybe we should go back to town." Not knowing what exactly to do to prevent her from saying such a thing, but knowing if she did, he was going to regret feeling only with his thumb what he badly wanted to feel with his whole hand, he held his breath and let his hand slide onto her breast.

Suddenly she collapsed against him, melting into his side. "Maybe we shouldn't do this," she said.

He moved his hand, praying she would quickly change her mind.

"Or maybe we should," she said.

He inserted his hand into her T-shirt again, swearing since she couldn't make up her mind, he'd make it up for her, and he almost assaulted her. This time the kiss wasn't at all tentative; it could have been scheduled to last a week. He lost track of what was happening, but when he closed his eyes, Amy was dressed, and when he next opened them, she had lost both her T-shirt and bra.

Never had he opened his eyes to such a sight. He stared in awe as if a painting had come to life beside him, an artist's conception of the beauty of a woman. He'd never seen anything quite as perfect as Amy's upper body. The lines and slopes of her shoulders and arms, skin that seemed barely cushioned, breasts with almost colorless nipples.

"You remind me of a living room chair," he said, barely, because he was having trouble breathing.

"A what?" She took a deep breath.

"Something with perfect construction. You're wonderful. You're beautiful." He looked but felt guilty, as if he'd snuck a peek at the back of God. And he knew that within two seconds, the biggest pecan tree near the car was going to suddenly fall and crush them. Quickly he moved, sitting on his knees facing her, straddling her legs. For the next unknown number of minutes he touched her bare skin.

Inspired to poetry, he said, "You're Eve, the first woman,

total perfection. Ivory soap but purer. Untouched snow. Rain a mile up in the sky. Oh, shit, I want to die right now because I'll never see anything like this again. This is the best moment of my entire life, the moment I've lived for."

He couldn't believe what was happening, couldn't believe that on a basic level his body was talking to him. "Screw her brains out, Page." He could tell things were changing and he didn't want them to. He had too much trouble with lust. For years he'd spent so much time exercising it that he figured one day the plumbing would explode and he'd enter the presence of God with his pants down around his knees, a well-worn centerfold from *Playboy* in his hand. "God, the kingdom welcomes Michael Page. In his natural state."

"Tell me if I should stop," he said, his hands lightly traveling over her torso, arms, under her arms.

Amy said nothing but his body did. "You're a fool, Page, a wimp of a preacher's kid unless you whip it out now."

He started to unzip his pants and for the first time in some minutes, Amy spoke. "Unh unh." She picked up her bra and started to put it back on, but he stopped her.

"No, I just want to look. I won't do anything else. Please."

She seemed uncertain and slipped the bra over her right arm.

"Please. I beg God to strike me dead if I do anything but look."

But something had happened to her as well. She put her bra on and wiggled beneath him, asking him with her shifting legs to move. Reluctantly, he dismounted and returned to the driver's seat. Once she was dressed again, he put his arm around her. He didn't know whether to apologize or again affirm his belief that his life had just peaked. He didn't say anything.

For a long time they sat without talking, looking beyond the pecan trees. The land there was the flattest he'd ever seen, ready for planting with cotton. It ran all the way to the creek and the treeline, which he could see only in configuration. Halfway to the creek in the middle of the field was a solitary cottonwood tree that had been left standing, its trunk so thick that two men couldn't have circled it with their arms.

The only sounds he heard were the wind and his body saying, "Face it, Page. You're a disgrace to real men everywhere."

3

After Michael dropped her off at her house, Amy went upstairs and immediately started running water for a bath. It was something of an unconscious act. She wanted to sit for at least an hour in the tub, soaking in sweetly scented oil, and watch her hands slide down the top sides of her legs, returning beneath her legs, again and again and again, stopping only long enough to add hot water when the bath cooled.

Oh, Amy, she thought. You have definitely messed up.

She stepped into the tub, where she had spent a good part of her life, because it was there, eyes following the motions of her hands, that she could put her mind in neutral.

Only one thing in life worked for her, and that was a vision. The vision was always the same. Several spotlights on the ceiling swished back and forth, not stopping on anything but briefly flashing across and illuminating members of a band. The musicians were well into an introduction, something with a repetitive beat in a holding pattern that would either end or change when the singer came on stage. Amy stood back in the darkness, waiting for the right moment, feeling the emotion rise, feeling the music that lived within her, music that had been ignited by the steady driving beat of the drums. Intuitively, she moved across the stage toward the microphone, and the crowd near the stage saw her as the light randomly flashed across her. Applause, cheers, screams spread steadily throughout the auditorium, and then she stepped into the circle of light at the microphone. She sang. She released her music for those who had come to listen.

The vision was a dream, not destiny. Any time she assumed something would happen, it never did, and the quickest way to hex a dream was to assume something *should* happen. Once she dreamed that her own dog, a German shepherd, rescued her from a murderer, and she got up the next morning with a safe and secure feeling, believing her life was protected. And then her mother had run over the dog as it slept beneath the car, breaking all four of its legs.

Her mother now rapped on the door of the bathroom and said, "*Why* do you want to look like a prune?"

Amy didn't answer. Each year she held an election for the least important person in her life, and each year Mrs. Hardin was the hands-down winner. She'd won every year since Amy was five, when her mother had squatted down in front of her, said she had to leave and didn't know if she'd be back to live with her daughter but hoped to work in a few visits. "Want to wish me luck?" Amy hadn't said anything in the past thirteen years she'd regretted more than what she'd said that day: "Good luck."

The only thing that had ever worked for Amy was her vision. It was an oasis in the desert, a place she fled to whenever she got thirsty. And she was working toward that vision. She was going to sing with a band at the end of school, not before the end of school because the keyboard player and drummer were both failing two classes and wouldn't graduate unless their grades improved. Their parents had prohibited them from accepting any engagement prior to graduation, a situation which Amy found sensible on the one hand, worrisome on the other. Had Carole King or Stevie Nicks ever experienced similar problems? Amy couldn't imagine that they had.

Every time she went out to play with Michael, she got the feeling she was being unfaithful to her vision. Whenever she wasn't rehearsing, writing a song, or simply thinking about her singing, a cloud of worry settled over her. Michael helped her sometimes, though. He was the first person who had ever understood how serious she was about singing. He'd asked a friend to make up a certificate that said Michael Page was the first president of the Amy Hardin Fan Club as though she were some sort of a star and not a nervous nobody. He'd written her notes during church after she'd sung the special music. "Mrs. Simpson told her husband that you could make it in Nashville. She'd never heard a voice like yours." Or he'd copy a magazine article and underline the significant parts, usually about a young girl who'd been singing in obscurity before becoming an "overnight" success. And every time he did such a thing, Amy was overcome with an unbelievably warm feeling. Someone else, another live human, believed in her.

She hadn't thought a great deal about her growing affection for him until she realized her desire for his touch was growing more and more intense, deeper within her. And then when he appeared, she didn't care if they talked about singing at all; she just wanted to play with him.

Now she looked at her watch on the tank of the toilet. She'd been sitting in the tub for an hour. After flipping the chrome drain switch with her wrinkled foot, she stood, getting a towel.

"How many songs have you written today, Amy?" her mind asked.

"I don't have to write songs every day," she answered.

"Not making much progress, are you?"

"I wouldn't have anyway," she said.

Before Amy could consider the threat—that Michael would

dump her and her vision would recede because she hadn't been working—she threw the towel down and ran more bath water, using three capfuls of oil.

Her mother knocked on the door so hard that Amy expected to see the lady's fist smash through the wood.

"I talked to the doctor about you, Amy. He said you're an anal personality. We should have let you play in your poo poo. Get out of that tub or I'm going to make an appointment for you."

Amy didn't answer. She got into the tub and lay on her back, wondering how it would feel to have Michael bathe her.

"Get out of that tub. Did you hear me?"

Amy hadn't planned on washing her hair, but she took a deep breath and slowly sank into the warm water until her head was submerged.

Brother Page was waiting at the parsonage, sitting at the kitchen table with his Bible open. He'd solved the big puzzle —what was wrong with Michael—but couldn't quite figure out, at this late date, 114 days before the boy's departure for college, what to do about it.

The problem was his son's name. Twenty years ago, when both Brother Page and his wife had wanted a child, the doctor had told her she had a fault in the womb, and unless it was surgically corrected, she would remain childless. Mrs. Page had chosen prayer over surgery, placing the matter in God's hands, and the subsequent conception of Michael had been a truly miraculous event. A *miracle.* Brother Page loved that word.

He had wanted to name the child Samuel because the faith of the mother, just like the faith of the biblical Hannah, had brought the child into the world, as surely as Hannah had delivered Samuel. But Mrs. Page, in some kind of postnatal swelling fit, had refused even to consider the name Samuel. Instead, she'd entered "Michael" into the records without so much as a brief consultation with her husband. Things hadn't been right since the boy had acquired that earthly name.

The father had erred by possessing and exhibiting an earthly pride in Michael's quickly developing mind, his secular abilities. Brother Page had thought the boy who could recite TV commercials at age three was funny. Ha ha. They should have been studying the scriptures (and would have been had the son's name been Samuel, a constant reminder for the father). And once started on the road to ruin, Brother Page hadn't been able to turn Michael.

Once, when Michael was twelve—this was just a random example that came to mind and Brother Page hoped God didn't think he was trying to build a defense or anything—Brother Page had set his son on the couch and tried to explain his ambition. "All I want is to enter the presence of God and hear him say, 'Well done thou good and faithful servant.' That's all. Now think about that and tell me if you can think of *anything* more wonderful than hearing God say that."

"Well, yeah, I can think of one thing—going to see *The Godfather.* Everybody I know's seen it but me. Why can't I go? Because it's about Catholics? President Kennedy was a Catholic and we used to watch him on TV. Why can't I go?"

How did you teach a child to be dead to sin and alive to God when all he wanted to do was watch "The Courtship of Eddie's Father"?

Brother Page tried not to think about the unbelievably few days remaining until Michael left—114, as compared to the 15,700 days Brother Page had already lived—because joy wasn't an appropriate response to escaping responsibility. (But just look at the numbers on the calculator! Michael would be gone in point zero zero seven two of the amount of time the father had already lived. Now, that was something.)

He was feeling better when Michael walked in the door, a look of contentment on his face.

He had returned to his grandfather's farm after dropping Amy at her house so he could contemplate the events of the afternoon, and when he saw his father at the table, the events of the morning came blundering into his mind. In an instant, Amy was gone because he could tell by looking at his father that the man now had everything straight. He sat across the table with a sinking feeling, hoping his father would get mad. When the man grew angry, shouted, jabbed his finger, he could handle the confrontation, but if his father expressed great sorrow and talked about God, then he couldn't fight back. He said a silent prayer that Brother Page could find sufficient fuel for anger. Maybe God would call him a liberal intellectual or something, really piss the old man off.

Brother Page cleared his throat and scooted his chair up to the table. "I don't understand why we have to have this conversation all the time. I mean, since you were four, we've talked and talked about it. You know it, I know it, most of all God knows it—you just never have learned reverence and respect. Never. It's the greatest mystery of life as far as I'm concerned."

Things weren't going to go well; he could see that immediately. Why, he wondered, did good things and bad things have to happen on the same day? Why couldn't he have preached yesterday and gone to the farm with Amy today?

"You're going to preach again," Brother Page said. "You're going to preach with an attitude of reverence like you were supposed to this morning, and you're going to wipe this abomination off your record before the church."

His jaw dropped. Preach again? The entire problem was that he had preached the first time. Surely his father saw that. He started to protest but his father didn't give him a chance.

"We're going to pray now, and you're going to ask for God's forgiveness. You're going to—"

"I don't—" he started to speak but his father cut him off, a good thing because he had been about to speak blasphemy. He'd been about to ask why he should ask God for forgiveness because he had never once suggested to anyone that if some person possessed a tiny amount of faith, he could make a mountain uproot itself and jump into the ocean. He had never in his life purposely tried to confuse anyone. Well, not many times. And then only girls.

Brother Page was already praying. "We approach you, Lord, with humble hearts, grateful as always for Jesus' death on the cross, that atoning act you owed no man. That act at Calvary, Lord, was one that should instill absolute awe in us. If our hearts. . . ."

He knew what was about to happen, and he tried to stop listening. He wanted to suggest that the answer to his problems was excommunication. Boot him out of the church.

"If you keep your eyes on Jesus, Michael, if you always remember that act of supreme sacrifice, if you picture Jesus— Almighty God come to earth to live as man—if you picture God, creator and ruler of the universe, hanging on a cross with spikes in his hands and feet, the crowd below jeering, if you can imagine God lowering himself to become as us, if you can imagine the pain in his human heart, if you can remember his divine grace, you'll never have a problem with reverence."

He had already closed his eyes. The name of Jesus brought pain into his memories, and he rubbed his forehead as if he'd been butting a brick wall. He couldn't deny anything; he was guilty of everything. He'd prepared a sermon while listening to "Jazzman"; he had called Peter stupid; he believed in doubt, not faith. He was a lowlife ingrate.

"'For God so loved the world that he gave his only begotten

son,'" Brother Page quoted. "He owed us nothing but he gave us everything. I'd start looking at my salvation experience if that didn't break my heart, Michael. I'd look at why I call myself a child of God. There have been so many times I've wondered if you *are* a child of God. I'm wondering that now." He sucked up a breath as if on the verge of crying.

The room seemed to have lost its light, as though the sun had been covered by thick clouds, and suddenly nothing else mattered to Michael except his own failings. He'd never wanted anything but a world of flowers and songs and people who loved God and one another, and he was doing nothing to make it that way. All he thought about was himself and fleshly gratification, and with each day that passed, with each hour, he was failing God, failing Jesus.

"How else could God demonstrate his love in such an emphatic way, Michael? Humiliation, pain, death. How else?" His father stopped again to inhale. "Don't you know that Jesus loves you? How could you stand in the pulpit and *laugh*?" There was a long silence and then Brother Page said, "You used to sing 'Jesus Loves Me' when you were little and I could see the love of Jesus radiating in your face. It gave me real confidence, Michael, and when something like this morning happens. . . ."

He was already crying, grieving over his inability to undo the day. If only he could start over, could prepare for a different sermon, if only he could remake his relationship with Amy and excise the afternoon from it. Never, ever would he touch her again anywhere except on her arm from the elbow down, he swore it. He'd never lose control. In a whisper at first, he began to sing. "Jesus loves me, this I know." He wanted to once again have the faith he'd possessed when he'd first sung that song. He would again believe that Jesus would reach down and touch him. And he realized that when he couldn't feel the love of God, when he felt a world of sin around him, it was his fault, pure and simple.

He sang louder.

Simultaneously father and son stood. They hugged. He continued to sing, watching his tears fall onto his father's suit coat. He could smell his father's hair, the fabric of his clothes. Never again would he purposely antagonize the man. Never.

In a logical world, he thought, the evidence of God's love would have been as plain as the signs that his mother loved him—bacon and eggs on the table in the morning, a kiss before he went to school, true concern for his well-being. To date, he hadn't been kissed by Jesus nor had he felt any real concern for his well-being. He'd prayed for hours and hours for assistance in controlling lust and in return he got erections in Sunday school when the director, a divorced blonde with a button undone on her blouse, stood up to lead them in singing, "When We All Get To Heaven." He suddenly hoped the song went on forever because every time she lifted her right arm, he could see almost the entire cup on her bra. He would never deny that Jesus' death on the cross had been an act of real love, but since he couldn't see any need for hell—why not just let unbelievers remain unmolested in their graves and forget about them?—the act of love didn't mean as much as it should have. What about a few signs of immediate love? A few less children starving to death, a few less earthquakes and floods and mean bastards?

He hadn't always entertained such thoughts; he had in fact refused to let one reside for more than a moment in his mind until his grandfather had died.

The old man, his mother's father, had suffered a series of strokes that had taken him farther and farther from the realm of the functioning, right into the nursing home. He had been at first fascinated by his visits to see the old man, even though the nursing home smelled a lot like a sewer. His grandfather had been the first person he had ever seen utterly confused.

Restrained by padded wrist straps, the old man would smack his toothless gums and look fiercely at him. And with a clarity that was truly amazing, the old man would accuse him of any number of crimes, thinking that his grandson was really the old man's brother Henry, his cousin J. L., his son Alvie. And the grandfather would say, "Now I seen them goddamn crooked rows you been planting, Alvie, and you don't care shit about them weeds neither. And I'll warrant you this, you little son of a bitch, that when I come home this e'ning, if I see one speck of Johnson grass in that cotton, I'm gone tear your ass asunder." This was the same kind old man who had taken him dove hunting every fall even though the old man didn't hunt, who had taken his grandson on excursions to surrounding towns in search of candy he hadn't yet tried.

His amusement died when he discovered that the old man was calling his daughter, his own mother, a "fat little bitch" and screaming whenever she walked into the room. When he saw his mother grow depressed, when she began to engage in fits of crying or to sit in the living room staring out the picture window for hours, he got confused. His mother was the kindest, most selfless person he knew, and he couldn't imagine that she deserved such treatment.

What was the purpose of the man's present existence? If, as Brother Page said, there was a plan for every life, if God moved behind every event, what was the point? Why would his grandfather, whose only function was to lie in a bed and let his loose bowels dribble into a big diaper, continue to cause his mother such sorrow? He began to work on the puzzle, fitting all the pieces together, and once he had assembled the entire puzzle, he discovered it spelled unhappiness. God's plan was for everyone to be unhappy.

Wonderful.

He didn't like the answer, couldn't believe it was possible, so, he decided, God would give him the real answer and allow him to remain faithful. God wouldn't let him slide headlong into infidelity like he was some sort of communist. So he prayed. At night in bed, he squeezed his eyes shut, begging for a different answer. He prayed nightly. And each night he got the same response. Nothing. The God who had taken such an active interest in earthly affairs when people had only one name—Moses, Joshua, Noah, et al.—had chosen to remain silent.

One night when he was about to fall into utter despair over God's lack of interest, he suddenly realized the method in which God would speak—through his grandfather. The old man, who a few weeks ago had been capable of speech—even though it was almost always profane—would tell him the great secret. The prospect caused his heart to throb.

He started spending more and more time at the nursing home as the doctor forecast the end. Each morning, he would pray that his grandfather wouldn't die before he could return to the home after school, and for the first time in his life, he had faith that something was going to happen. His faith was greater than a mustard seed. Much greater.

When the end came, one night when rain was spattering against the window of the room, he was with him, sitting in a chair near the head of the old man's bed in the darkened part of the room. He could plainly see the drawn orifice of a mouth that had been shrinking without its dentures, the beak of a nose that seemed to grow as the mouth shrank. The old man made a noise and he scooted his chair toward the bed, hearing a sound come from the open mouth that sounded something like a creak, the closing of a door in a haunted house. This is it, he thought. He's about to say something. "Michael, keep the faith even though you don't understand." At least that. Preferably, "Michael, God wants us to. . . ." He wasn't sure of the ending, but it wouldn't be "be unhappy." Not that. He drew as close as he could to his grandfather's face until he was repelled by the breath, the stale scent of illness.

And then, without ceremony, the old man stopped breathing.

It was several minutes before he was willing to believe that his grandfather wasn't going to speak. He expected him, after resuming his breathing, to tell him something, anything. But the obvious finally sank into his brain, and then he wanted the old man to sit up and cuss, to give one more "Shit!" over his wasted end and his daughter's unmerited tears.

"Say something," he ordered the old man.

He checked and felt his grandfather's arm, which wasn't warm but wasn't deathly cold either. He checked for a pulse in his wrist, found nothing, then his neck. He stood, bending, and placed his cheek near the old man's open mouth but couldn't feel even the slightest wind of breath. "Say something."

He stood up straight, giving the old man, and God, another thirty seconds in the dark room. The rain fell against the window but nothing else happened. And then suddenly he was so mad he was crying, so mad he didn't understand his anger. "Say shit mother fucker son of a bitch piss ant. Say it."

He left the room, found enough self-control to tell a passing nurse's aide, an elderly black woman, that his grandfather had died, and lost the self-control before he got to the front door, which he kicked as hard as he could, breaking the metal release bar. He cussed all the way home, all night, and into the next day. He hadn't asked for a miracle, hadn't asked that his grandfather be healed or that his mother stop crying. He hadn't asked for personal enrichment, hadn't made any overtly selfish request. He hadn't asked for fire from heaven, as Elijah had, as Elijah had received. And neither had he asked for the total betrayal he had received. Oh, yes, he had asked, as the Bible instructed, and he had received, as the Bible assured him he would. He had asked for faith and he had received one more instance of evidence that God had disappeared and planned on making no statements to any fool whose address was the planet Earth.

When the nursing home administrator sent his father a bill for repairs to the door, he was unable to explain his behavior.

"You broke the door?" his father asked.

He nodded.

"How?" Then, "Why?"

"I don't know. I kicked it and it broke."

"You *kicked* the door?"

"Yes, I kicked it, it broke, so just give me the bill and I'll pay it."

He got more than the bill, of course. He was ordered to apologize to the nursing home administrator for his irresponsible behavior and was then deprived of the use of his mother's car for a month. When one of his friends picked him up on the way to school one morning and asked why he had been seen afoot for several weeks, he merely said, "God's will."

Occasionally he thought the only place he could find the proper orientation toward life was at his grandfather's farm, but he never seemed to feel the same way on consecutive trips. If Amy was with him, he felt the old man's absence more acutely than at any other time. His grandfather would have liked her (before life had mutated him without the assistance of Hollywood's special effects), and every time he and Amy visited the farm, he longed for the entire family—aunts and uncles and cousins—cooking and playing and laughing as they once had.

Other days he went alone to watch the sun rise, and if the clouds were just right—as they had been the other morning when the horizon had glowed as if it were burning golden gases and the sky above had turned royal blue—then he could only feel his good fortune at finding himself in such a spectacular place. "Magnificent!" he wanted to cry out. "Bravo! Hooray for God!" And on yet other days, he could only remember the time his grandfather's cotton crop was just sprouting and ten inches of rain had fallen over three days and the entire crop had to be replanted. And the world seemed nothing more than a bad practical joke on people who surely didn't deserve such treatment.

Some day he'd get it figured out.

4

School had acquired an entirely new dimension, that same dimension a Monday acquired when it fell on December 25, because any day he saw Amy was as good as Christmas. He moved as if under the influence of the scent of pine needles and the sight of candle bulbs merrily bubbling on the tree. As he entered the hall at school, Amy was standing at her locker wearing a rust-colored skirt and white blouse. Such beautiful and unadorned wrapping, the first present under the tree his eyes fixed upon. It contained what he had always wanted, had dreamed about, had considered at great length in the catalogs of his youth in the privacy of the bathroom—two jiggling lumps of powdered flesh, as mysteriously suspended in the air as a star. He had to get the present unwrapped as quickly as possible. Off would come the ribbon, the shining paper, the lid of the box. Then, with both hands, aaaahhhhhhhhhhh.

Was he the same person as the one who had sat in church last night, right hand on his Scofield Reference Bible, swearing that he would never again touch Amy's breasts, that he would always remain a faithful child of God? Then why was he steaming toward Amy as a child on Christmas morning uttering a prayer of gratitude that went, "Thank you, Jesus, for being born so I could get all this good stuff on your birthday"? He'd think about it later.

Amy stood at her open locker, the door at a right angle to the wall, blocking the view from the other end of the hall. He walked up and placed his hand on her breast and felt the Christmas spirit ricochet around in his loins. When his hand landed on her breast, Amy squeaked a sound of surprise and jumped backward.

He said quietly, "I want to touch you all over and start right there." He stared at her right breast.

She looked around for eavesdroppers and spies and said, "Michael, we're in school."

"Our bodies are in school, but my mind is in yesterday. At the farm." He closed his eyes, trying to conjure up the image of Amy naked from the waist up. "I thought yesterday was the peak, but I was just on the first step. Oh, God, how many steps? Let there be hundreds, thousands, tens of millions. I want a stairway all the way to the sky." He added, but only to himself, "and forgive us, Lord, because only one of us pricks knows what he's doing."

It seemed absurd to Amy that she be standing in the middle of Ashworth High School listening to such things. How many times could she change her mind? Only last night she'd eaten supper with her parents and been subjected to a long discourse, spoken to no one in particular, by her mother about anal personalities. Amy had thought if she'd heard the woman use "poo poo" one more time, she was going to take a butcher knife and field dress the woman right in the kitchen.

Amy had gone to her room depressed, suddenly certain that Michael was going to discover one of her secrets—that she was basically unlovable, that nothing was really important to her except her vision—and dump her without ceremony. In fact, she had convinced herself that he was never even going to speak to her again, and she would therefore quit thinking about him altogether. So she and Stevie Nicks had passed the night together.

And now here was Michael not only speaking to her but speaking poetically.

"You know what we could do at lunch?" he asked.

Amy gave him a brief look, then returned her gaze to the coat hook in the locker. She could tell by the look in his eyes that he wasn't going to invite her to the Dairy Queen. Now she was sweating, little drops trickling down her sides, and she couldn't remember putting on any deodorant. Surely she had, but she couldn't recall the specific act of applying any.

"We could go to the farm at lunch," he said. Yes, indeed, they could because he'd seen on his way in that Amy had brought her father's car. And at the farm, he could finish opening his present. He had only seen into the upper part of the box. What could be down deeper? Lord love a duck. He hadn't even thought about the depths. The only real question was: could he wait until lunch? He put his lips to her ear, hair tickling his face, perfume causing him to levitate, and he said, "We could go to the farm and I could take off your panties and touch your pussy."

Amy backed up as if winched away from the locker, pushing the door closed as she went. Why had he said such a thing? Weren't there rules that governed what boys said? If there had been any such rules, they probably wouldn't have applied to Michael because he appeared on the verge of ecstasy. His mouth was open and his eyes were nearly crossed.

He pulled her to the wall of lockers and held her hand. "You know, yesterday was nothing now that I think about it. Remember listening to the "Prologue" on *Hot August Night*? You know how it starts slow with just strings? Then the guitars come in, then the drums, and then, bam, it's a full-blown band?" He cleared his throat, his head dipping, looking into her body as if he could see her naked. "Let's go get that tape and we can listen to it at the farm, and I can lift your dress up and pull down your pantyhose and then your panties, and when Neil Diamond comes on stage, there it'll be, oh, God, it'll be great and wonderful. Something I'll never ever forget in my entire life. Can we, please? Please?"

Amy was surely dreaming. She had to be. Never in her entire life had she imagined a boy would ask that he be allowed to undress her to music, appropriately timed. She had to leave and think but suddenly she couldn't come up with an excuse to leave. Michael, I have to go make the punch for Civics. I have to trim the rose bushes at the band hall.

"I'd always listened to that music and thought about the sun rising, not something like this. Can we? Please?"

Amy knew for certain: between putting on her slip and blouse, she had skipped a step and forgotten to put on deodorant. And by now she had to be at the stinky stage, as much as she was sweating. Something terrible was going to happen; she could feel it coming. So she turned and walked off.

He followed and caught her, walking beside her. "Amy, I'm sorry if I offended you. I don't know what's come over me. Forget everything I said. Everything. I think I'm going crazy. But I just never saw anything like I did yesterday. It was . . . it was indescribable. What's the greatest thing that ever happened to you? Well, for me, it was better than that. It was better than good, better than better, better than best. I hope I don't sound like a commercial."

Amy thought if only she could freeze the world, make everything stop but her, so she could take one clandestine sniff at her armpit, and then run home if she needed to . . . this was the strangest day of her life. She was happy indeed when she saw the door to the biology lab and thought about the over-whelming scent of formaldehyde in which she could hide. When they arrived at the door to the lab, she turned in and said to Michael, "We can talk later." Inside the room, she took a deep breath. Normally the smell of formaldehyde made her nauseous; today it made her insanely happy.

By lunch, Amy had settled two matters. The first was that she had managed to verify, through scratching the back of her scalp and reverently bowing her head, nose tilted slightly to the right, the presence of Secret on her underarm. And the second concerned her plans for lunch.

She knew enough about her response to Michael and of her body in general that she was going to have to deprive him of listening to *Hot August Night* at the farm. And the biology teacher had inadvertently solved the problem while discussing the body of a cat and the estrous cycle. While the class was giggling, suddenly Amy remembered everything she'd learned about boys during her terrible years. When a boy went into heat, as Michael had, even if only temporarily, the cure was common and quick. And the fact that Amy had forgotten the answer made her doubt her own intellect. Amy told herself: boys are simple creatures, and don't you forget it.

Amy was very nearly happy on her way to the car, even though she felt deceitful about her plan, when she was hit with problem number three. Eventually she was going to have to tell Michael about the band. Several times she'd come close to revealing her plans, and she had in her mind. And it was those imaginary conversations that were preventing her from engaging in a real one. Amy would sit Michael down and hold his hands and say, "I'm going to sing with a band; my career is finally going to get started. Isn't that wonderful?" And Michael would throw her hands off as though they were disgusting giant slugs and scream, "Well, that's just wonderful. You just go ahead, but you won't have me to kick around anymore." Why he would say that, and why Amy would imagine that he had, was a total mystery to Amy. But in every one of her rehearsals with him, that very response had seemed to come to her as if predestined.

He appeared at the car at lunch in a state similar to that of the morning—eyes glazed, his breathing shallow. He did retain the presence of mind that enabled him to look through the glove compartment and find *Hot August Night*. He sat on the passenger's side of the car, looking at it as though his life really was about to peak and the plastic case holding the tape contained the secret. He was a child who'd always wanted a BB gun and finally knew he was about to receive it.

"This is great, Amy. It really is."

Amy smiled and patted the seat beside her. Michael responded to her invitation and slid over. Part one of Amy's plan was under way as they left town; Michael's hand was already on her breast. Amy drove and checked with one eye for the sign that part two could commence, the sign being a definite protrusion in the denim fabric of Michael's crotch.

My goodness, Amy thought. Is that it already?

It certainly appeared to be.

Trying not to think about little boys deprived of BB guns, she went to work. Michael was so surprised and pleased and dramatic that Amy had to bite her lip to keep from laughing. A pickup passed them, coming into town, and Amy wondered what the old farmer thought, seeing the girl driving and the boy writhing in the middle of the seat, stretched out and trying to push his thing right through her hand. Michael's eyes were closed and his mouth was wide open, and he was holding his breath although he frequently uttered a little cry as though he were going to explode.

And then with a gasp and a mighty spasm while they were

still a mile from the farm, Michael was through. By the time Amy pulled into the pecan trees behind the old house, Michael looked as though he were recuperating from a long and wonderful illness.

So why was he inserting *Hot August Night* into the tape player? And rewinding the tape? And why was he turning toward her, eyeing her skirt as though he were a man possessed? Didn't he know what had just happened? That his battery had been discharged? Oh, she was a stupid little bimbo, again making assumptions that the world didn't care about. Before she could thoroughly chastise herself, she watched Michael's eyeless monster stirring in the dampness of his supposed grave. Well, she'd just have to be very careful.

The string section of Neil Diamond's orchestra played music as soft as the breeze floating through the pecan trees over the car as Michael took the hem of her skirt in hand and began sliding it up her legs so slowly that the act didn't seem as perverted as it probably was. The music built in substance and then the strings held a long note; they were joined by an organ. Amy swung her legs into the seat so Michael could remove her pantyhose. Down they went as guitars chipped in, then drums. The percussion seemed to somehow assume control of Amy's breathing, and Michael, working like an artist, very carefully, dropped her pantyhose into a pile beside him and then looked at Amy to verify the music was affecting her as it should.

Back came his hands beneath her skirt, searching for the waistband on her panties. How could he time this method of stripping her so perfectly? When the orchestra suddenly transformed its music to full-blown rock and roll, and when the crowd began to cheer and applaud because Neil Diamond had come on stage, he had managed, without changing his speed, to have her panties far enough down her thighs to have fully exposed her.

"Oh, happy days!" he shouted. "Happy days!"

Amy was almost irrational, both emotionally and sexually, and when he stabbed her with his finger, she immediately moved it to the point where she wanted it and showed him what to do. He was obviously inexperienced but willing to learn, and while Neil Diamond sang "Crunchy Granola Suite," Amy hoped that if she were ever reincarnated, she could return to earth as a cat.

Life had to make more sense to cats.

5

For once, Brother Page didn't mind sitting in the kitchen waiting on Michael. Even though he was normally at the church at 4:00 P.M., he'd been at home since 2:30, ever since Missy Harris's visit. He had a difficult time counseling some of the women of the church, Missy representing the most difficult case by far. She was a twice-married woman in her late forties who was having trouble with her second marriage. Her first husband of twenty-five years had departed for California with a nineteen-year-old blonde and her second marriage wasn't working out as she'd hoped. She started her visit with the same sentence every time.

"He just doesn't love me like I want him to love me."

And Brother Page always adopted the same pose—expressionless face, a careful nod, and eyes that didn't see either Missy's red hair or her well-preserved body. Invariably, as she sat in the chair across the desk from the preacher, she started crying, her face wrinkling, lips tucked inward.

"There doesn't seem to be much love in the world."

Brother Page always remained seated even though he knew

what would happen. Missy was going to ease around the desk and stand tearfully beside him, and then Brother Page could remain seated and safe or offer some repressed physical comfort. He wasn't cold enough to ignore her, so he'd take a few deep breaths and stand, allowing Missy to wiggle into his arms.

"Why won't he love me?"

Looking at the frosted glass window of his study, Brother Page would say to himself, "Our father, which art in heaven. . . ."

"I have so much love to give."

. . . hallowed be thy name. . . .

"I just want a man to love me."

. . . thykingdomcomethywillbedone. . . .

Brother Page, reciting whatever scripture came to mind, would slowly start guiding Missy toward the door, trying to peel his body away from hers. If she was feeling exceptionally deprived, he often quoted three or four chapters from the book of John before Missy had cried herself out.

Then, once she was gone, he'd sit at the desk with a live current running through his body, unable to concentrate, unable to do anything but wonder if he should go visit his wife for what she whimsically referred to as afternoon delight. The Apostle Paul would surely have approved. Today a call had calmed him though.

"I just wanted to let you know I love you," he'd said.

Mrs. Page had giggled. "Has Missy been to see you?"

"Uh, why, yes, she was here earlier."

"How much earlier?"

"Oh, I don't know. Five minutes maybe."

"You can sneak out the back door and nobody would see you."

"Just talking to you is nice," he'd said.

"That's too bad."

His distractions today had come from a second source as well. He had caught Amy Hardin's father at home during lunch because he needed to visit with the man, to find out what kind of girl Michael was involved with. The living room of the Hardin home was littered with ranching magazines, *Wall Street Journals*, *People*, almost any periodical found in a Presbyterian doctor's waiting room. You couldn't have found a Bible with a search party.

Mr. Hardin hinted at past troubles—hunger strikes and a Mexican dope dealer—and mentioned, almost in passing, as if it were insignificant, that Amy wanted to sing rock and roll. "I think she's doing all right now," Mr. Hardin had said.

"Sure," Mrs. Hardin had said from the kitchen. "She eats Jello three times a day, makes C's in school, and bathes at least four times a day. She's doing just fine."

Brother Page had seen Amy's mother around town but never up close and didn't during his visit. She remained in the kitchen and injected comments but never appeared. And Mr. Hardin sat listening with a tightening jaw, each time continuing after the interruption as though no one else had spoken.

"She's—" Mr. Hardin waved one hand feebly. "Artistic."

"Autistic," Mrs. Hardin corrected. "She's an anal personality and needs professional help."

Mr. Hardin rubbed the temple of his head with his fingers and resisted contradicting his wife. Then he escorted Brother Page onto the front porch and stood with him. "Amy's had a hard life, and your son's the first decent kid she's been around in a long time. I was glad to see them get together."

Brother Page was impressed with the man's sincerity and didn't know how to tell him that his daughter was going to soon be in need of a new friend. The thought Brother Page had was this: if Lenin and Trotsky had conferred on their affairs, they wouldn't have arrived at a plan to take Christ to the world, and neither would Michael and Amy. Therefore, the alliance had to be aborted. Michael wasn't going to date a girl whose ambition was to waltz with the devil.

Brother Page left the Hardin house shaking his head. Amy's father brought her to church because he thought she needed moral instruction. There was probably no question the girl needed moral instruction in the worst way, but obviously neither father nor daughter had listened to any of the sermons Brother Page had been preaching.

Did anyone listen?

The church was filled every Sunday morning with those wanting to go to heaven, also wanting, while awaiting transportation, to call the educational director a fool for ordering insufficient literature, to squabble over whether the church needed a van for the youth, and to demand the removal of one person or another from a position of perceived power. Brother Page wasn't able to bring them together as a church dedicated to serving God. He could spend thirty exhausting minutes preaching that a Christian wasn't to conform to the world and immediately after the benediction, he saw three hundred people rushing forth into the world to conform.

The commitment of Brother Page had been lukewarm until the death of his younger brother fifteen years ago. The brother, the baby of the family and much more a son to the preacher than a brother, had been hauling cotton to the gin one summer afternoon when he'd been killed by a drunk driver. Brother Page, naively enough, had expected man's law to serve justice on the drunk, who was a banker in Halton, but he discovered the man had plea-bargained a two-year probated sentence.

Brother Page had gone on a one-man campaign to expose the lack of justice in the county, but the newspapers had turned him away. His friends and church members were so sleepily apathetic they could only shake their heads and mouth apologies. He had approached several Christian lawyers and beseeched them to run for district attorney, but they were all too busy paying for their big cars to devote their time to justice. Even Mrs. Page had finally suggested that he forget the entire matter because he was driving himself to an early grave.

After a while, his rage and indignation gave way to sorrow. He seemed to regress. He was plagued with self-doubts and doubts about God and the world he lived in. Doubts about the woman he had married. He was acting like a child but couldn't shake the feeling. He wanted to see another person grieving for his dead brother, for the living brother. He wanted someone to spontaneously hug him. He wanted someone else to acknowledge that he hurt as everyone else did.

He began spending long hours in the church study with the door locked, often staring at the ceiling, just as often crying and talking to his dead brother. At times he wondered if the death of his brother was his fault, punishment for sins. And one day he fell onto his knees and for the first time in his life made a full confession to God. He confessed his doubts, his weaknesses, his lack of real faith, the constant lure of temptation. The longer he prayed, the more he began to feel the blessed assurance that God loved him, that God forgave him. And although he had been preaching for years, he only then began to understand the personal nature of God's love. It wasn't love from a distance, wasn't a lonely ray zooming in from the outer reaches of the galaxy; it was love that had brought God to earth as a participant in human suffering, that had taken on all the sins of mankind, that could lift a lowly preacher into a personal relationship with the almighty and living God.

It was the most important point of theology that Brother Page had ever discovered, and now, these years later, he couldn't convey it to his congregation in a meaningful way. Even when they were suffering, they couldn't see the answer, and when they weren't suffering, they didn't care.

His own son didn't care.

When Michael came home—frowning: he must have had a particularly bad day, unable to find even a stray demon —Brother Page handed him a Bible opened to Hebrews chapter eleven and told him that the text of his next sermon, to be preached a week from Sunday, was that famous portion of scripture that dealt with the great men of faith.

Michael accepted the Bible without comment, thinking that somewhere—in heaven or elsewhere—there existed an ongoing conspiracy to ruin his days. Here he was, flush from meaningful contemplation of real wonders in the presence of Neil Diamond and Amy, and he had walked in to find his father waiting on him. Mostly what he wanted was to escape to his room without thinking seriously about the upcoming sermon, another one of God's jokes. He could hear God saying, "Hey, angels. What say we throw this kid a curve. If he thinks faith is impossible, let's see how he handles a sermon on Noah and Abraham." But he didn't take two steps toward the hall door before he heard, "Michael." He didn't turn because the tone of his father's voice told him bad news was headed his way like an arctic cold front in January.

Brother Page sighed; he'd hoped they could have a short discussion on faith, but of course Michael wasn't interested. Wouldn't it have been nice to sit and talk about Abraham? Wouldn't it have been nice to sit and talk about anything? Except Amy Hardin. Brother Page would draw the line on any discussion there because the thought of the girl would probably inspire Michael beyond his normal capacity for irrelevant objections and twisted argument. So Brother Page simply bunched his fibers, inhaled deeply, and said, "You're not to see Amy Hardin anymore."

He turned, wondering what his father had said. The words

had been jumbled, spoken too fast, and had sounded like, "You don't see many hard-ons anymore." Obviously his father hadn't said such a thing, but he almost wished he had. Maybe they could talk about lust. Maybe the old man could tell him how to get lust back in its compartment. Out, it was like a monster that wouldn't die.

"Did you understand me?" Brother Page asked.

"No, not really."

Brother Page's antennae twanged, picking up a strong signal: Trap ahead. The boy's trying to trip you up. If his son had been a nice respectful boy, he would have already agreed to abide by his father's wishes and maybe offered to take out the trash. "You can't see that girl anymore."

"What girl?"

"Amy Hard-on." Brother Page turned away, wondering how the devil could wrench control of any conversation the father tried to have with the son. "Amy Hard*iiinnnn*. You know who I'm talking about."

Michael almost laughed because his father had used a name tossed about at school, but before the laughter formed, the reality of his father's typical method of overreacting sank in. And somehow the unexpected edict, which was so absurd that it failed to even worry him, caused not anger but sadness. The world was really an incredibly stupid place.

"Why?" he asked.

"Because I said so."

"I know you said so. I heard you. I want to know why."

Brother Page looked at the window in the den and scratched his eyebrow. Because, he thought, Eli did a wonderful job of bringing up Samuel in the ways of God but he was punished by God for failing to restrain his own sons. They stole offerings and seduced the women of the church, and their modern-day equivalent was a preacher's son who won other children's Sun-

44

day school offerings by betting on Bible trivia and who was dating one of the members who happened to be amoral and probably desirous of seduction. "Because, Michael, God doesn't want you dating a girl with emotional problems who wants to sing rock and roll."

He nodded, unwilling to enter into any discussion about God's will. He'd end up dropping to his knees as if he'd been shot in the heart and singing "Jesus Loves Me." Today he wasn't going to sing; the only song he wanted to consider was the "Prologue" on *Hot August Night*. And although he wanted badly to get into his bedroom, alone, for the further consideration of the noon-time events at the farm, he felt obligated as a son to ask a few questions. "Who told you Amy was the world's worst sinner? I assume we're talking about the same girl, the one who brought the special music at church this past Sunday."

"Her parents."

"You talked to her mother?" he asked, surprised.

Brother Page hesitated only a second. "Yes."

"Well, if you did talk to her mother, then you know how weird the lady is. I don't know, I may be wrong, but I always thought it was a Christian obligation to provide a good influence wherever you could, and that's what I've been trying to do." He said this with a straight face, in keeping with his argument. Actually, he *had* been a good influence until the past week. "Telling me I can't see Amy because she's had problems is like saying we can't send missionaries to Africa because the natives are pagans."

Some day Brother Page was going to sit down and review the history of his son's life and determine exactly where the boy's mind had gotten warped. It had to have suffered from watching television years ago. "The Three Stooges," probably.

"So the next step for the Southern Baptist Convention is to disband the Foreign Mission Board, rewrite the Great Commission, forget about the Annie Armstrong offering, and recall

all the missionaries from Africa and send them out to convert members of Baptist churches. Then we can—"

"Michael!" Brother Page shouted. He was going to point out the fallacy in his argument but couldn't remember the first stupid words. Instead he said, "You don't even know what you're talking about."

"I know what I'm talking about. It's what you're talking about that bothers me. You're saying I can't see a girl because she's—"

"A problem child whose heart belongs to the devil," Brother Page said, finishing the sentence.

"So singing rock and roll automatically excludes you from being a Christian. Well, let me make a call to Billy Graham and tell him because he obviously doesn't know that. And I guess I should tell my own mother because I've stood in this house and heard her singing popular songs." He shook his head. "I can't imagine that you want to blacklist Amy, because you don't even know her. I'll tell you what: I'll bring her over here and you can talk to her as long as you want. Then you can decide what kind of person she is."

Brother Page sighed and moved toward the den window, which looked out over the yard at the back wall of the church. Eventually he would figure out why God had created a father whose ears couldn't keep up with the mouth of his son. Turn him on and he wouldn't shut up. "Well, that's the way it's going to be. Besides, Mr. Hardin said Gary called her almost as much as you do. She probably needs to be dating some other boys. No kid needs to get serious."

"Gary calls her?" he asked.

Brother Page shrugged. "That's what her father said."

"Almost as much as I do?"

Brother Page tried not to acknowledge the childish pleasure he felt over Michael's abrupt collision with a stump and his sudden fall from his high horse. "I told you everything I know."

"Gary calls her," he said to no one. "I'll be—" He censored the obscenity and saved himself additional problems. Gary, his former best friend, the guy who had gone wacko when his father was killed in an automobile accident a year ago, the guy who had an endless supply of sacrilegious jokes and a complete lack of respect for other people, was keeping Amy's phone hot. And he had never suspected it. He wouldn't have expected to hear such news from Gary, but what about Amy? "How long has he been calling her?"

Brother Page shook his head. "Years maybe. I don't know. But Mr. Hardin didn't make it sound like a recent development."

"I'll be dipped in. . . . What'd he say to make you think it could have been years?"

Brother Page turned from the window. "There's no point in discussing something that doesn't matter. I'm serious when I say you aren't to see her anymore. And you've got a sermon to prepare, so you may as well start preparing."

Michael, carrying the Bible, turned to go to his room. "Well, at the least I'll just keep my eyes closed in any class I have with Amy so I won't see her, and at the worst I'll get a nice clean ice pick and poke my eyes out."

He left the room successfully, without hearing further words from Benito, and dropped the Bible on his bed. He found *Hot August Night* in his box of tapes and sat to listen to Neil Diamond beneath the headphones but soon discovered he wasn't hearing any of the music. Undoubtedly Amy had a good reason for failing to inform her alleged boyfriend, Michael Page, that Gary had been calling her seventeen times each and every night for God knows how many years. It wasn't an issue he could immediately settle because Amy was off on a mysterious mission to Waco with her father. He'd ask tomorrow, Saturday, but not before.

The conspiracy to ruin his days was much more involved and extensive than he'd known.

It occurred to him that the reason he wasn't hearing music was more basic than an inability to concentrate; there was no sound in the headphones. He hit the eject button on the stereo, and the tape popped out of the little door, dragging behind it shining brown ribbons of tape. He groaned, then discovered that about ten miles of tape was tightly wrapped around a tiny spindle. He worked for a few minutes releasing the ever-lengthening ribbon, then slowly went in search of a pencil with which to rewind the spool in the cassette.

What else can go wrong? he wondered.

The answer came as he reached the dresser—he'd left a glass of Coke beside Amy's framed picture, and the glass had properly sweated all over the wooden surface of the dresser, leaving a sickly white splotch three or four inches in diameter. He moved Amy's picture so the spot would be hidden, thinking if his father ever discovered such desecration, he would be paying financially and emotionally for the remainder of his life.

He fell onto his bed to take a nap, no longer able to remember if he had actually been at the farm with Amy earlier in the day. A listless depression began to filter into his system, the same lack of feeling he always got when he discovered the world and those in it paid no attention to the boundaries he wished to impose. And his father's demand that he stop seeing Amy was so ridiculous and unreasonable that it reminded him of the first such surprise of his life, one that had come eight years ago. The day Michael Page was initiated into the real world.

Having finished the fifth grade, he walked into the house one afternoon in early summer after a baseball game and found his mother at the sink, crying. Only one thing could have happened, he reasoned. As his mother washed dishes, she had looked through the window over the sink, witnessing the old rusted clothesline pole finally fall like a chopped tree, landing on a cat and killing it. He withdrew his Log Cabin water bottle from the refrigerator, tilted his baseball cap back, and took a long drink of cold water, toasting the death of another cat. He hated them all.

"Why're you crying?" he asked.

His mother didn't answer. Instead she dried her hands on a dish towel and walked to the phone. Her conversation on the phone consisted of two words: "Michael's home."

"So what're you crying about?"

His second question lacked the confidence of the first. His mother had obviously just called his father, and she wasn't even concerned that he was standing with the refrigerator door open while he got a drink. Bad sign. Very bad sign. To further test the waters, he asked, "Can I go see *Midnight Cowboy* with Gary this weekend?" When his mother failed to even respond, he knew that he was in major league trouble.

He walked into the living room to consider past sins that could have reared their ugly heads, but once in the living room, he felt a twinge of disorientation. Something was wrong. A bookcase had been shifted, pictures moved, the couch now sat against a different wall. And something was missing.

The television.

"What happened to the TV?" he asked. "Is that why you're crying, the TV broke?"

Still no answer. And when his father came home, Mrs. Page began to sob, which was the noisy signal not of trouble but of bad news. The last time he and his father had held a conference while his mother had cried in an adjoining room was the day that Brother Page had informed him that his dog, a little terrier, was in the custody of city officials and had been condemned to death for the crime of tearing the mailman's pants.

Brother Page walked into the living room, where Michael sat in a chair by the picture window, thankful he no longer had a dog, trying to think of reasons he couldn't possibly be guilty of breaking the TV. At the age of ten, he was experienced in proving he had not committed crimes he hadn't even heard about. That was what being a preacher's kid meant—existing in a state of guilt from which escape was only temporary and irregular.

Brother Page explained: the family would henceforth live without a television. Every time Michael turned it on, he was being exposed to all sorts of behavior unbecoming to God— sex and violence and drunkenness and drinking and cussing and lawbreaking and liberal newscasting. The family would benefit immensely, immediately, and if he only stopped to look at the situation with eyes that were growing more and more mature—he was almost eleven—then he would agree wholeheartedly. If he was sensible, he could do nothing but agree.

It was several minutes before he could get his mouth closed. The father was going to require the son to exist in a house without TV? Every family in the country had a TV. They came with infant care packages that mothers got when they left the hospital with their newborn babies. They came in cereal boxes and Cracker Jacks. They were a birthright. The only reason to live in the United States was television. Since he decided his life was at an end, as surely as if his father had removed his brain and heart, he wailed, "Shiittttttttt."

On the way to the bedroom, Michael hanging at the end of his father's arm, his father pointed out while removing his belt that his speech was a prime example of why they would live without TV.

By now reckless, without any reason to continue living, he said, "I heard that word at school. Are you going to close it down too?"

The father's answer was a series of lashes that set the son's butt on fire. For ten minutes afterward, he danced and bowed his body as if he could push the burning stripes through his body and be done with them. He cursed and gritted his teeth. But he didn't cry.

The days of summer were quiet without the Brady Bunch fighting or the Partridge Family singing in the living room. He spent as many days as possible at Gary's watching TV, even soap operas and game shows which had never interested him. He knew his mother was aware of his activities because she'd call and Gary's mother would say, "Oh, they're just watching TV." His mother was apparently keeping the secret of his violations—she had to be, since he had no new bruises on his posterior—so he asked if she'd discuss the possibility of the Page family rejoining the civilized world by acquiring another TV.

"Your father doesn't change his mind very easy."

"Even wetbacks have TVs."

"Your father does what he thinks is best."

"There's even TV in prison. I'd be better off murdering somebody so I could go to jail."

"I don't think that'd be a good idea."

"If you'll talk to him, I promise I'll be good. Just please talk to him."

He spent the next days determined to demonstrate such exemplary behavior, to exhibit such charm, that his parents wouldn't be able to resist getting another television. He brushed his mother's hair, helped her set the table for meals, dried dishes, carried out the trash without being reminded, asked, or threatened. He openly studied his Sunday school lesson and told his father knock-knock jokes.

His birthday was Friday and he'd suggested several times to

his mother that the ideal gift would be a small black-and-white television for his room. The new model of responsibility that he was, he could absolutely guarantee that he would watch only redeeming programs. If a Billy Graham crusade happened to be on, he'd invite all his friends over and collect an offering, which he would send, without deduction, to Billy himself.

And then an amazing thing happened. He got up one morning and his eyes fell on an ad in the newspaper that was lying open on the kitchen table. There was just what he wanted—a small portable TV. Now on sale. It was a sign from God: now that he was living an upright life, indeed a godly life, the good Lord was giving the all-clear for a new TV.

Praise God. Suddenly Michael, who was spiritually deep and in tune with the holy, saw that Brother Page had been right all along. All those people on "Let's Make a Deal" and "Sale of the Century" were being blinded by the devil of greed when they should have been in church learning how to get saved. Or if they were, by some slim chance, already saved, they should have been at home reading their Bibles and praying for the missionaries. Probably not a one of them tithed their winnings. God was obviously long-suffering to allow the networks to continue engaging in such sinful programming.

He prayed for divine guidance in the use of his new TV. "Please, dear Lord, give me the wisdom to know, as I watch, who is saved and who isn't because I want to pray for those who aren't. Give me enough strength so I can stay awake and watch so I can pray for that many more lost souls. You and I both know, dear Lord, that I'll watch this TV only after I've done my homework and studied my Sunday school lesson. Forgive me for all the bad things I've said about you and my father. I didn't mean to say those things but the devil blinded me. Thank you for your help in battling the devil."

On Friday morning, he leapt from his bed, full of good cheer and high spirits. Mrs. Page kissed her birthday boy good morning and sat with him at the table while he ate. He asked if he could have his present. Mrs. Page sat across the table and made funny shapes with her mouth and tapped her fingers together and said his father would be home in a few minutes; he wanted to give Michael his gift.

His poor father, he thought. He was going to make a special trip home just to instruct him on his future viewing habits, ignorant of his son's mature spiritual condition and prior arrangements with God. Well, his father was only human; he didn't understand everything.

When Brother Page entered the house, carrying nothing, Michael was elated. The TV would be a difficult parcel to carry all wrapped up, and unwrapped, wouldn't be a surprise. While his father made a short speech about his now attaining the age of eleven and able to understand responsibility, he started bouncing in his chair. When his father said they'd spent slightly more on his gift than normal because they weren't going to be able to take a vacation, he received a revelation from God— somewhere hidden in the house was a nineteen-inch Sony color TV with remote control. Oh, what sweet sense life made. With remote control, he could instantly turn off the set as soon as anyone started drinking or cussing or . . . no, not taking off her clothes. That took longer to verify. Remote control was God's gift to Christians who wanted to watch television. He was going to spend the remainder of his days praising God's wonderful name.

"It's out in the garage if you want it," Brother Page said.

He knocked his chair over backwards getting up and ran for the door, checking the clock as he went. "Sale of the Century" started in ten minutes, plenty of time to get the new set hooked up before the big sale began.

Sitting in the middle of the garage was a brand-new tenspeed bicycle, its bright gold paint sparkling.

Michael passed it by on his way to Gary's house, where he was going to watch television without ceasing, without regard to content so long as there was plenty of cussing and drinking and gambling. For the next two hours, he used the Lord's name in vain in a variety of interesting ways.

When he considered the course of his life, he saw it as the point of a pencil attempting to draw a straight line while a great number of hands swatted it constantly off course. As a result, any attempt to follow the line on a graph would have caused a vomiting dizziness. For an epitaph, his desire was simple: "He was a nice guy." He wanted to be a nice guy. He loved it when the ladies of the church hugged him for no reason and wished for daughters he could marry. He liked the opportunity to provide a genuine service for a needy person —running errands, mowing yards, changing tires, or just providing company. But the image he carried was usually not that of a nice guy; it was that of a preacher's kid.

Preacher's kid. Better Yankee son of a bitch or deadbeat nigger than preacher's kid. It was an image that combined the worst parts of a Catholic nun, a Hare Krishna airport solicitor, a flaming faggot, and a vibrator that was actually used for back massages. Never did he meet anyone when he didn't see that look, that look which said, "Preacher's kid, huh? Why you little lithping fairy, I think I'll hit you juth to make you turn the other thyeek." And when he saw that look, he started doing any or all of several things—drinking whiskey out of a bottle, cussing like a seasick sailor called upon to describe his symptoms, or starting fights. There were any number of trained observers around town ready to report his sins and those sins they wished he'd commit. He had been blamed for teaching the mongoloid man at church how to cuss, for writing extemporaneous accounts of sexual liaisons in the hymnals, for driving through

54

carefully groomed yards, and for selling dope on streetcorners to toddlers and retards. The recipient of these reports, his father, was always more interested in appeasement than in actual guilt or innocence, and he had once punished him for throwing rocks at children when he had actually been drunk in Dallas. And since there was no means of appeal, he learned to protect himself.

When he was sixteen, someone had emptied a bottle of dishwashing detergent into the baptistry while it was being filled for an evening baptismal service. When Brother Page arrived at the church, he discovered suds cascading over the glass of the baptistry and filling the choir loft. Arriving on the scene shortly thereafter was a kid named Billy, a wimp his own age whose list of friends was very short. Billy told Brother Page that he truly hated to be the bearer of bad news, but he was obligated to reveal that Michael Page had added the detergent to the water.

He was relieved of the keys to his mother's car so swiftly that he hardly had time to detach them from the keychain he had won in a pinball tournament at the Fina station, the keychain with the plastic disc in which was encased a picture of a naked woman. He'd only had the keys a week. The father was in an intense blathering fit, but Michael did hear the man say that he would pronounce formal punishment as soon as he regained his sanity, sometime in the next month, which Michael would spend in his room staring harmlessly at the walls.

He wouldn't have known the identity of the guilty party had not his mother approached him later that night and asked, "Is Billy telling the truth?" He listened with real pleasure as his mother told him several other people had seen Billy in the vicinity of the church earlier carrying a brown paper bag. He said he couldn't identify the guilty party because he didn't know who had done it; he knew only that he was innocent. His father disagreed. Case closed.

He and Billy had been enemies for several years, ever since the weekend his parents had left town and entrusted the care of their son to Billy's parents. Since the family had no extra beds, he ended up sleeping with Billy. Sometime in the night, he awoke to find Billy humping and fondling him with real vigor. He was offended because Billy had not only assumed he would be agreeable to such perversions, but when he turned over to choke Billy, the boy had feigned deep sleep and total ignorance. Billy thought he was stupid as well as queer.

He decided a simple choking wasn't sufficient punishment so he also smashed Billy's head against the mattress, an action which brought Billy up into a sitting position, from which Michael bounced him several times onto the mattress, slowly working Billy's head toward the headboard. There had only been two good smashes of skull against wood when Billy was rescued by his mother.

With the knowledge of Billy's accusation over the baptistry bubbles, he found himself in a unique position, that of being able to plot revenge. Normally he never knew his accuser; sometimes he was ignorant of the supposed crime as well. So he was limited to relieving his frustration on the neighborhood cats. Ever since he had watched the hammer-throw in the Olympics on Gary's television, he had been flinging cats. After some practice, he could place one in an open trash can from fifty feet, and more than once he had hidden behind the parsonage, cat tail in hand, waiting for the mailman to deliver the mail out front. The letter carrier had been surprised to see a whirling, howling cat come flying over the roof. But with a target for revenge, Michael sat in his room for almost a week, plotting revenge. The thought was so sweet he was almost reluctant to act.

On Saturday morning, he got up and asked his mother to make waffles, knowing she had no waffle mix, and after watching Mrs. Page search the cabinets, offered to go get some. Money in hand, he left, driving directly to the Ag Barn and pulling from beneath the seat a box of waffle mix he'd already purchased. He knew Billy went religiously to the Ag Barn each morning to care for his only friend, a pig he was raising as an FFA project. Sure enough, he found him there. Having already decided to commit mayhem without drawing blood, he walked up to Billy as he stood beside the feed room door and stared at him.

Billy said, "So what do you want?" and looked around for help, possibly hoping for an attack piglet.

He said nothing, watching Billy's darting eyes, and when Billy started to turn away, he hit him in the stomach, noting with satisfaction the grunt and spit that exploded from Billy's mouth. While Billy was bent at a right angle trying to regain his respiratory functions, he grabbed him by the neck and cowboy belt, dipped him several times into the water trough, and then ran him toward the spot most cluttered with cowshit. Billy tried to maintain his balance as if he were an airplane about to take off, but Michael had provided him with too much momentum. He slid hands first through the hay and dirt and dung.

Just getting into his task with enthusiasm, he was suddenly stumped. He couldn't go jerk Billy up and get contaminated, and Billy sensed the dilemma. He sat up and called names, some obscene, some childish, like "dummy head ox." Michael threw a few dirt clods at him, bouncing only one off Billy's knee, and in return Billy spit and sobbed and threw stalks of hay back.

Having worked up a good appetite, he returned home and ate two waffles, drank a quart of milk, and was in the midst of digesting both feat and food when his father appeared.

"Where have you been?" he shouted.

He shrugged. "Eating breakfast."

Brother Page went off in search of a reliable party, his wife, who was as surprised as he was with Billy's allegations. Michael had once again misjudged Billy because he hadn't thought the perverted liar would tell anyone about his latest humiliation. But that was the problem with one easily humiliated; he didn't care who knew.

Brother Page had already arranged a conference with Billy and his parents, and they drove to Billy's house. The memory of the midnight rape made Michael all the angrier as he walked in, and the sight of Billy with his damp hair combed in a twenty-year-old style gave him a strong desire to send an eyeball threat of severe retaliation. But Billy wasn't looking. He didn't look at him once as he stood before the three parents and made his plea. Michael, according to Billy, was insanely mean, formed gangs at school for the sole purpose of harassing him, tripped him as he rounded corners, poured Cokes on his head at lunch, and had once choked him in his sleep for no reason whatsoever. Of the charges, Michael was guilty of only one—the choking, for a good reason—and the longer Billy went on whining and lying, the more determined he was that he would not be out-lied by an old maid wimp.

When Billy finished, Michael declared that he knew, as did everyone at school, that Jerry McElvain had challenged Billy to a fight at the Ag Barn, and Billy was putting the blame on Michael for his refusal years ago to engage in perverted sexual relations in that very house. The truth was, and God was his witness, that Jerry McElvain and Billy had been involved in an ongoing feud over a girl for several months. That much was true, but he embellished. Jerry had been spreading rumors at school that Billy had been so torn up over losing his only girlfriend to a better man that Billy had been contemplating suicide, and Jerry's opinion was that the world would become a etter place once Billy had stopped contemplating and gone to committing. (Billy had been upset over the fickle nature of his girlfriend and had visited a doctor for his "nerves.") He could produce at least ten witnesses to a confrontation at school which had led to the morning fight, and he could produce at least twenty kids who had heard Billy saying, "McElvain is gonna feel pain." Jerry probably wouldn't have gotten upset if Billy hadn't called him a cocksucker in front of everyone. When Billy's mouth fell open at this revelation, he pointed at him and said, "Yeah, just look at him, so innocent, like he'd never say anything like cocksucker. Well, if you don't believe he uses that kind of language, just call the principal and see if he didn't catch Billy writing 'fuck' on the bathroom wall."

As both Billy and his parents knew, the principal had indeed caught Billy decorating the bathroom with four-letter words.

He detailed fabricated efforts to befriend Billy over the past years, making him sound like the shrew he was. Then he said, "And I'll give you another example of how the guy's got it in for me. He told my father I put soap in the baptistry, and he knows I didn't." He pointed at Billy and said, "You did it, didn't you, Billy?" Billy started to answer and he could tell by the look of desired flight in Billy's eyes that he was going to lie. So, using a thunderous voice that his father often used for scaring sinners from their seats, he shouted, "Tell the truth for once, Billy. For the sake of your Lord Jesus Christ, tell the truth."

Billy put his face in his hands and sobbed. "Yes, and I hate you. I hate you, I hate you, I hate you. I wanted to be your friend and you almost *killed* me. I moved here and didn't know anyone and I thought you were nice and I thought you'd be my friend because I didn't have any. I've never had any friends. Nobody has ever liked me. You were the only person in school who'd even speak to me. One day you sat with me after lunch and said, 'How's it going, Big Bill?' I've never even had a nickname and you called me Big Bill. And I thought we'd be friends and hang around and stuff, and then you tried to *kill* me."

Billy went on for almost thirty minutes, detailing a life so thoroughly pathetic that Michael almost cried. Billy could recall every word he had ever spoken to him, the two times he had patted him on the back, and the candy he had offered him in the prechoking days. He had never seen a person suffer an emotional washout, and he could only say, "I'm sorry, Billy," and squeeze his shoulder as he and Brother Page left.

On the way home, he had once again assumed the role of guilty party, and Brother Page said, "I just don't understand it. When you're presented with an opportunity to provide some real Christian service, you just go flying off the handle and all but *destroy* that boy."

He was too depressed to respond, first by the pitiful revelation of Billy, second by his own inability to claim innocence when he wasn't guilty. Brother Page not only didn't apologize for the unwarranted grounding he had experienced, but said he would not reclaim his mother's car keys until he exhibited a much higher level of maturity.

"I was thirteen when that happened," he had said, referring to the choking episode.

"And you're sixteen now."

Case closed.

When his mother called him for supper, he rolled off the bed as though his being were ancient and used up. The day had held a stupefying array of ups and downs, everything from the wonders of Amy at the farm to his father's cease-and-desist order concerning her. A second sermon, a dresser ruined by a forgotten but heavily sweating glass of Coke. As he sat to eat pork chops, mashed potatoes, fried okra, and black-eyed peas, he decided to tell his father about the dresser because it would then be one less sin, the eventual discovery of which would certainly ruin a good day. He'd probably be sitting with Amy at the farm when the sheriff would fly up the drive, scattering clouds of dust, get out his handcuffs, and say, "The state just issued an APB on you, Page. Neglect with the intent to destroy fine furniture."

Before even filling his plate, he confessed his mistake, and his father, in keeping with the tumultuous nature of the day, was unconcerned. Maybe even happy.

He looked at Mrs. Page and said, "Why don't you get some of that Contact paper that looks like wood and just cover it up?"

His mother thought possibly she had some on hand. She'd look after supper.

He should have felt much better. Instead he felt like a traitor for his intention to ignore his father's edict that he avoid Amy.

6

When Mrs. Page handed him the telephone receiver on Saturday morning, he made two discoveries: Amy was on the other end of the line, and he instantly understood the cause of his depression the previous day—Amy's failure to tell him about the calls from Gary. Well, forget about Gary, he told himself. Obviously Gary hadn't dated Amy since she'd begun dating him, so think about something important, like the old man's prohibition that he never lay eyes on Amy.

He gave his mother a quick look, trying to determine if she was going to assist in enforcement of the new law. But she walked from the room without a backward glance. Since she hadn't said, "If that's Amy, you remember what your father said," he assumed she had chosen ignorance over involvement. That realization should have given him at least a tiny surge of adrenalin, knowing he'd been joined by the forces of righteousness, but it did nothing to add sparkle to a downright flat mood.

Amy, however, was exuberantly happy. On Monday she was going to get a brand new Firebird. "Can you believe it? That's why we went to Waco yesterday. And I didn't even know why we were going." She invited him over to see the brochures she had collected from the Pontiac dealer.

He left the house without announcing his destination, driving his mother's car, and arrived just ahead of a storm. As he stepped onto the porch of the Hardin house, rain began splattering on the sidewalk, huge drops that hit the sidewalk like tiny pieces of glass, and within a matter of minutes, the morning reverted to night and the great black clouds opened.

He followed Amy up the stairs to her room, swearing he was going to act like an adult and share in her excitement, but when they entered Amy's room, he found his vow of maturity weak. Amy lay on the bed with her shiny brochures, inviting him down beside her, but he chose instead to sit on the floor, back against the wall, looking at the opened window across the room. The sill was wet and the yellow curtains billowed in the damp wind.

"You don't want to look with me?" Amy asked, turned onto her side.

"Maybe in a few minutes," he said in a kindly manner, knowing with that utterance he had exhausted his supply of kindness.

He had to get the matter of Gary settled. Unfortunately he couldn't ask directly because such questions would imply jealousy, which was stupid and childish—everyone agreed on that —and Amy's boyfriend wouldn't exhibit such an unworthy emotion. Also unfortunately, he knew exactly the kind of person Gary was. His fingernails were always dirty and he'd ignore the fact that Amy was beautiful and delicate. Think of his fantasies, which Amy was encouraging by talking to him. He'd squeeze her tits like pull-apart rolls and throw her spread-eagle onto the ground. The question was, what kind of fantasies was Amy engaging in? What was she doing while she was on her back naked in Gary's fantasies? Probably shouting words of encouragement: "Stick those dirty hands up me. Use both hands, Gary baby, use both hands. Come on, all the way to the elbow."

What on earth did she see in the guy?

She lay on the bed in a faded green housedress that had been washed so many times it fell across her prone body like a piece of cheesecloth. And he saw no telltale signs of underwear, no lines of panties or bra. (Amazing how a flimsy dress perfectly revealed the body beneath it when that body was free of underwear.)

Gary had once called her "Bubble Butt," and Michael, who had obviously seen much less of Amy than Gary had, only now realized she did in fact have a nicely rounded butt. Normally her clothes weren't all that revealing, so how had Gary known what he hadn't? Gary, who was so proud of his sexual apparatus that he'd once made an imprint of it in plaster of paris and carried the plaque around in the glove compartment of his car, and Amy. Gary and Amy had a better sound than did Michael and Amy, and everyone knew how much emphasis Amy placed on sound. Gary and Amy sitting in a tree, *k-i-s-s-i-n-g*. She was merely waiting for Michael to go away voluntarily. She'd probably thought at one time that she was attracted to the pitiful preacher's son and was now waiting on him to disappear with his feelings intact so she didn't have to destroy him emotionally. She didn't want a shell of a boy on her conscience. There was no love involved, just pity.

He'd just go ahead and ask outright. He opened his mouth to speak, then thought, you fool. What about the mountain of evidence in your favor that's against Gary?

But what about the gnawing in his gut, the rat of uncertainty that had him totally confused about something he'd been certain of twenty-four hours ago?

"Have you talked to Gary lately?" he asked.

"Gary who?" Amy asked, studying her brochures.

Crap, he thought. "Gary, the sleazeball who hasn't cleaned his fingernails or brushed his teeth in a year. Gary the scum-sucking pig."

Amy turned again onto her side and gave him a long look. She was excited about her car but she had invited him over for reasons unrelated to automobiles. This morning was the only time all weekend both parents were going to be absent from the house, and she and Michael were going to make love right on her bed.

She'd ridden all the way to Waco, thinking about her favorite poem, Yeats's "A Prayer for My Daughter," because she'd felt very fortunate getting to go look for a car, very fortunate to have a father with the emotional sensitivity of Yeats himself. And she had thought about the poet's desire that his daughter be given beauty, but not excessive beauty, not beauty that would make the girl an inadequate person. Amy had transposed talent for beauty and thought about herself. She made herself nervous even admitting she thought she had talent, as if by the admission someone would suddenly appear to prove her wrong, but she didn't want to be so obsessed with singing that she couldn't be a friend. She wanted to be Michael's friend, a warm and loving friend.

Or maybe, she thought, she was just horny and wanted to screw.

The morning was perfect, the weather just right for lying naked with Michael. So why was he sitting on the floor looking as though he were on his way to the hospital for major surgery?

"You never did answer my question," he said.

Amy couldn't remember the question. "What was it?"

Michael sighed. "Have you talked to Gary the sleaze lately?"

"He calls sometimes. I don't know when the last time was."

"What does he call about?"

Amy began to think Michael's disastrous mood was related to Gary but didn't understand why. Still, she hoped it was, because that was a matter easily dealt with. "He calls to ask me out. I tell him no and then he calls again. He doesn't understand I wouldn't date him if he was the last boy on earth. He's crazy and nasty and sacrilegious, the complete opposite of you. You're what I want." Amy made herself visibly nervous with the last statement because somehow the sexual connotations she felt had crept into the sentence, and her body vibrated.

"I wonder why he keeps calling," Michael said.

"Maybe he thinks I'll change my mind."

"There must be some reason he'd think that."

"Well, do you want me to call him and ask?"

The question went unanswered. Michael was thwarting her plans, and she was trying not to get irritated. All she wanted was to make love, and she'd chosen the time and place because she didn't want Michael staging a spectacle. Left up to him, he'd rent a rotating heart-shaped bed and hire a choir. It seemed as if Amy would have to resort to music herself though.

"Michael."

He rubbed his eyes as though very tired. "What?"

"Come over here."

"I have to figure something out."

"You can't. Nothing ever adds up."

"It has to."

Amy could think of three things that would add up—Fleetwood Mac, the weather, and Amy. Using her arm, she brushed all the brochures from the bed and then walked to the stereo, looking for the right album.

"I can only think of one thing that would make me feel better," Michael said.

"What?"

"To hear you say you hate Gary's guts."

"I hate his guts."

Amy found the album and started it on "Dreams." And while Stevie Nicks sang, while the vibrations of the drums echoed through the sound of the wind and rain, Amy walked to Michael. She stood in front of him singing with the record, inviting him up. For her, singing was freedom; she was a naked baby set on a beach to run and splash and roll in the sand, to laugh and cry as she felt the need. She never danced unless she was singing and then she didn't want to stop.

He watched as if hypnotized. Behind Amy the rain blew in the open window, the curtains swirled, and the air was heavy and damp. He never listened to "Dreams" when he wasn't transported out of himself into the presence of a solitary singer who knew all his emotions and wanted to help explore them. He stood, bringing with him, as he did, Amy's dress. It was light, as flimsy as it looked, and he held it while staring at Amy, at everything he wanted to see. And in the presence of two singers, he wasn't completely aware of his actions. He dropped to his knees and lightly kissed Amy's bare stomach. He ran his hands over the slight fuzz on her thighs, the dips at her waist. Seeing her naked brought an effect that was surprisingly opposite of what he had expected—a desire to keep their relationship at the level where they presently had it, stripped of everything unnecessary and confining and confusing, free of jealousy and suspicion and pressure.

He stood to walk with her to the bed, and when he did, he looked out the open window. There, on the next block, sitting framed in a lighted window that shined like a beacon in the dismal gray morning, was Lottie Swenson, her binoculars trained on Michael and Amy. The sight registered in his brain as one that would undoubtedly be troublesome in the future, but his thoughts weren't on the future. Within a few minutes, he was going to pass into a realm of wonder, and if he couldn't remain there the rest of his life, he didn't care what the future held.

When they were finished and holding each other, Amy felt a strange tenderness, hardly a sexual feeling at all, but an urge to just go right on holding Michael as though he were a newborn baby, someone who needed her. She had resolved to tell him about the band at this point, but didn't want to, didn't want to do anything that was going to break the spell of loving magic in which they lay. But thunder from the waning storm rattled the room and Amy took the sudden disruption as an omen that she should get on with the revelation.

"What would you think if I sang with a band?"

"Are you getting up a group?"

"I'm not."

"Somebody's asked you?"

Amy nodded. Michael, who was somewhat lower on the bed and whose head rested on her breasts, looked up at her face. Amy grew uncomfortable because he was looking right up her nose.

"Who asked?"

"Some people I know in Halton. It's real iffy right now. But I've always wanted to sing with a band."

"Are these people in Halton—guys?"

The conversation was proceeding along the lines that had kept her up nights searching the cabinets for Rolaids. Why oh why couldn't he just offer his encouragement and forget the questions? Of course, she'd been up nights before she'd unexpectedly recalled, during biology class, the tricks she'd once known. She sat up beside him and let her hand flutter like a butterfly over his body, starting at the neck and ending at his lower stomach.

"Yes, they're guys, but that doesn't mean anything. At least it shouldn't." Her butterfly flopped on damp ground. "You know, you were never the least bit jealous before we started getting sexual." She bent forward, her face over his, and said, "I think your jealousy has something to do with sex."

He shook his head. "Impossible. I'm not a bit jealous anymore. I hope the band goes places and does great things. If anybody deserves it, you do."

He reached up and kissed her, then dropped back onto the bed, contented as a cat warming itself in the sun. If Amy didn't want him to be jealous, he wouldn't be. He didn't have a jealous streak in his entire body.

7

Every time the phone rang during the remainder of the weekend, he expected to hear his mother or father say, "He was doing *what* in Amy's bedroom?" Rarely however did rumors come by phone when he was listening; they arrived silently, surprisingly, through the air-conditioning vents and settled in his father's ears. He never even knew the source of many, and he personally would have been embarrassed to repeat some of them to a preacher.

He got so tired of hearing about what all he'd done one summer that he and Gary fixed Lottie the Rumor Queen. They'd formed a yard-care partnership and had contracted with Lottie's best friend and chief rival, Ima Inez Randolph, to mow her yard and weed her flower beds. One morning as he and Gary were working on the petunias below Ima Inez's open kitchen window, they started talking about how surprised they'd been to see Lottie at a restaurant in Stanton with the director of the black funeral home.

Within a week, he had not only heard the original rumor repeated, but he learned that Lottie had always expressed an abnormal interest in blacks, that she had once sung in the choir of St. Paul's AME Church, and had carried, then aborted, the child of Martin Luther King's cousin. The rumors failed to damage her reputation as Queen of Gossip, however.

He went to school on Monday and found Amy at her locker. They had developed a feeling of intimacy and, like newlyweds, played a game of I-bet-I-can-touch-you-there-before-anybody-sees-me. Amy seemed as happy as he was, a wonderful turn of events for a girl who often seemed to fear happiness, and she touched him in a spot not normally touched in the halls of AHS. At the precise moment she touched one inch below the bottom of Michael's zipper, Beth walked up.

"Whoa," Beth said dramatically.

Amy looked as uncomfortable as if she'd been caught pilfering pennies from her mother's purse.

Beth was something else, a beautiful girl with a terrible reputation. She'd had every obscene adjective in the language applied to her and her dark skin, to her hair that was so black it seemed tinted blue, to her eyeshadow that matched her blue-black highlights. She affected every guy in school the same way, by inciting the madness that resided below his belt. Usually good-looking girls were careful about the boys they associated with, but not Beth. Yesterday Michael had seen her sitting on a car beside a guy whose T-shirt inscription had read, "Gimme head till I'm dead." If the guy had died, the circumstantial evidence against Beth would have been overwhelming.

"Listen," she said. "I've got one hell of a party lined up for graduation. My folks are going to be out of town and we're going to party." In a purple dress, she swayed like a belly dancer and snapped her fingers over her head. Her dress bulged in all the right spots, and there was a body inside straining so hard to get out he could hear it groaning. "It's going to be at our lake house and you two are invited. Listen," she said and put her arms around their shoulders, pulling them into a huddle. "This is going to be a party to remember. We're going to party till we can't. One night? Oh, darling, we won't even get started. And booze? All your little bodies can hold."

His stomach had been filled with helium, and a little mouse darted around his groin, stepping on all the right spots. He was close to giggling uncontrollably. Every morning should start with a face-to-face huddle with two girls. His nose touched Beth's and his cheek pressed against Amy's. He could smell cherry Life Saver on Beth's breath. He could smell perfume, he could smell makeup and powder, he could smell an orgy. He tried to pull them a little closer together so he could suck Beth's red tongue right out of her mouth, but Amy jerked away and threw his arm from her shoulders as though it were a boa constrictor. What was wrong with her, he wondered. Every red-blooded American youth dreamed of orgies. But she didn't look happy at all.

Beth continued with the details of the party, and he visualized a conflagration of desire that would make Sodom and Gomorrah seem like Jerusalem and Mecca. Beth was giving him a titillating hint of things to come and he thought: all dreams come true.

"Think you can make it?" she asked.

Amy stood, jaws jammed shut, but he said, "Are you kidding?"

"All you got to bring are your bodies," Beth said. Then she looked at Amy but grabbed a handful of his shirt. "If you bring his, you gotta share."

With that admonition and a sly look at him, Beth walked off, leaving him with a wrinkled shirt and stupid grin.

Amy looked at him and he couldn't tell what she was going to do. First he thought she might cry; then she seemed ready to spit on him. And suddenly he realized—Amy was jealous. He couldn't believe it and never would have expected it. He'd been the center of a battle between two girls before, but only two girls nobody wanted fighting over him. One had a mustache that was envied by every fourteen-year-old boy in school, and the other reportedly spent her nights making imaginative uses of weiners and bananas. But Beth and Amy?

Amy passed through several emotions and landed on anger. "You make me sick."

He uttered a silent prayer that she wouldn't figure out why he was holding his notebook right in front of his crotch, and about the time the prayer fluttered through his mind, Amy's eyes fell. He might as well have been naked with nothing to conceal him but a price tag. She gave him a look of hate, slammed her locker shut, and then, with an almost incidental attitude, she swung her fist downward viciously and swiftly and hit him right on the notebook. An animal cry squeaked from his mouth and his eyes crossed. Amy's image went hazy, unfocused, and he feared passing out for a moment. He thought he'd been uncocked, the thing knocked out by its roots. It hurt. Oh, it hurt.

"Amy," he moaned as she walked off.

He looked around his feet, checking for the flesh and blood and nerves he'd been relieved of. Dang, she had hit him hard.

He was surprised at lunch to see her waiting for him in her new car. He'd expected her to leave him stranded, but there she was in that beautiful black Firebird, looking like something out of a shiny brochure. If she'd been wearing a white dress, if the scene had been that of a rain-slicked street at night, she would have been the perfect model in the ad. But he could tell as he got in that she was still hostile. He commented on the beauty of the car and then wondered aloud if the white upholstery would be difficult to keep clean.

"If you don't like it," she said, "get your own."

He knew they weren't going to the farm. Amy wasn't overly forgiving to begin with. But his entire being was screaming through the air toward the fulfilling fantasy of Beth's party, and it could only have been the demon of fantasy that caused him to say, "Gimme head till I'm dead."

Amy pulled away from the curb, stuck her tongue out, and made a gagging sound as though she were throwing up.

They went to eat at the Dairy Queen, and, as fate would have it, fate being only slightly more perverse than God but better-natured, he got sandwiched in line between Beth and Amy. He got the orgy feeling again, the one that made his hair stand up. Kids shouted and shoved and pounded each other on the back, and cars outside were doing doughnuts in the gravel parking lot. All the commotion gave him any number of reasons to turn as he stood in line so he could see what was going on here, over there. When he turned to his left, his hand slid smoothly, with one pronounced dip, over Beth's ass. If he turned to the right, his elbow mashed Amy's breast. When someone behind pushed, the three of them got mushed together and he had to catch his breath. An orgy hors d'oeuvre. He could snack the rest of his life.

Beth turned to face Amy and himself, looked Amy over, and said, "I love that blouse. Are those buttons pearl?" And Amy said, "No, it's just a blouse I found on sale." They chatted about their clothes as though they were old friends at a reunion, and the entire time, Amy was grasping a chunk of his upper arm, just inside the triceps. She pinched the crap out of him. He wiggled his arm, begged with his eyes, tried to move away, and

Amy just looked at him very openly and innocently while her fingernails drove toward the bone.

They moved toward the counter slowly, and Beth, unaware that he was being tortured, propped herself against him, resting her forearm on his shoulder and bringing her breast into contact with his arm. Her wrist was two inches from his nose.

"You know," she said, "I think it's rotten we don't get a senior trip. We're the first class not to."

Last year's senior trip to a dude ranch near San Antonio had been marred by the arrest of two students for possession of drugs. They'd been caught while galloping down the median of an interstate, shooting cap guns at passing cars. The school board had banned all overnight trips so this year's senior class was getting only a one-day trip to the lake.

Every time Beth spoke, her hand gestured to emphasize her words, and every time his eyes followed the movement of her hand, Amy increased the pressure behind her fingernails. He was about to lose a cubic inch of flesh to a little girl who didn't possess the quality of mercy. Getting weak and dizzy from the pain, he excused himself and said he was going to the restroom. His arm was paralyzed.

Amy gave him a sickeningly sweet smile and asked, "Do you want me to order for you?"

He nodded and left.

In the restroom, he checked his arm and saw two half-moon imprints deep in the flesh. Any more pressure would have brought blood. He'd been bitten by dogs, cleated in football games, and lost parts of his mouth in fights, but he'd never been on the receiving end of an act more meaningful and heartless.

When he left the restroom, Amy was ordering and Beth had already taken a seat in a booth with three other girls along the windows. Amy handed him the little slip of paper torn from the order ticket and said, "Gimme head till I'm dead," then flitted off to the last empty booth.

He sat opposite her and massaged his arm. "You're about half mean, aren't you?"

She leaned forward. "Sex is all you think about."

"It isn't, either. One day last year I thought about street repairs."

"That's funny, Michael. That's really funny."

He sat watching Beth. She was the speaker before her three-person audience, animated and certain of her listeners' attention. Her hands were hypnotic, and she smiled, she frowned, she turned faint with one hand over her heart. She threw back her head and laughed. A one-girl performance, a melodrama of life and love at the Dairy Queen. While he watched, he thought about something a friend had once told him.

This friend and Beth had been camping with their families at the state park, and one night the two of them decided to sneak down to the amphitheater at midnight and drink some beer they had earlier stashed. They sat in the dark, drinking cold beer and listening to the crickets, until Beth suggested they go take a shower. This friend told him that Beth dearly loved showers. And ever since he had heard the story, he'd thought about taking a shower with Beth in a concrete stall, water dripping from her, eyes closed in deep contentment. She was dark-skinned, a child of nature, earthy and sexual. He wanted to watch water trickle through the hair on her lower back. He wanted to catch it with his tongue.

"Michael."

"What?" he asked, jerked back to dry civilization.

"If you don't quit staring at her, I'm leaving."

"I wasn't staring at her. I was thinking."

"Yeah, and I know what you're thinking about."

"Amy, you can take my word for it, you *don't* know what I'm thinking about."

Their order was ready so he got the hamburgers and Cokes. One of the cups had been overfilled and Coke was trickling down the cup. He watched the erratic trek of one brown drop and couldn't get his mind off showers. He heard water, the spray from a shower head hitting the concrete walls of the stall at the state park. He and Beth were soaping each other down, foamy hands gliding smoothly over wet flesh. Lather. So much lather. Beth was white with it. When she stepped back into the spray, he watched white streams sliding down her rubbery body.

Beth's party was going to be the high point of his life, something so magnificent that in later years he'd say, "You know, this was great, but it just couldn't match Beth's party." His father had always taught him to set goals, and this was his goal—to get Beth into the shower at the party. He'd drop the soap and when she bent over to pick it up, he'd slap her cheeks and watch them quiver like slabs of raw liver. Then he'd screw her brains out.

"Good-bye," Amy said.

She walked out before he knew what was happening. Very calmly she got into her car and left.

Within a few seconds, Beth had assessed the situation; she knew Amy was mad although she didn't know why. Sitting across the room, she gave him a tremendous smile, and then, with a look of joy, she grabbed her neck with both hands as though choking herself. Her friends laughed but he didn't understand the gesture.

He wasn't hungry, so he picked up his Coke and walked to Beth's table.

She explained: "Amy's got you on a choke collar. Try to run away and argghhhhh." She choked herself again, her tongue sticking out. Her friends cracked up. They slapped their legs and laughed like hyenas.

"Hilarious," he said. "Really hilarious."

He returned to school afoot, working up a redemptive sweat in heat that felt more of summer than spring. Humid air caught between the low clouds and earth hung over the small town, and he began to sweat immediately. He was well aware of what he had put Amy through. If they'd been sitting together and she'd engaged in a fantasy about Gary, he would have gone off like a sonic boom and archaeologists would have been finding pieces of Ashworth in remote areas of Nepal in the next century. He could have drawn a fine line—his fantasies had been ignited by a concept rather than a person—but he decided that he needed to feel like the traitor he was.

Amy had been so cool walking out, he thought. What style she had, what steel in her soul. He admired that quality in her because for years he'd been watching people demean themselves in church. They stood before the congregation and told everyone what sinners they'd been and how God had brought them to their senses through one calamity or another, which they always took as signs of God's displeasure. Their continued existence was a sign of God's grace. He disliked these moronic attempts to make sense of life because he engaged in them himself. But the people he really liked were those his father preached about—the stiff-necked. Amy could have been tied to a stake, tortured and set afire, but she wouldn't have given anything other than the finger.

He skipped track so he could apologize to her. They sat in her car on the street beside the school, in the shade of a tree, and watched a rain shower form to the west. What he wanted to tell her was this—he was subject to fits of jealousy because he'd never thought Amy would be interesed in him for long. She was beautiful and talented and he was just a preacher's kid whose primary feature was unrestrained lust. She on the other hand didn't have to worry about his addiction to her. It was total. But he didn't tell her that because pointing out the truth could be dangerous. Possibly Amy thought he was more than he was, and he didn't need to be improving her accuracy. So he simply apologized and said that Beth was nothing but a couple of tits, that's all. And Amy seemed willing to accept the apology until he overdosed on honesty and said, "I can't help it if she gets my attention."

Amy scowled. "You don't have feet? You couldn't have moved?"

Hot dang, he thought. Why didn't she accept his sorrow, which was real, and forget about Beth? He sighed and considered the question, because Amy wanted an answer. So he conjured up an answer. He visualized the line in Dairy Queen and substituted another girl into Beth's place, some ugly broad without sexual definition, and he came up with a response. "I didn't move because it would have been rude."

Amy's eyes flashed. If he had been any closer to her, he could have been seared on one side, baked half through. Some people, he thought, don't want any answers.

"You were the one I should have moved away from," he said. "You were the one pinching the crap out of my arm."

"It saved me from having to hit you on the notebook."

He gave a short airy gasp. Amy saw the pinch as a preventive measure. Thank God the drug industry had never marketed Compound P, a remedy for bothersome erections, as they had Compound W. Michael Page found himself looking into the face of his father's daughter, a female Benito, a fascist who would deprive him of his tools if she found him asleep. She could do the deed cleanly, quickly, joyously, in the name of prevention.

"You're as bad as my father," he said.

"I don't know what you're talking about."

"I do."

He got out of the car and slammed the door so hard the car rocked. And Amy wasted no time in leaving. She cranked the

77

engine and in the same motion dropped the car into gear, flooring the accelerator. He turned his back on the car as she squealed off because her tires blasted gravel all over him.

Watching her go, he saw her back lights flash red as she slowed, but didn't stop, at the blinking light at the highway. He wondered, what are you, Page? A man of high principles or just a common sort of fool? You overreacted just like your father would have.

Amy drove, thinking that nothing was working. Nothing. She was in a band that didn't even have a name, and the other night they had sat around in the garage at Andy's house, Andy the bass player, brainstorming and trying to come up with a name, and no one had even bothered being serious. Amy and the Enemas. Four Niggers in a Chevette. The Sex Potatoes. BB (for belly button) Lint. Auntie Amy and the Munchkins.

And now Michael was acting just like her mother. They both went wandering off in search of sex. Her mother had never been happy servicing only one man, so she'd set off like a mechanic in search of cars that needed grease jobs. No matter what her mother said, people didn't leave their families for any other reason, just like boyfriends didn't desert girlfriends until they saw big floppy boobs.

Amy looked at herself in the rearview mirror and said, if you don't quit crying, you're a bow-legged whore.

8

Brother Page had, he was certain, stepped into the sinful relationship of Michael and Amy just in time. Judging from recent reports, he decided that not only was Amy waltzing with the devil, but Michael had cut in. Ima Inez had come to the church study, dropped her purse on his desk with the usual clank—

more than once Brother Page had tried to peek into the great purse to see what burdensome treasures it contained —and offered her solutions to the problems of the church, the world, life itself. All of these monologues were merely a prelude to the real story—Michael and Amy had stood in an upstairs window of the Hardin house and exposed themselves to passing cars. This was a mild variation; the other stories had Michael tying up Amy and tickling her with a feather, and the two of them prancing around naked trying to call down evil spirits.

The preacher had learned over the years that many times rumors could be distilled to a common element or two, and of the latest batch of stories, they all contained two naked bodies and the Hardin house. Brother Page rode around the Hardin house a few times, not as concerned about the location of any particular window as he was with the location of nearby spies. And Lottie Swenson seemed to have the best view of the back of the Hardin house.

He paid a visit to the town's most vigilant pair of eyes and found her at her post in a rocking chair at the front window. Her enormous binoculars, obviously of military quality, rested on a small table that seemed to have been custom-made for its lone function. Lottie, unlike Ima Inez, thought preludes were a waste of time. Ever since she'd unintentionally witnessed an auto accident, the facts of which had been disputed by the parties involved, and she had been called upon to testify, she had seen her mission in life as that of a witness.

"That boy of yours is growing up, Preacher. I didn't see as much of him as the Hardin girl—and there weren't much of her I *didn't* see—but I can tell you this: they weren't playing pattycake."

Brother Page sat, thinking that visiting Lottie was preferable to calling upon some of her sisters because she required no pretense that the preacher was visiting for any reason other than to hear her sordid stories; on the other hand, the joy with which she made her revelations was always slightly painful for him.

"That window right yonder, that was the one. It was wide open even though it'd been raining buckets. I was thinking I might ought to call them and tell them they had a window open, when I seen the little Hardin girl just adancing like this." Lottie got up and, displaying a real sprightliness for an elderly lady, engaged in a sensual dance, pulling her skirts into a swirling motion that showed her stockings had been rolled just above her knees. She described the dance in a reverent tone. "I never seen anything like it since what's her name—Rita Hayworth —did that dance that cost St. John his head. That little girl's got some moves. And then, I don't know where he came from because I hadn't seen your boy until that very second, but he showed up and then that girl lost her dress like that." Lottie snapped her fingers and said, "The next thing I knowed, the girl was naked as the day she was born. She weren't wearing a thing but what God gave her, which for a little girl like her, was quite a bit. Then, as I sat there, I watched your boy disappear clean out of sight." Lottie held her hands over her head and slowly collapsed onto the floor. She got up and shook her finger at Brother Page. "But now, the girl, she didn't move. Well, she may have given it this with her shoulders, but what I mean is—she didn't change positions. I don't know what your boy was doing, Preacher, but I don't think he was fitting her for a dress, no more than she likes clothes."

Brother Page was feeling more and more demoralized when he had a thought that was enough to put him out of commission for good. "You said this was right after that storm the other morning."

"Shoot, I got the time written down." Lottie walked to her

chair and sat with a sigh, as if her demonstration had exhausted her, and picked a pad off the floor. She turned back a few pages and then looked through the bottom of her bifocals. "It was 10:37 A.M. Saturday morning when they both disappeared. I can hardly read my time because I wrote it real quicklike. I didn't want to miss anything if they showed back up. But it was 10:37. Yep."

Brother Page's shoulders sagged. If Michael had been in Amy's room on Saturday morning, he had ignored his father's edict that he stop seeing her. Brother Page shook his head.

"I wish Ted Mack still had his show on the TV," Lottie said. "I'd call him up and tell him about this girl. I've heard her sing, but I didn't know she could dance like that. Shoot, she could be a star, that girl could."

Brother Page rose to leave, thanking Lottie for her information although he didn't feel a bit grateful, and had trouble moving his feet. They were weighted, heavy, and he was tired.

"Listen, Preacher, if you see the Hardin girl, ask her what she was dancing to. I'd like to get the record." She giggled. "I would say ask your boy, but he probably don't recall the music."

Brother Page drove home thinking he should have been born in Boston so he could be a Catholic priest. No wife, no children, nothing but the good Lord to think about. He now had an additional problem—the propriety of a boy going from a forbidden rendezvous with a naked would-be Rita Hayworth to the pulpit of First Baptist Church. Brother Page may have grievously erred in ordering the second sermon. It was an unorthodox way of forcing his son to consider faith, but then, none of the orthodox methods had worked.

The one thing he knew for certain was that Michael was going to be grounded for some time. If he wouldn't voluntarily follow his father's orders, then the father would provide assistance. He would also provide a short prayer that Amy Hardin wasn't already pregnant. Any child born of that union would find his way into the history books under the section, "Revolutionary Leaders of the Twenty-first Century."

Mrs. Page's vision of heaven was this: a great dining hall where soothing music was softly piped in, where the tables were covered with white linen cloths and set with fine china and silver, and where every heavenly diner had a slightly humorous and very charming story to tell. This would mean of course that no men had been allowed in this particular part of heaven. She didn't disagree with the grounding of Michael, but she didn't understand why all the family upheavals had to occur at the dinner table.

Ten minutes after the grounding order had been issued, along with a request that Mrs. Page pass the liver and onions, Michael appealed to his mother. She coudn't very well tell him that she had already tried to reason with a slightly crazed husband who had been mumbling about Eli and revolutionaries and the "greatest mistake of all—not naming the boy Samuel," because she didn't want to tell him how disappointed she'd been to discover why father was clipping son's wings. How could a mother tell a son, "When I heard about what you'd been doing, I threw up all over the bathroom?" What had ever happened to holding hands?

Michael got a look in his eye that Mrs. Page had seen there before. She'd seen it right before he'd gone to the Ag Barn and beat up Billy, although she hadn't at the time understood exactly what the look portended, and she hadn't understood this time until Michael appeared the next day after school with a book on ESP.

He said, "I'm going to learn how to take out-of-body trips," and then locked himself into his bedroom.

Mrs. Page had never really known if a lock on Michael's bedroom door was appropriate, but he hadn't consulted with anyone before installing it a few years ago, and to date neither parent had found a good reason to demand its removal. But the very mention of out-of-body trips smelled a little sulfurous, evil, and Mrs. Page hoped Michael was only trying to demonstrate to his parents that when he was grounded, he had nowhere to turn but to the devil for entertainment. Surely he wasn't serious.

On the second day of the grounding, Michael told his mother, "Listen, the worst thing you can do to a person while his spirit is out of his body is to disturb his body. I may be sailing up in the sky somewhere, and if you knock on the door or call me, the jolt is terrible. I'm jerked back much too quick if my body is disturbed. So don't bother me."

Mrs. Page nodded agreeably and smiled and watched Michael lock himself into his bedroom. She wasn't overly concerned until she was standing at the sink peeling potatoes for supper and saw, through the window in front of her, Michael's spirit dart around the edge of the church and disappear. Help me, dear God, she thought and ran to his door, expecting to see sulfuric vapors oozing from beneath the door, to hear foreign tongues, to see the devil himself.

She beat on the door and screamed, "Michael, Michael." She tried to open the door but it was securely locked. Thinking the only method by which she could enter his room was through one of the windows, she ran outside. The first window she tried opened easily. Where's the screen? she wondered. The screen was standing against the house, just around the corner. And Michael's bedroom was empty. No body, no devil, no evil odors. She was so relieved to know she'd been merely tricked that she started laughing. Only Michael Page could make his mother think she'd seen a spirit.

She was going to have a talk with the boy. And she would

have told her husband about the spirit she'd seen, because he was in need of a good laugh, but he wouldn't see the humor.

9

Michael hadn't expected his ESP ruse to work forever, but he had hoped for more than two days. Amy had forgiven him for his accusations concerning fascism, and had presented him with a small blue piece of paper upon which she had written a poem. Smelling of Rolaids and looking haggard, she had made him promise not to read the note until she was in class.

The note had been a poem:

> I am an apple on a golden branch.
> Measure me with your fingers.
> Pick me.
> Put your lips on my skin.
> Taste my sorrow.

They made up at the farm. And after Amy picked him up two blocks from the house, for a second trip to the farm, he had returned home and was sitting on the bed, with the window closed and the screen reattached, when the door of his closet opened on its own.

A ghost, a *ghost* had appeared. His heart took one great twisting leap and started beating in his neck.

Luckily for him, his mother wasn't mean enough to scare someone beyond his capacity for fright and let him know it was her by asking, "So you want to commune with the spirits, huh?" She removed her sheet, laughing, and said now he knew what a good scare was and he should stop that foolishness. In return she'd retire her sheet.

When his heart had returned to its proper position and rhythm, his mother sat with him on the bed and said they needed to talk.

She kept asking, "What ever happened to holding hands?" And he assumed the question was rhetorical because he didn't know how to tell her hand-holding was still in vogue. He and Amy held hands all the time. But he understood what she meant. She meant, "What ever happened to holding hands?" in the same way he meant, "What ever happened to answered prayer?" Restraint and faith were usually misinterpreted. But Mrs. Page was worried that her son was going to become a premature father, and all her son could tell her was, "You don't have to worry about it." He started to be more specific and tell her Amy was on the pill, but Amy had taught him that people didn't always want actual answers.

Even though he couldn't quite comprehend anyone ever falling in love with his father, he asked, "Don't you remember how it was to be in love?"

She raised her hand as if to slap him and said, "What do you mean, was?"

"Then you know how it feels to have your life centered around another person. If Amy disappears, then I disappear. I can't just say, 'Well, since Amy isn't around, I'll be my old self,' because I don't even have a self without her. Being in love is like transferring your life to another person because when that person isn't around, you don't have any life. She has it. And she's the only one who can give it back." He smiled. "It only sounds strange when I think about it."

They sat for a while without talking, both of them smiling. And, thinking about Amy, who was only thirty minutes and one bad scare in his past, he fully expected his mother to say, "Oh, what the heck. Forget you were ever grounded." But she didn't say anything. She got up, unlocked the door, and left.

* * *

The grounding remained in effect, the meetings with Amy confined to school, so he had plenty of time to contemplate his sermon scheduled for Sunday. He started preparing for what was definitely going to be his last message from the pulpit. This was going to be a lawyerly smooth presentation, an uninvolved, unemotional speech.

While he sat in church Wednesday night and Brother Page asked for prayer requests, he flipped through his Bible and located Hebrews eleven, already distracted. How was he going to preach on faith when he didn't even understand why his father was soliciting prayer requests?

How many times had the church prayed for a sick person (including his own grandfather), only to watch the subject of the prayers die? He had heard an answer for that problem. If the sick person died after the church had requested healing, then the explanation was that the prayer had indeed been answered. The sick person had undergone "perfect healing" and now lived in heaven, suffering no more. And if the sick person recovered, then God had answered that prayer too.

It was easy for him to understand why Jesus' most famous illustration concerning faith centered around the tiny mustard seed. Anyone with faith the size of a canteloupe would develop a psychosis the size of a watermelon.

Hebrews eleven mentioned a number of the faithful—Noah, Abraham, Moses, Joshua, Sarah, and others. How could he understand these people and preach about them when he had had no similar experiences? Worse, some of the examples were not worth following, especially that of Abraham. Was he to believe a father's willingness to murder his own son was an act of faith? He had always assumed Abraham was either hallucinating or the victim of a practical joke. The voice of God, the one Abraham heard directing him to Moriah for a child sacrifice, had probably belonged to one of Isaac's enemies, some little kid with a big grudge and a handkerchief over his mouth.

He, Michael Page, was to translate this chapter into guidelines for life in the twentieth century. Right.

Sunday was a peculiar day. As he stood in the pulpit for his second sermon, looking out over the congregation, he suddenly became a preacher. Billy Graham, maybe, or his father, he didn't know, but he started *preaching*. With authority. He held his Bible open and shook it. He didn't understand what happened and couldn't account for it later, because his preparation had been careful but certainly not inspired. He had planned to speak, without laughing, for thirty minutes. But once he was there, he was transformed into the man of faith he proposed to the church. For thirty minutes, he believed every word he said.

"Abraham never questioned God, never asked, 'Well, are you sure about this? Have you thought it through, God? Let's talk about it.' Men of faith don't question, they act.

"Now look at this. Isaac was the son God had promised to Sarah. The child was a miracle, born to a woman ninety years old. And he was the son God had promised to continue the covenant through. So if anybody has ever had reason to question God, Abraham did. But he did a very simple thing, a thing as simple as it was difficult—he followed God's leading."

He preached. He told the congregation that Abraham's love for God was so great that he was willing to prove it in the most extreme way. He was ready to go to the wall because his trust was total and unlimited. How often had they wondered about another person's love? Had they ever asked someone they loved to perform an act so significant that they forever would know that the person loved them totally? How many wives had asked their husbands to give up cigarettes and stick around into old age? (A few accusing glances in the congregation.) How many husbands had asked their wives to forego remodeling in favor of a bass boat? (Accusing glances returned.) How many of them could even conceive an action on the level of Abraham's?

Of course God hadn't required the sacrifice of Isaac. The story wouldn't have made sense if God had done so. Then Abraham would have been worthy, but the object of his love wouldn't have. But didn't Abraham make them all seem foolish with their petty doubts and questions? Didn't his example make them see their lack of trust and faith?

After the sermon, he was engulfed by a crowd of hand-shaking, shoulder-slapping church members who thought he sounded just like his father, who thought he'd been filled with the Holy Spirit, who believed that he could be a great preacher. Amy took his hand and said, "I'm so proud of you, Michael." And his father was so overcome with emotion that all he could do was hug him. Once started, he couldn't stop.

No one knew how confused he was. Did he believe his own sermon or not? Suddenly he didn't know. Maybe he had never known. But he had the feeling that he was standing on the verge of a momentous event. After begging God to speak for years, to provide him with a sign, to confirm he hadn't disappeared, after losing all faith and becoming a regular infidel, after finally finding Amy and the pleasures of the flesh and the pleasures of the spirit outside religion and having the prospect of a life away from his father and the church, he was finally going to hear God speak. Because that was when you heard God—when you no longer wanted to. That was why the surface of the earth was covered with water that couldn't be drunk, why there were more flies than flyswatters and more feet than shoes, why God told Abraham to kill and not to honor his miraculous son, why his own shy and insecure father had been called to preach. *Everything worked in reverse.* That's why evangelists had been heroin addicts and criminals and winos.

And since everything worked in reverse, the only people capable of faith were infidels.

Now he, Michael, lover of the flesh, would be called to preach. The first words he would hear from God wouldn't be, "Here I am, my son. I'm here, with you through all time." No, the first words would be, "Go now to the seminary and take this chubby little girl for your wife. She shall press the curl out of her hair, refrain from French kissing, and will know you carnally only because it is her wifely duty. She shall recite scripture while doing so, so she won't engage in demonic displays of human lust." He would spend his life telling people they were bound for the pits of hell because they were rational. He'd be nuts within a year, trying to determine if people were dying because of God's will, perfect healing, divine error, or simple coincidence.

Things changed with blinding speed.

But what bothered him most was this—in the crowd of people who had congratulated him for his sermon and who must have assumed he was on his way to the seminary to find his chubby little girlfriend had been Amy Hardin. Amy, a socialite Baptist. She must have known all along that he was going to be a preacher, but she'd never said a word.

He sat at the table eating roast, trying to swallow food that kept lodging on one great question—had Amy known what the victim hadn't? Suddenly he had to know, had to find out, because his life depended on it. At the moment, nothing else mattered.

He dabbed at his mouth with a napkin and said, "I've seen the error of my ways. I need a few hours to pray by myself."

His father nodded, smiling, and he wasn't sure what his mother's response was. He wasn't about to look at her.

Into the bedroom, lock the door, out the window into a warm

spring day. He went into a running crawl outside, headed for the cover of the church building. He breathed a bit easier once he was moving unmolested in the shade beside the great brick building, but when he arrived at the front, beside the steps that went up into the auditorium, he met the chairman of the deacons, an hour early for deacons' meeting.

"How are you, Brother Pierce?" he said and kept walking.

Of course Brother Pierce called him back. The man had an hour to kill.

"Did you see me poke Doris during your sermon? I tried not to laugh, but I want to tell you, I've been after her for years to give up the soaps. I'm talking *years*. I get so tired of hearing these women talk about. . . ."

He stood shifting his feet and wanting to run, because any minute his father could round the far corner of the church. How was he going to explain his presence here? Well, you see, Pop, I was praying and fell asleep and just rolled right out the window. I guess I'd still be going if Brother Pierce hadn't stuck his foot out and stopped me.

"And she said, 'Harlan, soaps ain't a bit worse than playing Forty-two every night of the week, now is it? So you give up Forty-two, and I'll think about giving up the soaps.'"

Brother Pierce nodded and talked and smiled as Michael inched toward the street. And Brother Pierce followed because he wasn't through talking. Michael had to think of a reason to leave. But they had moved into the middle of the street that passed before the church, and Brother Pierce had switched to his grandkids. Michael knew without a doubt that in ten seconds his father was going to appear.

"Brother Pierce, I hate to leave you like this but the coach told me to run between twelve and one today and I think that's him coming in that blue pickup. He'll kill me if he sees me standing here. See you later."

"No, Michael, that ain't the coach. That's just Wister Lewis in that pickup."

He was gone. Amy's house was only four blocks away, but he couldn't take a direct route. The direct route passed in front of Ima Inez's house and would place him in full view of Lottie's binoculars. So he cut down an alley, hid in shrubs to avoid another of the deacons headed for church, and snuck between two houses. He approached Amy's directly from the front, placing the house between him and Lottie.

He was panting when Amy opened the door. She smiled and stepped backward, allowing him to enter, and he asked the question before anything could prevent him from doing so.

"What'd you mean this morning when you said you were proud of me?"

Wearing cutoffs and a T-shirt, Amy looked at him closely, squinting, as if she might diagnose his condition.

"Hurry and tell me."

Amy gave a nervous laugh and sat on the couch. "All I meant was that I was proud of you." She shrugged.

"But *why* were you proud of me?"

"Because you did such a good job."

This task was tougher than he had expected. He couldn't ask directly if she expected him to heed a call to preach; doing so might plant the idea.

"I always thought you were a good speaker, and this morning you did a really good job."

Progress. Blessed be the progress.

"You were very persuasive."

Praise the Lord.

"I was impressed."

Amen. Thank you, Jesus. Still, he had a great sigh held in reserve, waiting to be expelled, and Amy wasn't being specific enough. Amy believed she was through explaining, and now he would have to ask straight out.

"Amy, have you ever thought I was going to be a preacher?"

Amy snorted, her mouth closed, and then laughed. She fell onto the couch and pounded one cushion with her hand. "You? A preacher?"

He fell onto his knees and grabbed a waving foot, kissing her toes. Ah, he was so happy, so happy. There was only one thing to do, just to be safe. In all his years of listening to sermons and testimonies, he had never once heard a person say that God had called him to preach while he was engaged in fornication. God could speak out of the flame heating a spoon of heroin, from the base of a wine bottle, or from the bullet in a gun, but he apparently maintained silence during illicit sex. Fornication was like base in a game of tag. You were safe.

Since Amy was home alone, he led her upstairs, and once in her room, crawled along the floor to close all the curtains. Then he went crazy. He was overcome with lust and fear and dread and love, and he wanted Amy to be his mother and lover and friend all at once. He wasn't sure what he was doing but soon the bed had been stripped of its covers. His feet and hands just wouldn't stay still.

It was only afterward when he was breathing as though he had actually run the imaginary hour supposedly required by the coach that he could ask, "Amy, I didn't hurt you, did I? I didn't mean to."

She pulled his head onto her bare breasts and said, "No, you didn't hurt me."

For the next week, they spent their lunch hour at the farm without even kissing. He talked. He couldn't remember ever feeling as emotionally weak, as reclusively reticent. He wanted to set up housekeeping in his grandfather's deteriorating house and live the rest of his days with Amy, without ever leaving. And when she was out of his sight, he grew nervous, anxious over her return. And for once in his life, he had to tell another person about his problems with religion.

"I'm telling you, Amy, it was like sitting in a room with another person. You see him take a breath and turn his head toward you, and you know, you just know, he's about to say something to you. Well, I heard God take a breath, and I knew I was about to hear something."

And he had run, had purposely deafened himself. Amy wasn't a biblical scholar, so she didn't understand why he should be worried. She hadn't studied numerous characters in the Old Testament who had been hideously punished for some supposed offense. She didn't believe that God had sent a plague that killed 70,000 people just because David took a census, didn't believe that God's bloody hands knew no restraint.

He offered her example after example and her response was, "Oh, you don't believe that, do you? Or do you?"

"Amy, some part of me does. I can read that God threatened to kill Moses for forgetting to circumcise his son, and I can say, 'Oh, Page, you don't have to believe that.' But Amy, when you're told over and over and over from the day your father thinks you're capable of listening that everything in the Bible is true —everything—then you don't just suddenly decide you don't believe it. Because there's some part of you that does believe it. It's the same part that used to tell me there was a monster in my bedroom doorway when I was five. I didn't believe that voice either. I'd say, 'There's no such thing as a monster.' And the voice would tell me, 'The hell there ain't. You better start screaming while you can.'"

Brother Page would have been proud of him, he thought. Every day he was studying the Bible and instructing Amy. And talking to her seemed to relieve the terrible burden that had descended onto him. Besides, he'd lived for almost a week without being transformed into a leper or causing a plague, and the sky was still blue, without cracks or freakish lightning.

In fact, he was feeling better and better. He was just about ready for Senior Day at the lake.

10

Senior Day was faithfully attended by forty-one students, many of whom felt cheated over having been deprived of an overnight trip by some overzealous policemen and an overly strict school board, which had banned overnight trips following last year's drug bust. The four teachers who were sponsors for the event this year were sympathetic to the students' feeling of deprivation and had arrived early at the lake to help make the day a memorable one. They had erected a gaily striped canopy on the small beach to protect the students from the sun and had built a small bonfire even though the county had prohibited fires from being built anywhere but within the iron pits already provided. The teachers had even chipped in to buy extra Cokes, which they had iced down in washtubs. The teachers thought they were ready for the students.

The first car on the scene hit a stump, throwing two boys riding on the hood into a creek bed, where they became stuck in the mud. The second car drove beneath, and pulled down, the canopy the teachers had erected, and the third car drove down a boat ramp and into the lake. Within a matter of minutes, the small beach was pervaded with the sound of laughter, profane greetings, and generalized racket, and the sight of open containers of liquor or beer was as common as that of hand-rolled cigarettes. One group of students arrived by water on a deck boat under the command of Beth, who was wearing a purple bikini.

The four teachers conferred and recognized too late that they should have put the students on a bus, after thorough body searches, and taken them to a previously undisclosed location. Now, however, the teachers lacked alternatives. They couldn't suggest the senior class be expelled *in toto*, and they couldn't control students who were already drunk and/or stoned. So they made a pact that their version of the event would be a fun day at the lake with wonderful, well-behaved children who loved splashing and playing in the sand. Any word to the contrary would simply be the result of a malicious rumormonger. That decided, they took account of what was going on around them.

The student who specialized in the manufacture, and release, of chlorine gas in the chemistry lab had produced a water pistol filled with gasoline and was sitting on a picnic table shooting flaming arcs into the bonfire.

The history teacher thought he was being mooned by a student in the back seat of a car, only to find upon investigating that two students, one of each sex, were engaged in sexual intercourse. The teacher interrupted them because the boy was on top and the teacher couldn't get a good look at the girl's breasts. The boy ordered the teacher away from the car and threatened to sue him for invasion of privacy, and the teacher, who was after all a sponsor, said, "So sue me, you little creep."

The home economics teacher, a pretty young lady in her first year of teaching, was propositioned by the dumbest senior in school, who, she found out, was older than she was. He came to the proposition circuitously by telling her that he had an enormous "dong, which I call Pal," and he'd be mighty pleased to let her have a look if she cared to step behind a tree.

Michael had ridden with Amy and arrived in high spirits,

partly because he had already drunk the better part of a six-pack, partly because his father had neglected to include in the sentence of grounding any school activity that transpired during the day. He had worn his swimming trunks beneath his school clothes, which he'd stripped away and thrown in Amy's back seat. He thought Amy looked wonderful in a one-piece bathing suit with orange and red and green and yellow stripes. Her body inside could have been compressed plastic, perfectly formed. Overall, she couldn't have been improved upon.

Amy had drunk one of his beers but didn't think she needed any help getting excited. She'd heard the night before that Andy, the bass player, had got the band's first gig, a birthday party at the Halton Country Club. They were not only going to perform but they would be paid as well. And Amy, who hadn't slept at all, was still sailing strongly with the wind, feeling she was what she had always wanted to be—a singer. Every few minutes, she grabbed Michael by the arm and said, "Hey. Don't forget you're with a singer." Michael wanted to stand on a car and announce to the sprawling, inebriated class that Amy's band had their first gig lined up, but she thought that might be considered engaging in excess, a sure hex, and asked him to keep the news to himself.

She wore a white sheath that Michael kept suggesting she remove, and she was leaning against a car, engaging in, behind her sunglasses, a short fantasy, one in which she was singing. He brought her back to reality by tugging on her hand.

"You want to take a ride in the boat?"

"What boat?"

"Beth's."

The name hurt her ears, and the sight of Beth, showing excessive flesh, hurt her eyes. But Amy didn't want to poop Michael's party spirit, so she agreed. The day was clear and warm, the sky endlessly blue, just right for speeding across the lake on Beth's boat. Of course, Beth decided to make the trip in circles so the boat could bounce over its own wake and splash all the passengers. Well, Amy didn't care if she got her hair wet. No matter what Beth did, she couldn't affect Amy's band.

Amy took Michael's hand and held it in her lap because Beth kept looking back to make sure Amy's hair was getting sprayed, and she could see Michael was looking at her great hairy body. Michael, however, seemed to be cold, wiggling around and clearing his throat as though he wished he were out of the wind.

"Are you cold?" she asked, watching his hair blow, the water splashing as the boat bounced.

"Umm, yeah."

"We can leave in a little while and I'll make you warm."

"I wish we could go right now."

He was having trouble concealing, with only one arm, a condition in his swimming trunks that would earn him the death sentence when Amy realized what was happening. Beth kept looking back at them, and every time she did, she swiveled to her right, her left arm rising as she gripped the wheel of the boat, and the purple cup of the bikini top opened like a flower over her left breast. With another quarter-inch clearance, he could see her nipple. And he was trying his best not to look, but he felt like a birdwatcher who'd spent a lifetime tracking the brown-crested shuttlecock and had finally located one hiding in its nest, and although his spirit was willing not to look, his body wasn't. So he had developed an erection which he had only one arm to cover, the other arm being in the custody of Amy.

She squeezed his hand and whispered, above the wind, into his ear, "I'm going to sing, Michael. Can you believe it?"

He wanted to sit up straight and respond with equal enthusiasm, but he couldn't. So he nodded and smiled, reclaimed his hand from Amy, and said, "I think I'm getting seasick." He leaned forward.

Into the corner of his eye crept another sight—Beth's lower back. The black hair just above the bottom of her bikini made a ducktail, and he wondered how it would feel to move the hair around with his finger, sweeping it this way and that, brushing it backward and making it stand. He dropped his head onto his arms, which rested on his knees, and closed his eyes. Amy, his kind and considerate friend, knelt beside him, her forearm lying lengthwise on his thigh.

"Are you going to get sick?" she asked.

At exactly the wrong moment, Beth abruptly cut the throttle, throwing the passengers slightly forward, and Amy's elbow discovered his secret.

"You're not sick at all," she said, and with the sudden reduction in power, her voice was no longer competing with the wind.

"Is Page sick?" someone asked from the bow.

"You poor baby," Beth said.

Michael looked up. "I'm not sick."

Amy saw, in the elongated lump trying to rise in Michael's bright blue swimming trunks, the source of all problems. She picked up a fishing rod lying against the side of the boat, and with the cork-covered handle tried to kill the troublesome reptile. Swat, swat, swat. Michael stood, trying to push Amy away with one hand, and leapt out of the boat.

Michael had bobbed to the surface when he saw, through water-blurred eyes, a body flying toward him. Beth missed his head by only a few inches and clawed his shoulder as she tried to drag him under. And then he was under full attack by a girl determined to drown him. She kicked and scratched and attempted to climb on top of him, her foot gouging his ear in an effort to gain a toehold. Without considering what he was doing, he sighted through the murky, bubbling water the purple top of Beth's bikini, grabbed it, and jerked. The top came away in his hand. He surfaced and threw it into the boat.

Relieved of her top, Beth quit fighting and started splashing. Her hair matted to her skull, she appeared radiantly happy and pushed water at him. The movement brought her out of the water and her buoyant breasts into view, and there before him was what he had wanted to see a few minutes earlier. Two nipples. Nipples that had wrinkled in the cold water and were as ugly as pigs' snouts. Full of tiny crevices, they were esthetically appalling.

Somehow they reminded him of reality. They reminded him of all the parties he'd gone to, thinking he was going to get wildly drunk and have a time to remember, when he'd ended up on a bathroom floor, barely able to pull himself up to toilet height so he could vomit on something besides himself. Within a matter of seconds, as he was treading water and watching the boat bob in the lake, he had lost every ounce of alcohol that had buzzed him through the day.

Suddenly everyone who had been in the boat was shucking swimwear and leaping into the lake. Plomp. Plomp plomp plomp. Everyone except Amy, whom he couldn't see. The lake teemed with skinnydippers.

Amy was in the boat receiving a revelation. The answer to all her problems was unbelievably simple—celibacy. Since she had always known that Michael wouldn't work out to anything, she no longer had to worry. She was free. There would be no more sidestepping distractions, no backwashing complications in her life, and she would become single-mindedly ambitious again.

She was the cat all the way back to the shore, sitting with its tail wrapped around its legs, the translucent green eyes unblinking. Even when Beth ran the boat aground at the beach, trying to throw everyone out, Amy steadied herself and calmly stepped from the boat.

Word of actions afloat spread quickly, and a crowd gathered near the boat.

99

"You ain't gonna believe what Page did."

"What'd he do?"

Whispers among the crowd that seemed to converge as if on a bloody accident. Wide eyes. Shrieks. Turn and tell your neighbor.

"Beth?"

"You're kidding."

"You're lying."

"How big are they?"

Amy leaned against her car, watching without interest. Beth, wearing a gray T-shirt that had been cut short of the waist and that was wet and clinging to her breasts, walked up to Michael and handed him the top of her purple bikini, surrendering her flag as the class cheered. Michael stood swinging the top and smiling.

Never again would Amy let a boy sneak up on her and work his way into her heart. Never. Not in a hundred years, not in a thousand would she even look at that slimeball son of a . . . she took a deep breath and calmed herself, remembering she was the cat, unreadable, unreachable. She adjusted her sunglasses.

The cat watched Michael wander off in search of a drink. When he turned his back, the cat hissed.

11

Brother Page was confused. Here was Ima Inez standing in front of his desk in the church study, assuring him she wasn't one to gossip, but she'd heard that Michael had gotten a teeny bit tipsy at the lake and stripped the pretty little Home Ec teacher of her clothes. "I also heard he was in the boat with Sandpaper Simpson's daughter and they were so drunk they wrecked the boat. Just ran it right up on the land like it was some kinda car, and they was both passed out and naked as the day they was borned." The preacher slowly rubbed both eyebrows. If he'd been keeping track of the calls and visits, he would have worn out several pencils. What he couldn't understand was this—he had talked to all four sponsors and all four had assured him Michael's behavior had been exemplary. One had said, "He built the nicest little sand castle I've ever seen. You know how the county put that sandy beach over there? Those kids had the best time trying to outdo each other's castles." The entire matter was so confusing and murky that Brother Page wanted to go home and sleep.

He got rid of Ima Inez and then locked the door and removed the receiver from his telephone. From the center drawer of his desk he took his calendar and counted days again. If he was very careful, he might find he'd made a mistake thirty minutes ago when he had counted eighty-eight days until he delivered Michael to Stanton University. Instead of being able to account for his time like a good steward, he was counting days. He almost cussed when he counted, once again, eighty-eight days.

Well, he thought, that really isn't so very many. If a bricklayer was just starting his job and he laid eighty-eight bricks end to end around a new foundation, he probably wouldn't get around two sides of a normal residential foundation. Eighty-eight days, when you looked at them, weren't many at all. In fact, a man who was eighty-eight years old had told Brother Page just the other day that his fifth birthday had seemed only yesterday. So if that many years passed like one day, then eighty-eight days would seem like the blink of an eye.

The preacher was well aware of his problem; it had also plagued the children of Israel. They had been denied entrance into the land of Canaan because of their unbelief, and Brother Page was unable to rest because of his unbelief. (Eighty-eight days was longer than a world war, was long enough to wear out ten clocks. Admit it.) He had been so concerned with his image as minister, he had attempted to do God's work himself, had tried to turn Michael around, because he had never believed that God could handle the matter of Michael as any other. (If eighty-eight glasses were stacked, one on top of the other, they'd reach the moon. If he spent one dollar every day from now until Jesus came again, he'd never be able to spend all eighty-eight dollars. Eighty-eight was more than ten million.)

He decided to take a short nap and lay down on the carpeted floor. How was it that he could dispense such sound advice to his members, yet ignore it himself? It had only been yesterday when one of the newer members, a lady from Connecticut in her thirties, had stormed into his study and demanded replacement of her Sunday school teacher. "Either that or I'll sue her for defamation of character. I'm telling you, Father, I've had it." After correcting her—he wasn't a priest (although he certainly thought again about those lucky Catholic bachelors)—he determined that her Sunday school teacher had called her an infant in front of the class.

Brother Page had gone to visit the teacher, Mary Martha Matthews, an older lady who believed her surfeit of biblical names qualified her to be named Executive Sunday School Instructor, even though the Southern Baptists had no titles. Mary Martha had indeed called "the damn Yankee, if you'll pardon my French" an infant, hoping to convince the girl of her ignorance on biblical matters because she argued with every point Mary Martha made. "She even believes in purgatory. Talk about your blasphemy, your basic pagan ignorance. I'll tell you this, Preacher, when you get to heaven, you won't hear any Yankees up there running their words together." Brother Page told Mary Martha that she couldn't change the new member, that only God could, and she should turn the matter over to the

Lord, whose love was great enough to include Yankees.

Brother Page heard his own advice (even though Mary Martha didn't. She was God's spokesperson in her class) and the words of wisdom he had offered were exactly the ones he should have been giving himself. Only God could change a person. Only God could change Michael.

He got up from the floor, put the telephone receiver back on the base, and listened to it ring immediately. When Ima Inez told him that her granddaughter's best friend had heard the Home Economics teacher whispering in the ladies' room at the café that all the reports of Senior Day were true—especially Ima Inez's reports—Brother Page said he had turned the matter over to the Lord.

"Well, why in heaven's name would he care?"

Brother Page assured her that God cared about everything and everyone, even idle gossips. And as soon as he had actually relinquished Michael into the hands of God, he was guided to a brochure in the stack of recent mail on his desk. He picked up a circular announcing an evangelistic conference in Fort Worth, which coincided with the week of high school graduation. Graduation. The word made him shiver; it conjured up more images than a Halloween night staged by the most warped minds in Hollywood. Fort Worth. An evangelism conference. Brother Page stuck the brochure in his coat pocket. It contained instructions on how to register for the rest God had promised.

Every time Michael thought he was growing somewhat adept at predicting the events of life, life surprised him. He was certain, after Senior Day, that the senior class would be punished in some way, that his father would hear so many rumors that he would finally be pushed over the brink of acceptable conduct, and that Amy would never again even glance his way.

Wrong on all counts.

The four sponsors, all apparently human and in need of regular food and drink and the money to pay for such, all refused to acknowledge that anything even slightly out of the ordinary had happened at the lake, and started trading conspiratorial grins with the students as they passed in the hall.

Brother Page's attitude toward him had changed somehow, and he started praying about his son as though the son was another person, absent from his presence. His prayers at mealtime were often long enough to outlast the steam rising from the cooling food, and now he was one of the lengthier topics. "We remember the words in Hebrews, dear Lord: 'For he that is entered into his rest, he hath also ceased from his own works, as God did from his. Let us labor, therefore, to enter unto that rest, lest any man fall after the same example of unbelief.' And so today, Lord, I am once again renewing my vow to cease from my own works and I am entrusting my son unto you. . . .'"

The prayers worried him because they seemed to carry the implicit promise that the father was going to kill the son, thereby delivering his soul into God's care. Brother Page's behavior was rational, for the most part, but most likely Isaac had harbored the same hope and thought. "Naw, the old man would never really consider sacrificing *me*. No way." Noises in the night caused him to wake up, however, and wonder who might be creeping down the hall. Was it his father, come to exorcise demons with a ten-inch butcher knife, or merely a burglar, who would kill only if forced to? He hoped for burglars, thinking their attitudes were at least comprehensible.

And Amy. He passed her in the hall the day after the events at the lake, wishing there were some way to tell her that preacher's kids were not normal and could be entitled to a more tolerant standard of judgment, should the judge be exceptionally loving. But he didn't bother. In fact, he didn't even bother greeting her because he was certain she was going to ignore his existence.

"Hello, Michael," she said.

He had taken several steps before he realized she had spoken, before he realized she was wearing the same clothes—the white blouse and rust-colored skirt—she'd been wearing on Neil Diamond day at the farm. He swallowed, trying to return his heart to his chest, and chased her down the hall, dodging bodies and catching her just before she entered the biology lab.

"Did you say hello?" he asked.

"Yes, I said hello."

He recognized something new in her tone, a formality that would have been more characteristic of an English schoolteacher addressing a child in short pants. He wasn't sure what to make of this new tone but thought if she was willing to communicate at all, even formally, he had hope.

"So. Everything still looking good for your gig at the country club?"

"Oh, yes. And we're all very excited. I would invite you, but since you aren't a member of the band or the country club, you can't come."

The Teacher rapped the schoolboy across the knees, sending him reeling backward. Aha, he thought, this is the way we treat Beth's friend. She couldn't kill the appropriate portion of him at the lake, so now she was going to spit in his eye, which by now had fixed on the lace of her bra, the shadow of which could be seen through her white blouse. He tried not to look because he loved that little butterfly pattern, had rubbed it with his nose, had kissed the floating symbol of her mystery and softness. Maybe, he thought, just maybe he was misinterpreting her tone. God knew he was an expert at misinterpretations.

"Where're you eating lunch?" he asked.

"In the cafeteria. It'll save wear and tear on my car."

"Not to mention your body."

He watched, wanting to see a reaction, and he did. The burning coals flared, then disappeared.

"Well, the bell's about to ring," she said, "and we both have class."

As she entered the room, he said, "Cheerio now."

He knew he had only one means of salvation—the CIA. If they would let him borrow an exotic, noncontagious disease germ, he could inject it and land in the hospital, just out of the reach of death's clammy fingers. Otherwise, he'd never be able to humble Amy. There was no basis for feeling the immense amount of indignation that was causing his nostrils to flare—he freely admitted he was the sole cause of his present fix—but on the other hand, what could he do? Well, he'd just go with the flow and hate her right back.

Hating her was almost as much fun as loving her. In the chemistry class they took together, the teacher asked her a question, which she correctly answered, but Michael snickered anyway. Half the class turned to look at him. He made a noise in the back of his throat that sounded like muffled laughter, and the class was certain something funny was afoot so the laughter spread, first here, then there, until an ignorant observer entering the room would have assumed a very funny joke had just been told.

Amy didn't have to look to determine the identity of her snickering enemy. She sat without expression, adding a hundred years to the last hundred years she had sworn to pass without befriending Michael. As it stood, their friendship could resume somewhere near the end of the fiftieth century.

She was more determined than ever to ignore the two great sexual offenders in her life—Michael and her mother—because two weeks after graduation, at the Halton Country

Club, part of her dream was going to come true. After the business at the lake, Amy had gone home and taken a four-hour bath, emptying the hot water heater three times, determined to wash her mind clear of all distractions, a difficult task considering one of the distractions kept beating on the bathroom door shouting, "If you don't get out of that tub, I'm calling the doctor and asking him to commit you, Amy. Do you hear me? If you don't answer, I'll call the police and tell them to break the door down."

The band had been newly inspired since getting its first gig, and now even had a name—Heat Lightning. Not a great name, but Amy had never thought of a name exactly right, and Heat Lightning was better than BB Lint. Amy didn't want to think about the lake, nor did she want to think about her mother's complaints. She wanted to hear the music she'd been hearing before the disgusting boat trip had taken place.

She was making out just fine until PE class, and right in the middle of a volleyball game Beth found out about Amy's band. Beth was about to serve, had her arm drawn back, and yelled, "Amy has a band? They can play at my party." And before Amy was certain that Beth was serious, she had agreed, sending two volleyball teams into a frenzy. Amy had agreed only because Beth's party would give the band a chance to tune up two weeks before a real gig, but when she saw the reaction of twenty other girls, who all suddenly seemed to lose their minds, throwing the volleyball at the ceiling and tearing the net down, she began to wonder about the wisdom of her decision.

Within an hour, Amy was certain she'd made the worst decision of her life. The band wasn't that good, hadn't rehearsed enough, and Beth's party was the wrong place to demonstrate their lack of readiness. She had to make a trip to her car between classes—risking the wrath of the principal—for

Rolaids, because her stomach was eating itself. She could hardly stand up straight.

All through history, she talked to Michael in her mind. "What if we're no good? What if we sound like amateurs? What if nobody listens? What if everybody does listen and laughs? What if I've just been a silly little child thinking I could sing?" She could of course go find Michael after class and ask her questions aloud. He was still her friend, or could be again, regardless of his tendency to snicker in chemistry; he was only mad at her. She hoped.

Right in the middle of the history teacher's seventh retelling of how he had personally saved General George Patton's life— he had shouted "Sniper!" because he'd seen movement in a farmhouse window to his left, the movement being caused by a rooster, the rooster attracting some soldiers from Mississippi, who abandoned their jeep in favor of a sudden desire for fried chicken, which caused the column to halt and the general to jump from his own jeep just before it was raked with machine-gun fire—Amy had to run from the classroom. She recognized the tightening of her throat and tongue that always preceded throwing up, and she just made it to the restroom before losing all her Rolaids.

She remained in the restroom until a minute before the bell rang, then vigorously washed her mouth out and chewed three pieces of gum and applied an extra heavy coat of perfume to her neck. Since vomiting, she felt much better and hoped she exuded no offensive odors.

She went to find Michael.

He was the first person she saw upon leaving the restroom, and he was in the company of Beth, who looked like a bud about to blossom in her pink dress. I don't hate her, Amy thought. I don't hate anyone, because all hate derives from sex and I am celibate. I am therefore incapable of hate.

Beth, still excited over the prospect of having live music at her party, pulled on Amy's sleeve and said, "I was just telling him your band's going to play at my party."

Michael didn't look at all happy; in fact, he looked just like someone who would snicker at everything she'd say in chemistry. So Amy took him by the arm and pulled him away from the great pink bud and said, "I need to borrow him just a minute. I'll bring him back."

She steered him down the hall toward the little alcove near the janitor's supply room, suddenly feeling supremely silly. He wasn't nervous, Beth wasn't nervous, and Amy couldn't possibly tell him she'd just thrown up in the little girl's room. She couldn't even tell him the basis of her temporary fears without sounding like a nine-year-old nitwit. So she guided him against the locked supply room door and said without giving undue consideration to her words, "Listen, Michael. I don't care what you do with Beth; I don't care what you do sexual. I just want us to be friends like we used to."

Michael went from chief of laughter in chemistry to her kind and loving friend and took her hand. He smiled. "Sounds like a good idea to me."

Well, Amy thought, that was easy enough. She said, "I feel better now."

Michael squeezed her hand. "I do too."

"I guess we should go to class?"

"Can I touch your butterfly? With one finger?"

Of course he could. She didn't know how to advise him of her new status as a celibate; touching her butterfly was no different, no more arousing, than touching her elbow. She was simply an asexual person now. Watching Michael's finger near the second button on her blouse, she thought, I have no more response to that than a bedpost would. No, not a bedpost, which was probably a phallic symbol. What about, as unresponsive as a rock? A rock was hard, full of sexual connotations. A desk then. A desk had a flat surface where she could lie down and enjoy the sensations Michael's palm was causing, vibrations that caused the very center of her body to hum.

"What's your next class?" she asked, covering his massaging hand with her own.

"History."

"All you're going to hear about is how old man Sanford saved General Patton's life."

"Maybe we should just cut the next class then."

"What do you have after that?" Amy asked, pushing Michael with her body into the corner of the alcove, pushing still when his body had stopped.

"Typing."

"You already know how to type."

"If we cut both classes, we'd have two hours," he said, his arms now around her waist.

"But only if we hurry."

12

He should have been pleased when his father left town during the week of graduation because now the old man couldn't hinder his plans, but for once, he longed for hindrance, paternal intervention. The closer graduation came, the more he thought about this fact: thinking abstractly about Amy's singing with a band and then witnessing the actual performance was probably similar to the difference in contemplating war and fighting one.

This rather distressing bit of reality began boring into his head one afternoon when the drummer in Amy's band picked her up after school. They were going to Beth's to check out electrical plugs and the general layout. He walked out of the building with Amy, and sitting at the curb was a maroon van, driven by one of the sleaziest-looking, most repulsive-acting cretins he had yet seen. He had a mohawk haircut, and the sides had grown out slightly, giving him the appearance of a person who had suffered massive half-moon ringworm. He wore gold earrings and his clothes had been partly torn from his body.

"What the hell is that?" he asked.

"Rusty," she said. "And don't ask me any more than that. I tried and tried to find another drummer, but he's a friend of Andy, the bass player, and Andy's really good. Just remember, this isn't *my* band."

Rusty got out of the van, moving like a hyperactive pigeon, trying to keep the beat of his blaring stereo, head and fingers popping and bobbing. He opened the passenger's side door with a flourish, the gesture of a doorman who was practicing to be a derelict.

"This is Michael," Amy said.

Beside the door of the van, Rusty did a little dance—best described as an upright seizure—and offered the palm of his hand. "Cut the jive and gimme five."

He ignored him and told Amy bye.

"Don't do five, you ain't alive," Rusty yelled. "You be pain, don't come a-gain."

Leaving the two of them at the van, he stepped into a disorienting sort of sickness, the kind he'd have felt if he'd seen his mother enthusiastically checking a biker's crotch for nits. Amy was voluntarily entering into an association with such a person? Amy Hardin?

Come back from Fort Worth, Pop, and enforce my grounding, he thought.

He spent the day of graduation drinking beer with friends, hoping to get sick, but by the time of the commencement exercises, all he'd developed was fatigue and a headache that roosted over his right eye. He sat with forty black-gowned seniors and listened to the local Methodist minister deliver an address in which he told the seniors that this was the first day of the rest of their lives, a profoundly depressing thought for him. He tried not to listen and got dizzy watching the tassel swing from the mortarboard atop his head.

Afterward, he drove his mother home, listening to her say that many parents took for granted their children's school attendance and eventual graduation, but she realized that he still had to possess self-discipline and ambition to graduate. At the house, she reached over and kissed him.

"I told Amy I'd come listen to her band out at Beth's lake house, but I can't do that. I'm still grounded."

Mrs. Page waved one hand at the insignificance of the past. "Go have a good time. You deserve it."

He cut the engine on the car. "I'd just feel guilty, knowing Dad wouldn't approve."

Mrs. Page slapped him lightly on the arm. "And the moon is made of green cheese."

She walked to the house, turning at the porch to wave, and he left. He drove so slowly the speedometer needle didn't budge off zero, feeling just as he had when as a child he'd been ordered to leave his baseball game or hide-and-seek and was ushered into a car so he could attend a revival service his father was leading in some nearby town. Then and now he'd had the same feeling—a perfectly good summer night was about to be ruined.

Before he got to the lake, the sun had set. The few clouds in the western sky hung there like short pieces of yarn, going slowly from luminous orange to gray as the sky lost its color. At

Beth's, two tables had been set up in the grass near the pool, and on top were three kegs of beer and an assortment of liquors and mixes. Two stereo speakers by the sliding glass doors of the house blared Blondie's "Heart of Glass." I wish my heart was made of material as stout, he thought.

Beth, wearing a black bikini that was wet and sagging, left the swimming pool as he approached and gave him a kiss as wet as she was, leaving the damp imprint of herself on the front of his clothes.

"What're you doing by yourself?" she asked.

"All my friends just graduated from high school."

The maroon van was parked near the house and Amy's gang of four was unloading equipment. The drummer, who had shaved his skull along the brush of a mohawk, was giving orders that went unheeded. "First the amps, don't need no lamps. Now the bass, don't make that face."

Amy wore a diaphanous dress that showed nothing but certainly seemed to. Her face radiated good health and a joy over being alive; in fact, she seemed to have been infused with an additional spirit. She could have been an advertisement for spring—life busting out all over. Without a word, she took his hand and pulled him toward the lake. They crossed a long lawn of freshly cut bermuda grass that stretched all the way to the water. The farther they got from the house and the floodlights on the eaves, the more ghostly Amy seemed. They stopped when they reached the lake and stood watching the reflection of the moon being chopped into pieces by the movement of small waves.

Amy kissed him, then took his hand. "I've been wanting to call you all day but I never know whether I should call your house."

"I wasn't at home, but you can call whenever you want."

After a brief silence, she waved one hand at the house. "I

just—I don't." She hesitated, stymied."When I was little, I sang all the time. I didn't want to perform, not really, not like this, and the strange thing is, sometimes I still don't. Mostly what I want is to *not want* to perform. Does that make sense? I want to be content to sing in my room because when you start wanting to perform, you just become one of ten million people wanting to perform. Sometimes it seems like everybody wants to. And I can't figure out if I'm any better than those other ten million. I don't know but I wish I did, I really do, because do you know what happens when you invest so much in wanting one thing? If you don't get it, it's like suicide. Like killing yourself because there isn't anything else you want to do."

She stopped for a moment, a look of concern on her face, concern for the future maybe, when she discovered she was just one of ten million, indistinguishable. He didn't speak and Amy searched the stars for answers.

"I want to know how good I am. I want somebody to tell me. I want to know if I'm wasting my time. My nightmare is this—five years from now singing in sorry little bars where everybody's drunk and nobody's listening. God, oh, God, oh, God, I want to make it, more than anything."

She redirected her gaze at him and looked more serious than he'd ever seen her. "Michael, how do you stop *wanting* so much? Wanting this much makes me afraid. What'll happen if I don't make it?"

For a moment he thought she might cry, but instead she seemed to have embarrassed herself. She walked toward the lake and started to dip her foot into the water lapping the shore but remembered she was wearing shoes. He was amazed and touched by her extensive revelation; he never would have expected such a revelation from her. She'd just said more about herself in the last two minutes than she had in the previous two years. He walked up behind her and put his hands on her shoulders.

"You know what's funny?" she asked. "Tomorrow this'll all be over. Tonight's a dream, but dreams don't last."

He pulled her against him and clasped his hands before her waist. This time the right words were there. "No, it's not a dream, and it won't end. Amy, you've got it all, everything you need, and this ought to be the best night of your life. The best of anything is always the start, and this is the start. Just like the "Prologue" on *Hot August Night*. It's the best part. And in five years, you won't be singing in dirty little bars; you'll be singing at concerts, you'll be singing on TV. People will pay fifteen bucks to hear you. It's going to happen because it's got to happen. What the preacher said at graduation is true for you. This is the first day of the rest of your life."

Amy turned and squeezed his hands, looking utterly euphoric, beautiful in the moonlight. He believed every word he'd spoken. He'd listened to her sing, and his tastes were universal enought to predict her future. Before long, everyone in the world would love her singing as much as he did. And as he listened to the band tuning up, he felt like a father about to give his daughter in marriage. The groom was going to love her as much as he did, and he'd have to share her. And although he wouldn't have held her back had he been able, he also didn't want the image of her face, as it burned brightly into his mind, as polished and smooth as a gem, replaced by one of her singing with four guys he didn't know.

"You're beautiful," he said. "You know that?"

"No, but tonight I feel beautiful. Tonight I think everything's going to be perfect. Everything."

She pulled Michael by the hand toward the house. Halfway there, she decided his reluctance was slowing her down, so she stopped and kissed him, hard and fast.

"Thank you," she said.

She ran alone toward the brightly lit patio, and he watched

her go. Amy, his Amy, was a phantasm running toward the light, in which she'd disappear, be swallowed up, and he'd never get her back. *His* Amy would become *their* Amy and nothing would ever be the same. An inauspicious beginning for the rest of his life.

After a few minutes of loitering in the near-darkness, he followed. The band had set up on the patio, between the house and the swimming pool, and the instruments were impressive, scattered over the concrete amid the snakes of electrical cords. As he surveyed the band, he discovered something worse than *Australopithecus* on drums. Much worse. The bass player Amy had mentioned, good old Andy, had long black hair and a face with features so clean and distinct and fine that he closed his eyes and murmured a short prayer on behalf of all the disadvantaged: "Dear Lord, if there is justice in this world, if there is even the slightest hint of equity, when I open my eyes, Andy will have the worst goddamn harelip anyone has ever seen."

Andy wore an orange T-shirt upon which was a silhouette of a man surfing into a huge sun over the words, "Port Aransas."

The noise of the party suddenly died and there was a brief silence as Port Aransas said, "One, two, three, four." And then there was music, full-blown and sudden. What he had expected to be an amateurish display of pretentious kids, possibly embarrassing for Amy, was much different. There were five people on the patio dedicated to making music, and there were fifty people listening attentively as they sat in and around the pool or in lounge chairs.

He watched from across the pool, standing at the edge of the light, and he was surprised because Amy wasn't moving when she sang. But her hands were; they were hypnotic, not at all stiff or manipulated. They were extensions of the music. And the longer she sang, the deeper into the music she seemed to sink, so deep that after a few minutes, he could have walked up to her and she wouldn't have recognized him.

Someone near him came out of his trance long enough to say, "Dang. I didn't know she could sing like that."

The scene was a strange one. What had been billed as an orgy was beginning on an almost reverent tone. But the band switched gears and went into a rollicking sort of blues number, and here and there hands started moving, feet tapping, water splashing in the pool. And although he had built up an almost instantaneous dislike for the band, he couldn't dislike the music.

But then Amy sang "Dreams," sang the song to which they had made love, and he couldn't have felt more violated if Amy had shown movies of the act. He wanted to leave, to go cry over the betrayals of life. He couldn't believe that she would sing that song in public as though it were just any song. For one moment, he hated her. But while he was hating her, while he was regretting every nice thing he'd ever said or done, he was also closing his eyes and listening to her sing.

Amy stood absolutely still as she sang, and she seemed to retain—or maybe Michael just wanted to think she was able to retain—that private part they had shared on several occasions. She didn't look at him, but neither did she look at anyone else. And when she sang, "I keep my visions to myself," he felt better. This girl, only part of whom he seemed to know, had shared her visions. With him. She had and nothing could change that.

He couldn't help but smile.

1 3

At 1 A.M., he was sitting in the parking area of the downtown section, a half-block that had been cleared and paved across from the main block of business. The day of graduation had been the longest and most tiring of his life. He felt as though he'd been to a bad party that had lasted a month, been involved in a wreck in which his car had rolled across a cotton field and into a brickyard pit, and been deprived of the care and cooperation of his father, only to be congratulated on beginning the rest of his life in this manner. He'd lost the alcoholic buzz that had fallen on him briefly about midnight, and the can of beer in his hand had grown warm as a piece of wood.

He was the only representative of the senior class among the dozen or so others gathered downtown to pass the night. Gary, his former friend, would have qualified but had quit school two months prior to graduating. The remaining seniors were either at Beth's continuing party or on their way to Nuevo Laredo or Galveston or Corpus Christi, doing something memorable. He had two options: he could go home and climb in bed or he could continue to sit in his car and feel nauseous, both exciting choices on what was now the second day of the rest of his life.

Gary, drawing near to drunken oblivion, was wandering from car to car in search of an audience that hadn't heard his repertoire of jokes, most of which concerned Jesus, all of which were sacrilegious, and he wasn't finding a warm reception anywhere. Instead he was shouted away with, "Go tell your jokes to someone who hasn't heard them, you dumb drunk."

"Hey, man, you ain't heard the one about the Last Supper. I ain't *ever* told you that joke."

"And you ain't *ever* going to, either. Go home and tell it to your mother."

Gary stumbled between the cars, looking for an open window, and Michael rolled his up. Faithless though he was, he still didn't like sacrilegious jokes. Gary noticed the appearance of glass in his window, stopped beside the door, and gave a look of shock. He rolled forward on his feet and then whipped drunkenly upright, his spine straightened by indignation.

"This preacher's boy don't like my jokes."

"Nobody likes your jokes," a voice shouted. "Go wreck your car or something."

Gary, ignoring the advice, knocked on the window of Mrs. Page's car with the base of a whiskey bottle, almost hard enough to crack the glass. "Get out here and preach us a sermon, boy. Tell us what Jesus has done for you. Just step right out and *testify.*" He said "testify" as if he were black, giving the word several layers of inflection. "Tell these boys how you tried to save my soul one time." He stopped and gave a pained look as though he were suffering a bad attack of indigestion.

Gary then began to recall, amid head-rolling memory lapses, closed-eye pauses, and mindless backtracking, the time Michael had attempted to lead Gary to salvation. They'd been ten years old, in the middle of a spring revival, and he had been mistakenly concerned about Gary's lousy soul. What surprised—and embarrassed—him was that Gary's memory was accurate, and he was inspired enough to exercise option number one, which was to go home and fall in bed.

He had adjusted his tired body behind the wheel and was ready to start the car when Amy pulled up directly in front of him. She blinked her lights twice, then killed her engine.

Seeing an extension to his endless day, he sighed and walked to her car.

Amy had that beatific look of someone who had been levitating and continued to hover above the routinely dreary residents of earth. He knew the emotion but hadn't experienced it since the end of football season. It was the elation that came from making a spectacular run, which caused everyone in the bleachers to go nuts and throw ice into the air and slap each other on the back, the elation that remained with the memory of a perfect run, when the cuts were precise, the acceleration superhuman, the opposition clumsy.

Gary arrived just after he got into Amy's car and stood in front of Amy's hood, staring at them through eyes that were only occasionally focused.

"Now what does he want?" Amy asked.

"He wants to tell us a joke." He looked behind them to check for traffic and said, "Let's get out of here."

Amy started the car but hadn't moved before Gary lay down on the hood of the black Firebird. Michael reached over and hit the horn, expecting to see the liquor industry's best customer rapidly eject, but he didn't move. He honked again, letting the blast continue for ten seconds. Gary stirred slightly, then raised his head and squinted with one eye. "Amy. Baby." He began to move forward, crawling on his belly toward the windshield as though trying to swim. His progress was slow.

"*What* is he doing?" Amy asked.

"Humbling himself. It's call prostration."

They sat watching as Gary's face reached the windshield. He looked in at Amy, then pressed his face against the glass. His nose flattened and his mouth, pursed for kissing, mashed open like an obscene sphincter.

"Gross," Amy said.

Gary was apparently unable to understand why Amy's face

was as hard as glass and began to pull himself up higher, swimming again. His face, pressed against the windshield, inched upward, but his lower lip remained in its former position, giving them a close-up view of Gary's lower gum and teeth.

Michael shook his head. "Have you ever noticed how life is just like a horror movie sometimes?"

He got out, rounded the car, and grabbed the wrist of Gary's right arm. Without a great deal of gentleness, he pulled Gary from the car and dragged him five or six feet away before he left him lying on his back on the pavement, singing in a slurred voice, "My Bonnie lies over the ocean."

He asked one of three boys sitting on the hood of a pickup to dispose of the body before going home, was assured Gary would be delivered to one of two homes—"His or the funeral" —and he returned to Amy's car.

They drove out of town as Amy squirted the windshield with the washer, trying to remove the residue left by the human slug. Before long they were whipping quickly through the night toward the river, falling gently into a valley. Amy wanted to drive and drive, faster than she ever had, wanted the night to last forever. Everyone at the party was probably puzzled by her disappearance, but she'd had to leave, to think, to consider the first perfect night of her life. She was living a fantasy. A dream had come true. Everyone at the party had talked about the band and about her singing, had pronounced her a future star. She'd been told that on various songs, she had given one girl chills, another tears, and yet another "the nicest feeling I've had since I lost my virginity." Amy had been complimented before, but never so enthusiastically, so thoroughly. (Surely the fact that everyone had been drinking was insignificant. Maybe the alcohol had just loosened some tongues without altering response. Sure. That was it.)

She left the party for another reason—to find Michael. She'd watched him walk off almost immediately after the band's performance, although he had said to her as he left, "You are so damn good I can't even tell you." All night he had seemed as somber as an undertaker, and Amy didn't want him to be unhappy, not on the best night of her life, and he wouldn't have been except for one thing—sex. Sex had wrecked their relationship. If they'd still been the simple but very good friends they'd been three months ago, Michael would be as happy as Amy.

Actually Amy hadn't even realized how disgusting sex was until a few days ago when the biology teacher had shown a movie on reproduction. All that screwing. Wing-beating birds and clumsy beetles, rhinos and rats and ducks and cows and horses with things like arms that even had fists. Yuk. Being told she was a member of the animal kingdom was bad enough, but to see first-hand that people shared the obsessions of big fat cows and unbelievably equipped horses, just as though Amy were like her own mother—well, that was all too much. Amy dropped the vow of part-time celibacy, accelerating into full-time and permanent.

The road climbed out of the valley, up and around a hill, and descended again, this time toward trees so thick that the claustrophobic builders of the road had been reluctant to let it settle into the woods. Instead they had built the road on a ridge at treetop level.

"So you liked the band, huh?" Amy asked.

She had to shout because the car was like a wind tunnel with both windows open. He rolled up the one on his side before answering, too tired to compete with the wind and road noise.

He nodded and said, "The band was good, but you were great."

Amy smiled.

"Why'd you sing 'Dreams'?"

"I had to, Michael. That's my favorite song."

"I thought it was our song."

"It is. That's why it's my favorite."

He nodded, thinking, it's going to be that kind of night. A night of relentless concession on his part. Winners, on the other hand, never had to concede, a fact which accounted for the direction of their travel. Away from his grandfather's farm. Obviously Amy was avoiding the farm for a reason, and the reason was a mystery. He slid down in his seat and closed his eyes.

The car dropped into the river bottom, the tires singing over a concrete roadway. It flew over several bridges, blowing through the cattails that leaned out over the road, and when it approached the levee, Amy braked. Before she reached the sharp little hill, she turned onto a dirt road, and then he realized where they were going—her father's ranch.

Within a few minutes they had climbed back into the modest hills and could see the lights of town spread before them. The ranch was a few hundred acres planted with coastal bermuda in a valley as open and rolling as the ocean. Amy slowed at the entrance, then turned, the car rattling across the cattle guard. She followed a gravel road into the center of the ranch and then stopped, killing both engine and lights.

"Why'd we come out here?" he asked.

Amy rearranged herself, sitting with her back to the car door, legs twisted primly in the seat. She let her head fall backward until it was extending from the car and she was looking skyward. "Because I wanted to thank my lucky stars. Because this night was perfect and I wanted to spend part of it with you. Quietly."

"The farm's closer to town."

Amy raised her head forty-five degrees so she could see him and send a message acknowledging his. "Can I tell you what

I've been thinking about? Without making you mad or hurting your feelings?"

Well, he thought, here comes the real graduation address. Welcome, senior, to this noncommencement proceeding.

"Michael, I loved you as a friend. You were the best friend I ever had. And I *hated* you when all that business with Beth started. I don't know why it is, but friends can't get sexually involved and then just stay friends. They start acting like husband and wife or something. They think they have to get married so they can watch each other like hawks. And it's not that way with just you and me. It's that way with everybody whether you want it to be or not."

He couldn't find fault in her argument because he suspected she was right, but she had no idea what she was asking of him. He couldn't sexually revert, he couldn't undo puberty, he couldn't fall out of love. How on earth was he supposed to look at her and not think about *Hot August Night* and "Dreams" and the rainy Saturday in her bedroom? How could he saw off the peaks of his little mountain range? "You want me to forget you're a girl?"

"No, silly. I just want us to think about something other than sex."

"All the time?"

The question seemed to make her uncomfortable. She reached up and touched the headliner, then let her head fall backward so she could again observe the stars. "How many constellations can you identify?"

He sighed. "The only one I see right now is Corliss, the cross-eyed eunuch."

Amy giggled and brought her head back into the car. "I'd forgotten how funny you are. See what sex did? It made us stop talking."

He reached and placed his hand on her knee. "Amy, can we please make love?"

124

Amy took his hand in hers and held it as though she were warming a hot dog bun. "Michael, I want to rehabilitate you. I want you to think about art or literature or anthropology."

He pulled her hands toward his mouth and held them against his lips. "We'll compromise. I'll buy a painting of a naked lady reading a book about the sex lives of aborigines if only you'll let me kiss you."

"I'm trying to be serious."

"And I'm trying to tell you something, Amy. It's impossible for me to see you as a regular pal. I wish I could if you want me to, but I can't." He shook his head and pressed her palms against his cheeks. "I want to tell you something. When I was little, there were things I thought were great—Christmas, summer vacations, going to Colorado—and they were great, but they were—I don't know, just worldly experiences. And I went to church expecting even greater things. I wanted great spiritual experiences. I wanted to feel a cosmic battle going on in my soul or something. I at least wanted to feel the presence of God. And I never did. And I never knew what a spiritual experience was until you came along. I just want you to understand this one thing—you may be talking about sex, but I'm not. I don't want sex. I can provide sex myself, and God knows I've about worn my hand out doing it. I've never got more than a few minutes' pleasure from all that. But, Amy," he said, wondering exactly how he could express the thought he wanted to make her understand. "Amy, you know the only thing that redeems this place, the only thing that ever allows you to rise above this rotten world? Love. That's the only thing. Not religion, not sex, not vacations, not anything else. Just love. And I finally figured something out when we made love. I suddenly understood the meaning of 'making love.' We were *making* love."

Amy maneuvered across the console into his lap and kissed him. "I want you to write me a song, Michael. Say all that in a hundred words, and I'll put it to music, and we'll both get rich and famous." She pulled her dress up over her waist so she could spread her legs, then straddled him just as he had done the first day at the farm, facing him, sitting on her knees. "Why do I always know what I want until you tell me different?" She kissed him again, this time rising up and pressing his head back against the seat. "You better not be tricking me, Michael, like you did with the butterfly the other day." She made a passionate sound and kissed him even harder. "Promise me you mean everything you just said."

"Promise," Michael said between kisses. He had been serious, although he couldn't have sworn one way or the other *why* he had said anything. But he did know this: on countless occasions he had been under the sky at this time of night, usually when he was camping, and he'd sit near a smoldering fire in the faint shadows of the trees, turning his head until he'd seen the sky from every angle. He'd lie back on the ground that was already covered with dew, and he'd know that he was in the right spot. And right now he knew he was in the right spot.

While Amy pulled her dress over her head, he reached over and turned the ignition switch on so that the tape player would function. A Fleetwood Mac cassette had already been inserted, and all he had to do was find "Dreams."

When they were both naked, touching, tasting, he said, "You've got to record that song with the band, with you singing it. I want to make love while you sing it."

"I will, I will," she said. "Just for you."

14

On the Monday after graduation, he started work for the state highway department, driving a dump truck on a highway construction crew. There were six truck drivers and one foreman, an older man thin as a whip who kept his eyes fixed on the sky. The dry but hot weather of summer was prime road-resurfacing season, and he spent the day worried about clouds and sudden showers. Always looking for an advantage, he accepted the drivers' speedy attempts to get finished and ignored the way the crazed and frustrated racers took the back roads of the county as if they were trying to qualify for a blue collar grand prix.

Since Michael was the junior man, he got stuck with the lousy jobs, the worst of which was taking a shovel and descending into a railroad car to clean up after the dragline unloaded gravel or premix. That rusted dented railroad car with its steel walls soaking up the sunlight was the hottest place he had ever been.

But the menial tasks weren't all bad. Between road jobs, the foreman sent them to a wooded area where the state was clearing right of way for a highway-widening project. The trees had been cut but the stumps remained, waiting to be uprooted and hauled away. The trucks backed up and the dragline operator dropped his line, on the end of which were two steel hooks. Michael fixed the line on the stump, then stepped back to watch the line creak and groan as the dragline popped the cork. As the stump came up, dragging roots and dripping dirt, he got a stick to knock off the copperhead snakes that were occasionally hidden in the recesses. While the trucks were gone, he'd grab the hooks at the end of the line and the operator would raise him twenty feet into the air. He would dangle, then spin in great circles as the boom swung him around.

When his father returned from the conference in Fort Worth, he assumed he was no longer subject to grounding since he was, after all, a high school graduate, employed, and about to leave home. Brother Page didn't press the issue. He came home full of renewed vigor and plans and ideas for revitalizing the church. He was starting a series of seminars on faith and asked Michael, of all people, to give his testimony at one.

The reasoning was this—a church member had set up a scholarship fund several years ago to enable one graduating member of the church to attend Stanton University in Stanton, ninety miles away, and obtain a quality Christian education at that Southern Baptist school. Since there had been four seniors in church this year with plans to attend college, Brother Page had told him not to apply for the scholarship, fearing, and Michael agreed, that if the pastor's son was granted the scholarship, those members prone to grumbling would have happily shouted, "Favoritism! Favoritism!"

Brother Page wanted him to attend some other Baptist school, but Michael, if he couldn't attend Stanton and Stanton law school, was going to a state university. And so he hadn't even applied to Stanton, lacking the necessary assurance of funding. He hadn't applied, that is, until his father told him to go ahead. "If God wants you there, he'll provide a way."

As it turned out, all the competition for the scholarship money dropped out of the race. The only graduating girl decided to move to Santa Fe and study art; one guy got a football scholarship to a junior college; and the third decided education could wait until he had personally visited France and checked out the women there.

An answered prayer, according to Brother Page. He asked

him to testify to the fact, and Michael said that maybe merely thanking the old gentleman who had established the fund would be more appropriate. He didn't want to tell his father that the development had failed to stoke his fires of faith.

"Michael, I don't understand. You see answered prayer in your own life and you don't want to tell anyone?"

"Actually, I'm having a hard time seeing it as anything but a default. A win by forfeit."

Brother Page's jaw dropped. "A default?"

"You mean God sent Cindy to New Mexico, Rick to France, and Bottlecap to football, just so I could go to Stanton?"

"Have you ever thought that God's plan may be unfolding in their lives too?"

If he had known God was recruiting graduating seniors and sending them to France to inspect women, he would have been praying up a storm. As it was, however, he told fourteen people on a Monday night about his good fortune and plans to attend Stanton University.

He called Amy, but she was never at home. She was either at rehearsal or off playing at some rich kid's birthday party. He talked a lot to Mr. Hardin, who was as concerned as he was over Amy's total immersion in the band. "You think she's doing the right thing?" he asked Michael several times. All he could tell him was that only Amy knew.

She returned his calls at 11 P.M., when she got in early, or at 7 A.M. before he went to work, and he was either half-asleep or still waking up.

"Michael! How are you?"

"Fine."

"What're you doing? How's your job?"

"It's fine too."

"Tell me about it."

"I drive a dump truck."

If she wasn't rehearsing or playing, she was off with good old Andy trying to line up gigs. Their paths crossed once, and they stopped in the road to say hello and to consider some real favoritism—Andy's looks. They made him wonder what on earth Amy had ever see in plain old Michael Page. Amy introduced them and Andy glanced at him and said, "Yeah," confirming his fear that he was as common as a turtle.

For a while he tried writing Amy a song, as she had requested, not for the riches or fame, but only so she would remember him. Since he knew nothing of songwriting, he listened to Stevie Nicks over and over and discovered there was an experience more humbling than comparing himself to Andy. His lyrics were hardly impressive. "I love you when you sing and I love you when you don't." He had never cherished degradation, so after one or two attempts at composing a pop hit, he decided to deprive the world of his songs.

He was also waiting on his song from Amy, the tape of her singing "Dreams." He asked her several times during their graveyard shift telephone conversations, and she always said, "I haven't done it yet, but I will. I promise."

He couldn't believe what was happening. The most exciting, most fulfilling relationship of his life was dissipating before his eyes. How many times, back when he'd even vaguely believed in prayer, had he said, "Dear God, please let us like each other for exactly the same length of time so no one will get hurt"? And now he was feeling the pain he'd wanted everyone to avoid.

He was all right during the day at work, but walking home from the highway department yard, listening to the cicadas blare in the trees like blast furnaces and watching oily waves of heat rise from the street, he saw an empty night and felt an acute longing for the girl who made the sun rise.

About this time, when he was learning he couldn't write music but could sing the blues, Judy reentered his life. Judy was his age, a girl with a rangy body, almost broad-shouldered, with dusty blonde hair that was parted in the middle and simply brushed down on either side of her head. The daughter of an alcoholic, she had always hovered in the limbo of social nothingness but could have told you the parking techniques of every boy in town. She'd been more used than the tackling dummy at the football field but had always managed to retain her virginity. When things got hot and heavy, she invariably said, "I can tell you one thing, buster. Ain't no boy screwing me till we're married."

She and her mother were fairly frequent in church attendance. The race to see who took her for "a Coke" after church had been as heavily contested as the Boston Marathon. And one Sunday night when he was wondering why Amy hated him, Judy sat down beside him and said, "I heard Amy dumped you for a guitar picker." While he was considering a response, Judy said, "I wouldn't have done that."

Looking at the girl's empty face, he remembered many Sunday nights on which he had won the race and suffered extensive guilt and dissatisfaction until he'd quit running. The poor girl was backward and dumb and kissed as though she were gumming applesauce, but she had taught a large number of Baptist boys the basics of female anatomy.

And on this Sunday night, she asked, "You want to take me home?"

"Sure," he said, intending to do just that, no stops on the way.

They were barely out of the church parking lot before Judy slid across the seat of Mrs. Page's car and put her arm around him. She kissed him lightly on the cheek. She smelled faintly of Kool-Aid.

"We don't have to go straight home, you know."

He had more problems than he wanted to count. What if

word got back to Amy that he wasn't remaining loyally pure? What if word got back to God that he was taking advantage of one of his less fortunate creatures? Would he be forever disqualified from receiving a call to the fertile mission fields of France? What if Judy's body throbbed with disease?

"I done decided a long time ago that the only boy I'd let screw me was you. 'Cause you're the nicest boy I know." She patted him on the back like an old buddy.

"I couldn't do that, Judy. You've saved yourself too long for me to do that."

"Well, I ain't saving myself *no more*." She cuddled up and rested her head on his shoulder. "You don't even have to marry me."

He remembered more than he wanted to. Judy's cooperation had always surpassed her enthusiasm and imagination. Undressing her hadn't been much different from stripping a corpse, and an aged one at that, because she wore full-sized panties and a heavy-duty white bra. And although she had a fairly nice body, he had never found a way to get her excited. Her response had always matched her kissing—just another function.

"Judy, I can't possibly be the first. The first is supposed to be the man you marry, and I don't ever plan to get married."

Judy giggled. "Well, you wouldn't really be the first. My cousin done beat you to it. When we was fourteen and playing in the backyard, he tricked me, that little fool. He told me, 'Now close your eyes and don't open them 'cause if you do while I'm taking your temperature, you'll go stone blind.' Well, I knew he wasn't taking my temperature, but I didn't know he was doing *that* till I opened my eyes, and when I seen what he was doing, I picked up a rock and flat knocked him out."

"That doesn't count then. You were tricked."

Judy lived near the river, and the last time he had taken that route, he had been with Amy on the night of graduation, not with a girl who was running her fingernail across his zipper to provide the music to a song he hadn't heard since childhood. "The worms crawl in, the worms crawl out, they play pinochle on your snout." They turned on the road that ran parallel to the river while Judy sang, and for three or four miles, they felt the air grow damp and cool.

Suddenly Judy sat up. "You're taking me home."

He looked sad. "I have to tonight, Judy. My mother needs her car. She's going to sit up at the hospital with Mrs. Jackson. But next Sunday night, you and I can do whatever we want. Unless of course Mrs. Jackson is still sick."

Judy stared at him for what seemed an hour, trying to judge his truthfulness, his sincerity about next Sunday.

In an effort to impress her, he said, "I can't wait till next Sunday. We'll have a lot of fun."

Apparently convinced, Judy returned to her former position, head on his shoulder, and kissed his neck. The kiss sounded like the opening of an air lock. "You was the only boy who ever told me I had pretty eyes."

He assured her that her eyes were as pretty as ever and turned into her yard, the lights of the car illuminating a weathered house with a long porch, also a father sitting in a rocking chair, hand on a bottle, the bottle resting on his leg. How would it be to come home always to a drunken father? His resolve to remain disentangled disappeared under the weight of Judy's apparently empty life. "You know, I bet my mother can use my father's car. Let's just go for a ride."

Judy, almost out of the car, hesitated, then finished making her exit. She looked back in, her hair swinging on both sides of her face. "Shoot, you don't want to go for a ride. You just want to screw me."

"Shh," he said, looking at the man on the porch.

"Don't you shh me. I can talk if I want to."
She slammed the door and walked to the house.

He worried about Judy all week. Either she had already called Amy—but she'd have to leave a message, just like everyone else —or she was going to appear at church next Sunday in a thirty-year-old Easter bonnet and white patent leather shoes. He wouldn't have to fabricate an excuse to get out of the date; he was going to be authentically sick.

After calling Amy on both Tuesday and Thursday, calls which she returned at 11:30 P.M. and 6:45 A.M., the latter causing the phone to ring simultaneously with the alarm clock, he began to wonder why he was the only one initiating the calls. She always seemed genuinely glad to talk to him, but she never called first. Never. And she didn't talk about the band unless he asked, and when he did, she wouldn't shut up. Every time he sat listening to her tales and plans, her enthusiasm occasionally running the words together so that between his stupor and her hyperactivity he often didn't even know what she was saying, he was repeatedly impressed with her sole desire. How many times did he have to learn this? How deep was his stupidity? Amy wanted to sing and that was all. So he decided to stop calling her and see if she ever called him.

The answer to his problems with both Judy and church attendance seemed abundantly clear on Sunday morning. He was old enough to determine his own course, and if he didn't go to church, then he wouldn't see Judy. Simple. Very simple. When his mother called him for breakfast, he turned over and covered his head with the pillow. When she removed the pillow a few minutes later and suggested he was going to be late for Sunday school, he yawned and said he wasn't going.

Twenty minutes passed before the pillow was hoisted again, this time by Brother Page.

"Are you sick?" he asked.

He wasn't asking a question; he was making a statement. God's children had but one excuse for missing church, and then only for the prevention of epidemics, not for convenience of the sick. Church members braved ice storms, ignored tornado warnings, and forgot the Dallas Cowboys when their schedule conflicted with God's. And obviously he couldn't tell his father he was avoiding church because if he didn't, he'd have to screw Judy.

"I'm not going."

Brother Page knelt by the bed and prayed. "Lord, forgive us our terrible weaknesses. Forgive us our desire to remain in the comfort of a bed in an air-conditioned house. Forgive us for even thinking that leaving the bed and walking a hundred feet to church might constitute a sacrifice. We see these minor changes in the position of our bodies as sacrifices, Lord, because we have forgotten yours. We have forgotten you made the ultimate sacrifice. You wore a crown of thorns and were nailed to the cross. We never think about the pain one little splinter can cause in our hand and then multiply it by a hundred encircling our head. We don't think about how it would feel to have a spike nailed in our hand. The point breaking the skin, tearing through muscle, breaking bones, severing nerves. . . ."

He got up and started dressing before his father had finished praying, even though his hand was hurting and he could barely manage the buttons on his shirt.

He didn't know then that Judy had already gone to San Antonio to visit her aunt and would stay, finding work as a meter reader. Neither did he know that Amy wouldn't call him once over the next two weeks but that he would see her at church the third Sunday in July.

15

Amy felt so good she couldn't believe it. She smiled all the time, felt almost no need for sleep, and thought even her skin felt more healthy than it ever had. She'd no sooner finish one gig before she was thinking about the next, about how to fill her time until they were again setting up in another place. Most of her days were spent in the contemplation of perfection, of the perfection of perfection. She rearranged their sets and their songs until all the transitions seemed logical and natural, until the two juveniles, the keyboard player and drummer, started saying with loud groans, "Here goes another change," whenever they saw her. Everyone was generally cooperative except Rusty, the drummer.

He was a rich little dope fiend who wanted to be a rock star but who wanted to expend the minimum amount of effort on the way to fame and the maximum amount of effort at making Amy mad. And he knew the quickest way to raise her ire was to start talking in rhyme.

"You switch songs, you be wrong."

"Are you too lazy or too stupid to go along?"

"Mess with success, never be blessed."

"We are moving this song."

"You make noise, bother us boys."

Amy would stare at his ridiculous mohawk and say, "Why don't you just shut up and get a haircut."

The conflicts with Rusty failed to distress Amy though; even her mother couldn't bother her. If Mrs. Hardin wondered aloud why Amy was no longer spending four hours a day in the tub, Amy ignored her, as she did when her mother asked of no one, "Why wouldn't a girl want to do something constructive with her life? What does it mean if she wants to run around with thuggy-looking boys?" Amy thought about moving to Halton but didn't want to spend the required amount of time or energy or thought on such an activity. She wanted only to think about one thing—singing.

At times her voice amazed her. She had done nothing to get it, didn't deserve it, and didn't even understand how it worked. But she had watched herself on a videotape that some rich kid had made when the band had played for his birthday, and she'd been so proud of herself that she'd gotten chill bumps, which she had covered with an afghan so no one would notice. Her pride had both embarrassed and thrilled her, and she immediately had tried to humble herself by asking, "If you're so good, why is Andy more important to the band than you are?"

He was more important. The bass player was responsible for most of their gigs, and the juveniles looked to him, rather than to Amy, for approval of any changes. Andy's only problem was that he kept talking about moving to Houston. "Hey, man," he said more than once. "You're looking at a guy who jammed with Billy Gibbons. What the hell am I doing hanging around here? Let's go to Houston, L.A., let's go to the top." Whenever he introduced the subject of moving, Amy reminded him that they hadn't yet conquered central Texas. One step at a time.

Her father said, when he and Amy saw each other, that she was disappearing from his life and he missed her. She didn't know how to explain that she didn't want to slow down, didn't even seem able, and when she occasionally sat to eat lunch with him, her mind was elsewhere, wanting to leap ahead, wanting to set up for the next gig, wanting progress.

He invited her to go to the hundredth anniversary service of the church and eat dinner there with him, and she agreed. And when she did, she remembered Michael. She needed to see him too.

He saw her enter the auditorium and blinked to clear his eyes. Amy at church? Why hadn't she told him she'd be there so he could have at least been looking foward to seeing her? The answer, of course, was very simple—she hadn't bothered to call him for two weeks. He followed her in, taking a bulletin from Mr. Hardin, who was serving as an usher and who seemed quite proud that Amy had chosen to attend church that day. "Finally got her to slow down for an hour anyway."

"Good for you."

She had sat midway down the outside aisle near the window, the same spot they'd once regularly occupied, and wore a pale blue sleeveless dress. When he got within ten feet of her, he felt something like a current enter his body. He had walked into her aura. His nerve endings were suddenly exposed and he could feel every breath she took, every movement of her muscles.

"So how's it going?" he asked, sitting beside her.

"Great. Really great," she said and smiled. She seemed genuinely glad to see him.

"How's the band?"

"It's doing great too. One week we played *every night*."

He was saved from having to respond to this depressing bit of news by the appearance in the pulpit of Brother Singer, an elderly white-haired man who had preceded Brother Page as pastor. He was spry for his eighty-some years, a living example of the wisdom of clean Christian living, a man Michael thought too reasonable to be a Baptist preacher. He'd once preached a sermon entitled, "The Folly of Prayer," in which he had enumerated the reasons not to pray. The only reason to pray, according to Brother Singer, was to attune yourself to God.

Brother Singer said, "I know some of you are wondering, so I'll go ahead and tell you: I *wasn't* the first pastor this church ever had."

He leaned toward Amy, the better to smell her, the better to feel her thin arm, and asked, "Why don't we go to the lake this afternoon?"

Amy gave him a helpless look. "We have to rehearse. We're doing a new song."

"All afternoon?"

"Probably," Amy said, realizing she was lying, realizing also that she didn't want to go to the lake with Michael. She was somewhat startled by the thought, because two months ago, she would have said yes without any thought at all. Her answer created a tension between them; Amy noticed because she had the peculiar feeling that her body had just been placed on alert, as if she were some sort of air force base.

Brother Singer was reading a church history. The first building erected had burnt down in 1898. "Some of you may have helped fight that fire. Some of you may have started it," he said, a reference to the continual feuding over building and not building, a reference that brought laughter from the congregation.

"So what's with you and Andy?" Michael asked.

Amy started to ignore the question but didn't. "Do you mean am I dating him?"

"That's a good place to start."

"No."

"I guess when you spend eighteen hours a day with someone, you don't have time for dates."

He withdrew a hymnal from the rack in front of him, then put it back, suddenly frustrated enough to cry. For as long as he could remember, he'd hated nothing any more than being ignored. When he'd been small, he had occasionally pulled a dog's ear to hear it yelp. Anything to make it respond. And right now he wanted to pull Amy's ear until she squealed.

"So you and Andy are just friends, huh?"

Amy nodded.

"I don't guess he's the kind of friend you'd have to give your little speech to, is he? You know, the speech about how you value friendship so much you can't stand to fuck a friend?"

The remark made Amy so mad she couldn't think of a response that would adequately convey her indignity, her anger, that would make him understand they would never again be friends. He sat there in a gray pinstriped suit looking like a decent human but he was really mean and vicious.

Brother Singer said, "And the great war to end all wars claimed that good pastor of ours. . . ."

Sounding just like Rusty, he said, "Be Amy's chump, you get dumped."

Amy hit him on the shoulder with her bulletin and said, much too loud, "I hate you." She rose and squeezed out of the pew, stepping on his foot as she did. He rose to follow.

Brother Singer said, "And it looks like a smaller war has claimed our pastor's son."

He followed her up the outside aisle, watched by everyone in the auditorium, including his father, who was seated on the podium and was suddenly interested in his Bible, and he followed her outside. She was already in her car and about to slam the door when he caught the handle.

"Let go," she yelled.

He had never heard her yell before, and although he was shocked, he didn't let go. Instead he moved between the door and car so she couldn't back up without running over him. Her pale blue dress had ridden up her legs, but she didn't move to adjust it, and the sight of so much lovely thigh encased in shining pantyhose reminded him of one day at the farm with Neil Diamond. Amy started the car and dropped the gearshift into reverse, causing the car to roll backward at idling speed. He walked along, pushed by the open door.

"You don't even know what a friend is, Michael. You think it's somebody you can use."

"I don't? I wasn't the one who said, 'Oh, I loved you as a friend.' You don't love anybody, Amy. You don't want friends. If you did, we wouldn't have gone two months without seeing each other. I didn't realize that night at your ranch that I was getting the axe. I didn't know that was it. Forever."

Amy ignored him, watching her rearview mirror and turning when she got to the street. She straightened her wheels, dropped the gearshift into drive, and said, "I've called you twenty times at least."

"Only because I called you first. How many times have you called me the last two weeks? None. Zilch. Zippo. Zero. Why? Because I didn't call you first and you never even thought about it." He leaned forward so he could speak into her ear. "I know what's happened. I know exactly what's happened. You've got your band and you're singing and everything's just great. So what use have you got for some shithead who paid five bucks for a fan club certificate that embarrassed you? What use have you got for a guy who loved your singing before you had your lousy band? None. You've got no use for him, so you just throw him away like an empty bottle. You've already sucked out everything you needed, so out the bottle goes. You're just like your mother—too self-centered to love anybody but yourself."

Amy watched a car coming toward them, hoping it would hit the open door of the car and smush Michael Page into goo, shut him up forever. He was going to make a great lawyer, because he could take words and twist them into something that sounded believable when they were nothing but lies. Amy Hardin *was nothing* like her mother, and Michael should be punished for saying she was.

But if she weren't like her mother, why, for the first time in two months, was Amy feeling sick, emotionally nauseated? Because even if she wasn't, Amy still wasn't a good person. What Michael had said was true: she had treated him terribly, had taken his encouragement and support when she'd been in need, then forgotten him altogether. Had she not just lied to him about being busy the entire afternoon? And she had indeed told him that she had loved him as a friend when she must not have. Otherwise, she wouldn't have forgotten him.

In the middle of the road on a hot July Sunday, Amy suddenly realized she was not only an inadequate person, but she was never going to succeed at singing because she didn't deserve to. And while Michael watched, she started crying.

Michael squatted beside her and touched her arm. "Amy. Amy, I'm sorry. I didn't mean any of that."

Amy didn't want to cry, didn't want to talk. She wanted to undo two months' neglect, wanted to relive those two months and find room for those who had loved her. She was emotionally deficient and deserved not success but oblivion.

Still squatting between the opened door and the car, he watched her cry, sorry now as he always had been when he'd pulled a dog's ear but knowing still that he'd again feel the blinding need because satisfaction came only with hearing the yelp. He started to get in the car and direct Amy toward the farm. All he'd have to do would be to find the Fleetwood Mac tape and play "Dreams." And he wanted to. But at the very best he'd only be reviving a dead affair.

Logic seemed to dictate only one course of action. He stood; his knees ached from squatting.

"I'm sorry, Michael," Amy said, fearful he was about to walk off.

"Good-bye, Amy," he said.

And he did walk off, all the way to the corner of the church, headed for the parsonage, without looking back.

II

16

The happiest day of Michael's life—and probably of his father's as well—came the day that Brother Page deposited him in the dorm at Stanton University. They had a quiet ride over, ninety miles of silence broken only by coughs and clearing throats. He kept waiting for words of wisdom (study to shew thyself approved) or warning (flunk out and you'll end up in the Salvation Army), but his father didn't say anything at all. And a strange thing happened—he got sad, not because they were parting but because they were parting so readily, so easily. He began to remember missed opportunities.

He'd had a small dog that slept on the foot of his bed a few years ago, and one night, the dog had experienced a nightmare, one of those trapped-dog dreams where its legs twitched and it emitted mournful sounds like squeaking hiccups. The little dog woke him up, and when he looked at the foot of the bed, he saw Brother Page standing in the doorway. He stepped toward the bed and said, "He must be dreaming," and patted the dog on the head, scratching him around the ears. The dog woke up and stretched, pleased to find a warm hand on its head and not the vicious pack of mongrels that had cornered it in the dream. Brother Page asked, "You all right? You all right?" Michael had had the dog for several years and had never seen his father touch it before.

Since he was awake, he got up and used the bathroom. Once finished and ready to return to bed, he noticed a light on in the living room. He went to investigate and found his father sitting in his pajamas. The man didn't have anything to read, no Bible, no commentary, nothing; he was just sitting there in the middle of the night. Michael wondered if he'd been awakened by a nightmare, if a terrible dream had brought him sympathetically to his son's room, and he started to ask. In fact, he wanted to sit and talk to him. How's it going, Pop? Everything all right? Are you worried about something? But he hadn't, just as he hadn't in the car on the way to Stanton, when they'd had nothing else to do but talk.

He wanted the man to admit he was human, subject not only to nightmares but to fits of jealousy and lust and envy, and Brother Page never exhibited any of those traits.

He'd almost done it once, on a vacation in Florida. They had decided to give golf a try and found a beautiful course with palm trees along the fairways. And Brother Page, who had always been easily frustrated, couldn't figure out why those stupid little golf balls were taking such great curving flights every time he smacked one. The longer they played, the tighter his jaw got, and then he began to miss the ball altogether and chop up the course like a rabid gopher. Michael thought the afternoon was funny although he didn't laugh, but his father had sworn never again would he touch a golf club. His lack of skill had brought him to the brink of losing his relationship with the Lord.

"I almost cussed," he'd said.

That's what Michael had wanted to hear, a hell or a damn.

Their communication was infrequent and accidental. The other day he had been eating a sandwich at the kitchen table and had watched his father walk into the den to return a magazine to its stack. He had tried fitting the magazine onto the top of the stack, but the curved handle of the rack wouldn't allow passage of one more magazine. It wouldn't fit any more than a loose brick would have fit into the wall of the parsonage, but Brother Page worked from several different angles, determined. When his efforts failed, he gave the magazine a hard shove. It folded up like an accordion and dropped to the floor. And as Brother Page walked off, leaving the crumpled magazine on the floor, he noticed Michael watching and gave him a small smile of guilt. Michael laughed.

But then they were in the dorm room and Brother Page looked around at the beds and desks and said, "Well, it looks pretty comfortable."

"Yeah, all it needs is a mother to keep it clean."

Brother Page passed up the opportunity to deliver a lecture on responsibility and Michael knew the man was in a hurry to get away.

"Want me to help you get settled?" the father asked.

He shook his head. "I can do it easy enough."

They stood looking at the window and he started to say, "I love you, Pop," but grew teary before the words reached his mouth. Suddenly he was incapable of speech.

Brother Page gave him a quick firm hug, leaving him with the smell of his dark blue suit, and said "Good luck."

Good luck? he thought. The man didn't even believe in luck.

He watched at the window as his father left the building two stories below. On his way to the car, Brother Page seemed to be walking more upright. His father's stride was rapid, purposeful. And he would have given much for Brother Page to have been blessed with a more suitable son, some little guy with a strong faith and a desire to follow his father's teachings. His birth had been a miracle; he'd been told that a thousand times. But a miracle for whom?

His roommate hadn't checked in yet, but he already had him figured out. Ron from Houston was going to be his opposite, not of small-town, semi-impoverished, Bible-thumping stock. He'd look like . . . well, he'd look like old Andy in Amy's band, but he'd think Brother Page's son was an interesting and worthwhile sort of person to know. His parents would have a huge house in River Oaks but wouldn't be a bit snobbish. Ron's old man would drive a Mercedes but wear gimme caps, and his mother would consider her maid a friend. They'd have a big swimming pool and Ron and he would spend more time there than they did at school, meeting all of Ron's beautiful female friends.

The door to the room opened.

Through it came a boy who weighed at least three hundred pounds, wearing a white shirt and black pants. Somehow his pants were too big; they were gathered at the waist as though he had been on a diet. The boy's black plastic glasses were about to slide off his nose, and almost did before the boy had set two suitcases down and let four thick books drop loudly from beneath his arms.

He introduced himself: Ron from Houston.

Ron shook his hand with his own catcher's mitt of a hand, and the small bald head of Ron's father peeked around Ron's side.

"So tell me," Ron said. "I want to know your dreams and aspirations. I want to know you inside out." He backed up and stuck his hands in the voluminous pockets of his black pants. "We're going to be good friends, I just know it."

Ron's father nodded affirmation and tried to smile but the smile didn't quite form. The man was a half-drawn portrait.

Ron looked around and said, "Hey, a nice room, huh? We're going to have some real bull sessions in here. Maybe we might even do some studying. How's your poker, Page? You ought to be great with those eyes. They're flat, a little hard; they don't give away anything. I bet you could bluff a New York cop. Hey, maybe we could get a game lined up for tonight. What do you think?"

"My father's down in the parking lot waiting for me to say good-bye. I'll be back in a few minutes."

"Take your time," Ron yelled after him, "but hurry back. So we can talk."

Walking down the hall, he watched his love life leap from a window and land headfirst on the sidewalk below. Baptists judged by appearances, and he'd be judged as if he had hand-picked his own roommate. "You know Page, don't you? He's partial to obesity." But after wandering the campus for a few minutes, he began to feel better. There were girls everywhere. Beautiful girls. Well-dressed girls whose skirts swung just right. He didn't see one with the perfect walk of Amy, the walk that said, "I could make the sun rise," but then he hadn't expected to.

As he looked at the castlelike administration building and saw all those unfamiliar faces, he knew he wasn't in Ashworth, Texas, anymore. He was starting brand new because no one with the possible exception of Ron knew he was a preacher's kid, and he'd swear Ron to secrecy. He stood there in the stifling heat, sweating but as happy as a slave with his own copy of the Emancipation Proclamation stuffed securely in his pocket. He didn't want to buy a plantation or ride a steamboat or rape a Southern belle. All he wanted to do was stand and smell the air of freedom.

(He didn't count on the ghost. Ninety miles from home, his mind failed to comprehend the distance. On Wednesday night as he was eating a quarter-pounder in McDonald's, he noticed it was 7 P.M., time for prayer meeting. He had the distinct feeling that his father was about to charge through the door with a big frown and chase him to church. His plans for church were simple—he was going to attend just once so he could tell his parents he'd found a church. On that Wednesday night, had he been at home skipping church, he would have congratulated himself for his daring and ingenuity; in Stanton, free to skip, he felt guilty. I guess that's life, he thought.)

He'd never been an exceptionally good student because he had disliked the lack of activity involved in studying, and he saw no good reason to change his attitude just because he was attending a university. Biology and history hadn't changed, just grown additional details, and algebra still drove him nuts. X and Y were now even more accomplished in their deceptions and he wouldn't have been surprised to learn they were Nazi war criminals.

He'd always made fairly good grades in English, and when the freshman English teacher assigned a paper to be written about any aspect of high school, he recalled from memory his prize theme from last year and wrote about two-a-day football practices. He did a good job of describing the sadistic coach who liked to see his players run again and again the length of the field, leaping spread-eagle onto their stomachs every ten yards, who demanded that they run the tires in the mud for indefinite periods of time, until they had all fallen to the ground and thrown up. He believed he had adequately described the agony of the heat and the misery of the mud and believed anyone reading the paper would understand why at the end of every summer, he had hoped the Russians would invade, thereby saving him from further football practices without the loss of face involved in quitting.

The teacher gave him a C and noted, "Far too much exaggeration to be effective." He started to protest but the teacher was a wan-faced and delicate-looking Yankee who obviously would never acknowledge the reality of class A football in Texas.

The course that interested Michael was Introduction to the Old Testament because he wanted the teacher to tell him how God could have devised genes and DNA and the immune system and why he had gone to such trouble to install them in man, a creature who could be so brutally rotten that no other animal alive could come close to matching his wickedness. The Old Testament exceeded modern newspapers in depicting man amok, and his favorite story was that of the Levite who had hacked his mistress into a sufficient number of parts to allow him to distribute portions of her body to the twelve tribes. He had always known the tribe of Judah was thrilled to receive, donkey express, part of an amputated arm.

He wanted the teacher to point out God's *real* plan. He believed that Jesus was the means of salvation. Salvation from God. After several thousand years, God had finally admitted his incredible error, that was, that the creation of man had been technically brilliant but morally absurd. And Jesus was much too late. By the time of his appearance, man had already learned how much fun it was to murder and rape and maim and wasn't a bit interested in learning to inherit the earth through meekness.

But the teacher didn't satisfy that longing. Instead, he stood before the class and disoriented him.

He wrote YHWH on the board and pronounced those initials a rendition of God's name in Hebrew. Vowels had later been added, transforming it to Yahweh. Michael looked around to see if anyone else was as lost as he was. Yahweh? Did the teacher mean God wasn't a Hebrew word? He had been in church all his life and thought he had heard it all, but he wasn't familiar with Yahweh. He checked the concordance in his Bible but couldn't find any such name. God with a name was a brand new concept. Was Yahweh his first or last name? Benny R. Yahweh? Yahweh Steinmetz?

He turned to the boy beside him and asked, "Did he say Yahweh?"

The boy nodded. "That or Elohim."

The first five books of the Bible, according to the teacher, combined the anonymous narratives of four traditions. He never even mentioned Moses as author or even as a possible alternate. He wanted to yell, hey, what about the guy who looks like Charlton Heston, but the teacher had moved on. He was saying that the Bible contained two different stories of the creation and they didn't agree.

He squirmed. He frowned. He wanted answers, not puzzles he had never considered. Immediately after class he went to the library and found one of the commentaries Brother Page considered reliable, and it disputed the two-version theory of creation. The "second" version was merely an expansion of the first, with emphasis on the creation of man. And Moses had indeed authored the first five books of the Old Testament. The record of Moses' death in the fifth book was a simple editorial insertion made later under divine guidance.

His mouth opened. In eighteen years, he'd never known Moses had recorded his own death. He was famous for a great number of acts, but this one beat turning sticks into snakes.

He sat in the library reading the first two chapters of Genesis over and over, and a strange thing happened. He began to see two distinct stories of the creation, and the teacher was right—they weren't in agreement. Two different stories, similar, but in the chronology of events, definitely different.

Suddenly he was giddy with excitement before he even knew

why, and he turned to a girl at the same table, a studious-looking young lady.

"Hey," he said. "I'm a Presbyterian. I'm a goddamn liberal, intellectual Presbyterian."

The girl looked concerned. "But have you been born again?"

"Just now."

He got up and ran for the door, for the future, seeing himself as a Presbyterian lawyer who went to church where people drank coffee and smoked during Sunday school and no one cried during the invitation. Anyone claiming to have heard the voice of God was placed on waivers and picked up by the Baptists. His life, which had been nothing but Sundays, went to nothing but Saturdays.

When he got to the front door of the library, he ran into the night shouting, "I'm free, thank God, I'm free at last."

The happiness over his liberation was almost enough to offset his disappointing social life, which, so far, had consisted of poker games with a bunch of guys and going to movies with Ron. He discovered something basic about Stanton society when he asked a girl for a date. She was shocked that he'd even spoken to her and acted as though she hadn't heard. The second invitee grew embarrassed and laughed, and the third waited until she'd heard he lacked a car before declining. Ron had to explain to him that he was dealing with "the Stanton girl."

Soon he became expert in spotting one. Her hair was usually highlighted or frosted and short, and her clothes were well-made if not expensive. Her body was slightly flabby, not from overeating because she was very conscious of her diet, but because she'd never broken a sweat. Her idea of exercise was lifting her legs into a car, right before someone else closed the door for her.

She knew what she wanted. She had plans, entire drawers

full of them, pages cut from *Better Homes and Gardens* and *Southern Living* showing the precise architecture and exact furnishings of the house she'd live in. She had come to Stanton to find the only cog missing from her scheme—the poor sucker who would obtain all these things while she remained seated in contentment on milk-white buns.

Ron said, "Don't try to fool these broads, Page. They've been taught by experts—their mamas."

Ron was a slob, stumbling around on misshapen shoes with his white shirttail sticking out through his half-lowered zipper, and was farther removed from the Stanton girl's charms than Michael was. A student of psychology, he analyzed everyone he saw. To him, behavior was a subject for analysis, serving the same purpose as blood or tissue samples, something that differentiated one person from another. So the strongest reaction a Stanton girl got from him was, "Ah, yes, there she comes now, Miss White Settlement, in her stunning ensemble of daywear."

He was at his best in the afternoon, when he occasionally disappeared, reappearing with a grocery sack containing canned martinis. He and Michael would pour them into white plastic cups adorned with the school mascot, a red eagle, and they'd sit on a bench in front of the administration building to "watch the masses" while smoking dollar cigars that came in silver tubes. Being the Presbyterian he was, Michael enjoyed sitting in the middle of that Southern Baptist property getting woozy on martinis.

One day they were sitting on their normal bench under a giant pecan tree when the president stopped by for a short chat.

"How are you fellows doing?"

"We're experiencing life in all its glory, sir," Ron said. "We're letting our spirits soar."

The president looked closely at their cigars and walked on.

Ron swirled ice in his cup, getting close to depleting his drink, and said, "Oh, this poor girl coming along now was only runner-up in the Miss Dime Box pageant. Otherwise she wouldn't be walking with a boy who appears to have stuffed his designer jeans with a ten-inch German sausage. She hasn't yet discovered that he's afraid of close relationships because he had a childhood conflict with his parents. They denied him warmth. So his crotch is his badge; don't get too close, it says."

They sat quietly for a while, watching the gray smoke of their cigars rise lazily in the afternoon heat. A boy and girl walking very slowly, swinging their clasped hands, stopped to embrace, then kiss.

"Ah, lovebirds, Page. Phenylethylamine at work. Better than speed, probably better than cocaine."

"What?"

"Phenylethylamine, the love drug. The chemical in your brain that provides you with feelings of elation and euphoria that you associate with love. It's amazing, isn't it? We're nothing but the product of electrical impulses and chemical reactions. As I always say, Page, we're just one short synapse from sainthood, a short circuit from schizophrenia."

Michael offered to play bartender and return to the room for refills even though Ron needed the exercise. He wasn't thirsty but was anxious to get away for a minute to think about what Ron had just said. He didn't believe man was nothing more than a circuit board, but what if falling in love was no different from adjusting the pH in a swimming pool? What if phenylethylamine could be synthesized and he could give some to Amy? What a wondrous place the world would be.

He buzzed slowly back to the dorm, thinking about Ron. One day he was considering relocation, the next congratulating himself on having a knowledgeable roommate. Ron's desire to analyze couldn't be stopped, and when he started profiling him, Michael was amused. Most of the time.

"You know, Page, you're very reserved around males. You must have a very formal relationship with your father."

He hadn't commented, and Ron had decided to prove his point by taking his hand into his catcher's mitt.

"Knock it off, Ron. What if somebody walked in right now?"

"You prove my point. I'm just trying to show you something. We're both afraid of intimacy. With you it's boys, with me it's girls. Don't you see? We can learn from each other. You help me with girls and I'll help you with boys."

Ron had crossed the room and put his arm around Michael, causing him to jump away and advise Ron that he should knock off the crap. But the words had bounced right off Ron's hollow head. He'd sat on Michael's bed like an obese prophet, smiling as though Michael were acting in a completely predictable manner and the light of knowledge was only seconds away.

"I could kiss you right now," Ron had said, "and it wouldn't mean anything."

"It would too. It'd mean sudden death."

"You're so hostile, Page. Does your father deny you respect?"

He had thought about asking for a change in rooms because he had trouble sleeping after that exchange, waking up every hour to make sure the hulk was in his bed across the room. But he didn't want to desert him, because Ron would probably run through roommate after roommate until he finally concluded that the whole world hated him. Then he'd commit suicide. He did tell him that he was considering a change of rooms because he wanted to impress upon Ron that he should never, not even in the interest of science, try kissing him.

"Page, Page, Page," Ron had said. "You can't change rooms. I'm the only person who can save you from yourself. You're an idealist and I need to be here when you discover there's no ideal. Idealists always end up with guns in their mouths. No, no, out of pure self-interest, stay with me."

He couldn't figure out exactly what Ron's sexual orientation was. Ron didn't like girls wearing tight clothes because they were emphasizing their reproductive parts, their nourishing parts. He thought Freud had got it all backward with penis envy; men resented women for their ability to reproduce.

Michael returned with their drinks to the bench before the administration building, feeling the pleasant effects of the previous martinis. He was ready to pass the evening in that spot. After giving Ron his drink, he picked up his cigar, which he'd left on the end of the bench, and relit it, sending great clouds of smoke into the holy air.

Then, like a miracle, coughing and complaining, coming through the smoke, was Andrea.

"Talk about pollution," she said.

Andrea sat next to him in English. She was a pleasant and rotund girl from the valley who wore sack dresses and who shouldn't have been any more threatening to Ron's sense of sexual deprivation than a roofing shingle. And she had appeared through obvious divine guidance so Ron could practice intimacy with a girl and Michael could sleep at nights.

"Don't ask her to sit down," Ron whispered.

"Why don't you sit down?" he asked her.

"You'll fry in hell for this, Page."

"I can't. I'm a Presbyterian and don't believe in hell."

Andrea sat, stacking her books on her considerable lap, which brought them to his eye level. Michael began to immediately doubt that her appearance was divinely inspired because she sat on the end of the bench, moving him closer to Ron.

Ron guzzled his martini and wiped his face with a blue plaid handkerchief. When Michael introduced them, Ron's greeting was an uncontrolled squeak. Ron switched glasses with him, taking one that was almost full and leaving one in his hand that contained nothing but ice and air.

Andrea peered around him at Ron. "I haven't met you but I've seen you around. Where're you from?"

Ron mumbled into his upraised glass, which he then lowered to reveal chipmunk cheeks packed with ice. He pointed at his face, explaining with his finger that he was temporarily incapable of speech.

"He's from Houston," Michael said.

Andrea looked delighted. "My sister's in Houston. Maybe I can catch a ride with you some weekend."

Ron suddenly spewed ten ice cubes onto the sidewalk, where they skittered in as many directions, leaving tiny trails of water. "Ahhh," he said, fanning his mouth with his fingers in an attempt to warm it. "Ah ont eer go hom," Ron said with his mouth wide open.

Andrea was watching Ron with worried eyes, so he told her that Ron had a toothache but couldn't get an appointment with a dentist immediately. Andrea opened her purse to search for aspirin, but he told her not to bother. Ron's tooth didn't hurt unless it got cold, and he'd been checking to see if it still hurt. To save both Ron and Andrea, he changed the subject.

Their next assignment in English was to choose one of several topics and develop a position pro or con. He asked Andrea if she had picked a topic yet.

"I think I'll take artificial insemination."

Ron made a sound as though he'd been punched in the stomach, rolled to his right off the bench, and lumbered off like a bear that couldn't decide whether he wanted to walk upright or travel on all fours. He headed for the administration building.

"I think you were wrong about the pain," Andrea said, watching Ron go.

"He may be having pain I don't know about."

He excused himself and went to check on his aching friend, finding him sweating just inside the door of the building, mopping his forehead with the blue handkerchief. He panted as though exhausted.

"Oh, God, Page, I just remembered where I saw her. I was following her up the steps of the Student Center and the wind blew her dress up. Talk about your reproductive capacity, talk about your wide hips. She could give birth easier than a chicken could lay an egg."

He didn't know what to say.

"Don't chickens just amaze you, Page?"

17

Ah, hindsight. Had the registration process for Stanton University been correctly carried out, he would have used a post office box as a home address and completed all the forms himself. As it was, university officials felt free to correspond with his parents at will, and even sent them an invitation to Parents' Day. Mrs. Page called to express her delight and to make plans, thinking the event would be like PTA Open House, a grand opportunity to visit his teachers, listen to how bright they thought he was, and to see his work on the bulletin board: "Our Friend, Mr. Cow."

And there on his new home ground were his parents, along with thousands of other interlopers. The strange thing was, not everyone seemed to feel as though his parents had violated some tacit agreement by coming and exposing themselves. Some of these kids were smiling and walking arm-in-arm and acting happy. Obviously some of them were simply engaging in a social charade required of gentlefolk and couldn't wait until their miserable parents departed, but some of the students were genuinely happy in the company of their parents.

When he saw his father, he thought about the past weeks in which he hadn't felt compelled to make silly excuses as to why he couldn't participate in some event on a Wednesday or Sunday night, ashamed to admit he had to attend church services. He hadn't eaten in a restaurant and been directed to bow his head while his father offered an audible blessing, nor had he heard his father loudly declare he *did not* drink and certainly had no need to see a wine list. He'd been free of the worry that they'd meet someone who didn't know Brother Page's position and would unwittingly make an off-color remark, receiving in return a mini-sermon on the need for a pure mind and mouth.

And when he introduced Ron, he hoped that his father would act like a normal person and maybe ask Ron about his family or his studies and not about his religion.

"What church do you attend, Ron?"

Michael's big roommate, whose own parents were in Mexico, wasn't at all embarrassed. In his black pants and white shirt, he rocked back on his heels and said, "My religion is science and my church is the laboratory."

What followed was another activity he hadn't engaged in for a long time—witnessing. He doubted that his father could have recited Ron's response two minutes later; all the man had heard was the lack of an acceptable answer, which set him off on his spiel—there was only one way to God, through Jesus and his saving blood shed on the cross. He outlined the steps of salvation—admit you're a sinner, repent of your sins, ask forgiveness, and accept Jesus as your Lord and savior. He handed Ron a small tract entitled, "Where Will You Spend Eternity?" and suggested Ron be saved on the spot.

Witnessing had always driven him crazy. It was the subject

of special clinics in which Christians condensed the stories of their own salvation down to a minute or less. In one of those clinics, he had been given a lapel pin, upon which was drawn a maze. When a curious person asked why he was wearing the pin, he was to suggest that the inquisitive person could find his way through the confusing maze of life by accepting Jesus as his savior. He had thoroughly hated that little pin. He appeared for breakfast each morning with it stuck in its proper place—on his shirt pocket—but upon walking out the front door on his way to school, he hurriedly stuck it in his pants pocket, hoping no one was watching him through binoculars and would ask him before other people, "Say, Page, what was that you stuck in your pocket this morning? Let's see it. Tell us what it means."

On his way to school one morning, he had thrown the pin into a cedar shrub that he could still see in his mind, and he hadn't got a hundred feet away before be began to feel truly ashamed. Was Jesus ashamed of him? Besides, didn't the Bible say that Jesus wouldn't confess to knowing a person who wouldn't confess to knowing Jesus? Didn't that mean the pits of hell for all eternity?

His last attempt at witnessing had been several years ago when one of his friends had gotten drunk and started crying over his lousy life. His parents didn't understand him, he wasn't bright enough to succeed in school, and he'd never get a job that meant anything. Life was an empty experience. He suggested that his friend could find hope in God. The friend's response was one he hadn't forgotten: "I prayed and prayed and asked Jesus to come into my heart, and nothing happened." He had proceeded to get much drunker than his friend already was.

Now Ron stood looking at the tract presented by Brother Page. "Do you think this is a way man combats cosmic loneliness?"

Michael expected his father to cry, "Infidel! Heathen! Bring forth the Grand Inquisitor!" But he wasn't upset at all. Instead he delivered a short monologue on the historical basis of Christianity and gave his personal testimony, how he'd come to recognize he was a sinner in need of salvation. Brother Page put his hand on Ron's shoulder and led him off—out of Michael's hearing and influence—leaving him with his mother.

She wore a navy blue dress with tiny polka dots. They stood, this small woman and her son, watching the strollers and gawkers and the parents who were reminding their children of all the changes that had occurred on the campus since they'd attended this wonderful school. He was glad to see his mother and listened to her questions—was he liking school, was the food good, did he and Ron get along—wishing he could offer her a hint of the homesickness she wanted to see and he didn't feel. He told her he missed her, he missed her cooking, and most of all, he missed her car.

She hit him with her purse.

He thought about what a large part she had always played in his life, and how little he thought about her, being obsessed, as he was, with her husband. He'd never given her the consideration she was due and he wasn't sure how to make up for it.

"You haven't asked me yet," she said.

"Haven't asked you what?"

"What I know about Amy."

My God, he thought. She's committed suicide, moved to Algeria, entered a nunnery, got killed in a wreck. He didn't know why he immediately expected bad news, but no news in Ashworth got spread unless it was bad. "What do you know about Amy?"

"Not very much but I expected you to ask so I called her father before we came. He said Amy's doing fine, living in Halton and still singing with her band. And he gave me her phone number in case you wanted to call her. You know, that man likes you."

Suddenly he was nervous. How could you distance yourself from someone, convince yourself that she may as well be living in Egypt, and then realize you were only a phone call away, a few seconds from her voice, a short bus ride to her front door? His reluctance was proof that he could never be a simple friend to Amy. He wanted badly to know how she was doing, what she was doing, but he didn't want to ask her himself, any more than he wanted to stick a pencil in his eye and ream out the socket. "I don't want her phone number."

Mrs. Page didn't mention Amy again.

While waiting on Ron and his father to return, he thought about one of Ron's theories—that sons search for the image of their mothers when it came time to marry. He didn't think so because he couldn't find any similarities between his mother and Amy, any more than he could between Bella Abzug and Billy Graham's wife. Maybe he'd never be happy with Amy, but he worried about coming home to find the little woman frying chicken. If he had a little woman, he'd treat her like one. He'd keep an extra box of doggy biscuits handy so he could pitch her one if she learned how to roll over. He'd unzip his pants and say, "Beg, Lucille, beg."

Brother Page and his potential disciple returned from their walk, and since the preacher's hand was no longer resting on Ron's shoulder, Michael assumed the pagan had resisted conversion. Still, he was amazed by his father's tolerance. If he had ever suggested that salvation through Jesus was nothing more than man's answer to cosmic loneliness, Brother Page would have assured his premature entry into eternity by a quick blow with that sword of the Lord he always carried, the Bible. They left Ron with the assurance that Brother Page offered—they would be praying for him, a signal to Michael that Brother Page was committing Ron into his son's slippery hands.

As they walked toward the center of campus, Brother Page said, "That's the most confused boy I've ever seen," implying, Michael thought, that if the son had been fulfilling his obligations, Ron would not only exhibit less confusion but would be teaching Sunday school and maybe even be leading the singing in a small church.

"He's so—big," Mrs. Page said.

They ate lunch in the student center with one of Brother Page's friends they'd met along the way on their tour, a fellow preacher who had a son Michael's age. He and the son gravitated, after years of conditioning, to a separate table. Sitting across from each other, they studied their reflections. In the wiry little guy before him, he saw what Ron professed to see in him—the flat look of a person seeking romance with rebellion, the discouragement of someone consistently thwarted by intervention from within and without. They sat and acted like two preacher's kids.

In a disgusted whisper, the other said, "What I wouldn't give to be drunk on my ass."

Michael assured him that within a few hours, he would be.

"Hey," the other said, sitting up straight. "You found anybody over here to fuck?"

"Nah."

"Me neither. You ain't got a car here, you ain't shit."

"You got that right, motherfucker."

While their parents asked the blessing, loud enough for the sons to hear, Michael stared at the ceiling and his reluctant companion picked his nose.

They parted after lunch without any plans to see one another. He thought they were both experiencing the same emotion —for the first time in their lives they had been living as normal people, but with the appearances of their fathers, their cloaks of anonymity had fallen to the ground and they stood exposed for what they were—eunuchs, little boy nuns. They didn't need each other as reminders.

Not long after lunch, the Pages left also, and Michael was relieved to see his father go. The good thing about the man was that he never tarried long in any one spot; he didn't like to observe dust settling. Michael watched them drive off, seeing also a father and son laughing. Laughing. He couldn't remember one instance in which he and his father had shared a good laugh. Not one.

He went to find Ron and a sack of martinis.

18

The first date he had—if it qualified for the tag—was with a girl from his history class. Donna sat beside him, and the first time he saw her, he thought, now there's a healthy broad. She could have stepped directly from a milk commercial, and even without a glassful in her hand she epitomized good health and sweetness. She wasn't fat, just big with wonderfully full hair, the color of which made him think of autumn. He wanted her to take him in her arms and nestle him between her ample breasts and tell him that everything would always be all right. He would have believed her.

One day when he was complaining about the tasteless food in the cafeteria—it wasn't really tasteless since it all tasted alike, from fried chicken to cherry cobbler—she invited him to her house for a home-cooked meal. She lived right there in Stanton, it turned out.

She picked him up on a Friday evening in her car, a four-door Chevrolet Malibu several years old. There was a—warning signal—Bible in the back window. When Michael approached the car, Donna slid across to the passenger's side so he could drive, and it took Michael a minute before he realized she wasn't moving to search the glove box for a map. The act threw him off balance because he'd never seen Amy do such a thing. In fact, he had never driven Amy's car.

"You want me to drive?" he asked.

She nodded. "Unless you don't want to."

He drove, following Donna's directions, to her house, where she lived with her parents and younger brother. The white brick house was set off the road about fifty yards on the side of a hill, several miles from town. There was a fence of rose bushes along the road, and as they passed through them, he thought, gosh, it's quiet out here. It was an appropriate entry onto the grounds of a place where he would spend one of the most pleasant evenings of his life.

Donna's father, who worked for a utility company, had built the house himself over a period of three years, and while they waited for dinner, the man showed him around, his childlike pride unconcealed. He was a small man with slicked-back hair, which he had probably been combing in the same manner for thirty years, and he kept up a constant stream of information. "Got these studs on sixteen-inch centers. The joists are two-by-sixes. And I hung every sheet of wallboard in the house myself, had to get stilts for the ceiling." Smiling, he reached for the ceiling, missing by three feet.

They ended their tour in the kitchen, where Donna's mother, exhibiting the same good cheer as the father and same radiant health as her daughter, said, "He is *so* proud of this house. If you get tired of hearing about it, just say so, but look how he put the appliances in first. This kitchen is a dream."

The food—fried fish and French fries and hush puppies

and homemade coleslaw—smelled like a diner's dream, and they moved into the dining room to eat. The table was set with silver and a white linen cloth, as though he were an honored guest. Only the son looked out of place in his Ted Nugent T-shirt. What happened to him, he wondered, but soon discovered that the boy called him "sir."

Donna' father advised him that the only way his wife's feelings could be hurt was by eating an insufficient amount, and over the course of the meal he saw more food than he had seen in any single month before. He tried to outeat little brother but knew when the boy asked for a loaf of bread that he was in trouble.

"The wife fries the cleanest catfish you ever saw," the father said. "You won't find a speck of skin on this fish. Of course, catfish aren't really all that clean to begin with, now that I think about it, laying in the mud all day—"

"More tea?" the mother asked, interrupting her husband.

"No, thanks," he said.

"They get down there in that mud and wallow around—"

"More tea?" the mother asked, more loudly this time.

"No, none for me, thanks," the father said. "You figure after spending all that time in the mud—"

"Daddy," Donna said, "I think Mother wants you to shut up."

"We don't want to talk about muddy fish," the mother said.

"Well, I was just talking, that's all. The wife does have an eagle eye though." He chewed a hush puppy reflectively and said, "She found worms in some bass I caught once that were so small—"

"Daddy," Donna said, "you're making everybody sick."

Michael didn't get sick until receiving his portion of a chocolate cake, about a quarter of it, and by the time he finished, he was beginning to feel like Buddha. He wanted to spend the rest of his life sighing and rubbing his stomach.

While Donna and her mother cleared the table, the father took him onto the front porch, which ran the length of the house and had a porch swing on either end. Between the swings sat several pieces of lawn furniture with cushions, and while he sat wondering whether his overloaded digestive system would get discouraged and shut down, the man beside him outlined the advantages of living in the country. He listened, watching the late afternoon sky, and thought, the world is out there somewhere, beyond the rose bushes. Miles away you could see wrecks and hear noise, but not here. Nothing happened here.

Donna came out and took him for a walk. Continuing on and over the hill where the house sat, they wandered into a valley beyond. The evening was still and quiet except for the whistling flights of doves headed for the stock tank at the bottom of the hill. He felt as though he had returned to his grandfather's farm and had spent too many nights crowded into a dorm with too many kids. Tense without having known it, he gave in to gravity and let his body sag. He uttered a long sigh.

Smiling, Donna took his hand and said, "I hope you enjoyed supper."

"It was great. I won't have to eat for a month."

Her smile was as sweet as a gumdrop.

They walked to the grassy dam at the end of the tank and sat. The sun was setting, an orange disc slipping into the trees above them, and the remaining sunlight glowed on Donna's hair. Her eyes were golden, but barely, because the pupils were huge, pushing the irises outward into rings as tiny as Life Savers that were almost used up. It seemed absolutely natural that she would sit and he would lie with his head in her lap.

Looking up, he asked, "Does your family ever have any conflicts?"

"I'm sure Mother's embarrassed to death about supper, the way Daddy was talking."

He asked because in class, Donna made excuses for him. If he got a grade that displeased him, she'd say, "Well, you can't study all the time when you're young and away from home." If he hadn't read an assignment, she'd say, "Well, it's impossible to read everything they want you to read," even though she always did.

"Will she get mad? Say anything to him?"

"Oh, sure. She'll say, 'I wish you wouldn't talk about mud and worms at supper.' And he'll say, 'Well, I was thinking about what that coleslaw was going to do to my gall bladder, and I didn't want to talk about that.'"

He laughed. "Do you ever get bored out here?" He asked because as much time as he and Gary had spent along the creek at his grandfather's farm, they had eventually followed their erections, like divining rods, back into town.

"No, I don't think I've ever been bored."

"Hmmm."

Donna stroked his forehead while watching his eyes. "You must have Indian blood in you. Your eyes are dark."

"Maybe that's why I've always liked white women."

He immediately regretted the statement because Donna bent forward and kissed him, at first catching her hair, then letting it slide over his face like a blanket. And although he felt comfortably covered, he knew they weren't, and he suspected his inability to respond stemmed from his sense of betrayal. He had come to the home of these fine people, eaten their food, then brought their daughter to the tank so he could ravish her. He worked an opening in the curtain of Donna's hair and looked at the top of the hill, expecting to see her father topping the crest, waving his twelve gauge. But all he saw was the empty hill, the trees, the clouds orange with the sunset.

They kissed and his hand roamed, finding no resistance until he hit a roll of fat at Donna's waist. Since she was bent over, she should have had some excess there, but his finding it made her squirm. She took his hand, squeezed it, and placed it firmly on her breast, which was as large as a canteloupe. And while he lay impotently, wondering why the signals weren't getting through to his body, Donna seemed to be getting excited. Her movements and breath grew sharper and more intent. He couldn't figure out what was wrong with him, so he sighed and broke the kiss as if trying his best to keep his outrageous lust under control.

Donna blinked a few times and regained her gumdrop smile. She appeared to be as content as she had when walking down the hill, and her ability to adjust so rapidly bothered him for some reason. Something was missing in her makeup, something that would have made her comprehensible to him, some grasping selfishness, some capacity for disappointment that would have made her think, if not say, "Hey, why'd you quit, boy? You kiss me some more, right now."

He kissed her fingers because she was so sweet, thinking possibly she was the nicest person he'd ever known. Then he held her hand on his chest, feeling secure in the twilight. The valley had fallen into darkness although the sky was still light and the trees at the top of the hill were reflecting the sun they couldn't see. They were in a hole that was filling with night, and it was as comfortable as being in a tub being filled with warm water.

He felt as he always did after he'd been exposed to a genuinely nice person—extremely fortunate and contented.

He fell asleep in her lap.

19

One morning he couldn't tolerate the thought of trying to keep up with the illusory transformations of X and Y, so he skipped algebra to engage in his favorite morning activity—leisurely reading the newspaper while he ate breakfast at a small café near the campus. He'd spread the paper out and read everything, even the personals in the want ads, while eating and drinking coffee for an hour. It was a much more satisfying way to spend time than watching magic tricks no one could explain.

He was looking over the entertainment page when something caught his eye, much as an X would, making him think he'd seen "Texas." He looked the entire page over, trying to figure out what had goosed his mind, when he realized he was staring directly at it—a small block ad that contained the name "Heat Lightning." The band was playing that night at the Mountain Creek Café. Everything—the clatter of dishes, the clinking of spoons, the shouting of orders—seemed to stop the instant he realized the significance of that ad. He put down his coffee cup and stared out the window.

He went from serenity to finger-quaking nervousness within a second, a dried-out alcoholic who had wandered into an empty room and found a full bottle of scotch sitting on a table, the seal broken. He rubbed his face and thought of all the reasons why he ought to walk out of the room and all the reasons he deserved a drink.

Good Lord have mercy, was all he could think.

He skipped his other two classes because he couldn't concentrate, couldn't think of anything but Amy's proximity. She was going to be in Stanton. It had to be a sign from God. He'd given him a hint that He wanted Michael to see her when Mrs. Page had offered Amy's phone number, and since he hadn't taken the hint, God had brought her to Michael's doorstep. He couldn't believe that God was really up there watching out for him, that he could once again possess faith.

Praise God's holy name, He wanted him to be with Amy. Faith was wonderful, easy.

Page, he told himself, you have gone absolutely crazy.

But what if it was just another band with the same name? Or if it was the same band but Amy no longer sang with it? He couldn't possibly wait until that night to find out, so he called the Mountain Creek Café and asked.

A voice told him, "Hey, this band is great. They've been playing all over the country and getting raves. Don't miss them."

"Where're they from?"

"From? Dallas or Houston."

"Do they have a girl singer?"

"I wouldn't know about that."

"What do you actually know about this band?"

"They're great so don't miss them."

He decided not to spit in God's eye and hoped for the best. He invited a guy named Blake to go with him. His room was down the hall, and he had a car. Blake was the male equivalent of a Stanton girl in his Izod-Jordache-Topsiders outfits and couldn't identify anyone without first being told of his social affiliation, and if a person lacked such a thing, he wasn't worth identifying anyway. He knew several guys with cars but asked Blake because he wanted the guy to see Amy. Sort of an eat-my-dust syndrome. Blake was actually a louse and they'd banned him from poker games because Ron had caught him cheating.

They arrived at the café just before dark. It was an eating

establishment in front, famous locally for its hamburgers, and the dance floor opened up toward the back. The floors were wooden and from the exposed ceiling joists hung assorted junk —kerosene lanterns, plows, stop signals, weather vanes. The place seemed to have noise built into it and he believed he could walk in when it was empty and hear a blurred roar of voices.

His faith was working. As he walked in the front door, he looked directly at Amy. She wore Levis and a long crocheted vest over a white blouse, and her hair was longer and unruly. She stood near the rear of the building talking in a serious manner to the keyboard player.

He began to shake. The wondering was over; he saw Amy a hundred feet away and suddenly felt very cold, trembling cold. He stuck his hands in his pockets.

Blake had stopped with him right inside the door, and he had followed his line of sight. Now he had Amy fixed with his eyes. Making pleasurable sounds in his throat, he said, "Hey, introduce me to her."

He shook his head, afraid if he voiced refusal, the "no" would sound like a high-frequency scream.

Blake decided to make his own introduction and swaggered and bounced across the dance floor. He watched him go, wondering why, when he had so little confidence in his own ability to attract Amy, he had brought Blake, who was certain all women loved him.

But God, who disliked Blake as much as he did, was in control. As Blake reached Amy, she turned and saw Michael. She looked twice, craned her neck, squinted, and then walked right past Blake on her way to him.

Oh, that walk of hers, that stride of confidence and grace.

"Michael," she said, smiling, "what're you doing here?"

Without wondering about the propriety of hugging her—but

well aware of the impropriety of an emotionally uncontrollable voice—he hugged her, sticking his face into her frizzy hair. He squeezed her, smelling her and thinking about how inadequate his memory was. She felt incredibly good, soft but solid beneath his hands. He stepped back and smiled.

She almost laughed. "What're you doing here?"

He took a deep breath and said in a voice that was only quivering a little, "I came to hear you sing."

She gave him a long look, then took his hand. Then, trying not to smile, she asked, "Are you nervous?"

He was ready to cry and couldn't do anything about it. He nodded.

"You poor baby," she said, taking him by the hand and leading him outside.

They sat out front on an old church pew that had been carved on by a great number of people proud of their initials and liaisons. The evening was Texas autumn warm, and a thick black cloudbank had built up on the horizon. The sun, having set behind those low clouds, created a brilliant nimbus in the sky. It reminded him of Easter. The Resurrection.

"How'd you get here?" Amy asked.

"Friend."

He wasn't so nervous that he hadn't figured out Amy was disoriented. She'd been playing with the band and hadn't seen him in an audience; suddenly he appeared and she couldn't fix his home port. Michael Page, Michael Page, now where did that guy go after high school? He had only told her a thousand times he was going to Stanton, and Stanton law school, and Amy, dear Amy, chasing so hard after the carrot, didn't remember he was in Stanton.

"Well," she said, turning toward him and taking his hand. "I'm glad you came. I haven't seen you since. . . ." Her voice trailed off when she remembered the last time—the day of the church's anniversary, the day he'd made her cry and then walked away. "Since the last time I saw you."

He had a question but didn't feel sufficiently calm to ask it. Andy had either been replaced or hadn't made the trip, because the bass player was a small red-haired guy. Rusty, the hyperactive drummer, had let his mohawk grow out but now had a burr; he looked like an escapee from a punk band in England.

Amy said, "I've never seen you go this long without talking."

"Well."

"Something terrible must have happened. When you got to college, they taught you, 'If you don't have anything nice to say, then don't say anything at all.' Is that it?"

Amy was getting an enormous amount of amusement out of his emotions, and if she hadn't been lovingly stroking his hand, he would have gotten upset.

"Don't you even want to know how I've been?" she asked.

"Of course I want to know."

She talked about the band. They were playing as much as they could, getting decent pay, and making progress. She bared the facts without one bit of real enthusiasm, and the disappointment, for one who knew where to look, was easy enough to find. She could leave him, she could forget him, but he didn't want her to get discouraged. He had never doubted she would succeed if only she wouldn't quit. Her talent had enemies —impatience, unrealistic expectations. He rolled the proper syllables over in his mind.

He asked, "Are you telling me you're making progress, or are you composing an obituary of this band?"

Amy looked mildly shocked; her output monitor hadn't warned her she was revealing so much. Sighing, she rested her head against the white wall of the café and looked at the sky. "You know the best song I've written is called 'Pipe Dreams'?" She looked as though she had delivered the punch line to an inside joke he should have remembered. "Pipe dreams. Things are so big."

"And you're so small?"

She shrugged. "I guess that's it."

He shook his head. "I hate to hear you talk like that. I always hated it. Nothing's changed but your perspective. Everything's the same, unless you've lost your voice, and I don't think that's happened. You may know more than you did a few months ago, and you may be more aware of the competition, but nothing's changed. You're still Amy Hardin, and you're still going to make it. Stop and think about how far you've come."

She slapped him lightly on the leg and left her hand there. His thigh muscles contracted as if he'd been stuck with a needle. Amy squeezed, trying to make his leg relax.

"What happened to Andy?" he asked.

She removed her hand from his leg and gave a double sigh, letting her head roll backward as though she were very tired. "He went to Houston. And nothing's been right since."

All the confidence he had gathered from her touches and smiles seeped from his body like sweat. They sat in silence and he tried to measure the gap between them. Amy had always been too good to be true, too much like a dream, and now she seemed as far away as the past, as irretrievable. He'd lucked out once but never would again. He may as well have been sitting with Stevie Nicks because nothing he had to say was important. He didn't know music and wasn't part of her life. She'd forget everything about him before she got back inside.

They talked for a few minutes, but he couldn't enjoy her company. The band was tuning up and she was going to leave and he wanted at least an hour with her. In an hour, he could discover what was possible, what wasn't.

She stood and said it was time for her to go in. He followed her, watching as she passed Blake. Hunched over at a table, his engine started when he saw her, his fingers tapping the table as if typing two hundred words a minute. He sat down beside him, and Blake glared, obviously angry over his refusal to serve him Amy on a platter.

The band was ready, and he was ready to hear them. The guitar player hit some well-amplified notes that passed an electronic verve into the crowd, and the new man on bass ran off several blues-flavored riffs. The mood of the crowd went from one of beer-drinking revelry to a quietened sense of anticipation. And then the band burst into a fast blues number and the bar came to life in response. He couldn't help but sit straight up, his legs bouncing, because he was with them. And the band knew they had started right because each member smiled. It was the kind of song Amy liked because it required her to fall immediately into a role, that of a woman faced with more desires than time.

He listened with renewed admiration and old awe because Amy's voice did things it shouldn't have done. It could scrape the gravel or soar with the birds, stretch out a line and give it more nuances and twinges of emotion than any nineteen-year-old girl should have been capable of. He forgot about drinking and slid deeper and deeper into that state of trance from which he seemed to listen so intently and in which he nursed memories, memories designed to create emotional aches. He knew what was happening—he was falling in love all over again—and he was powerless to stop it.

After a few songs, Amy conferred briefly with the band, then turned back to the microphone and said, "This is a song for an old friend, so everybody think of an old friend they haven't seen in a long time, somebody they want to see again." She sang "Dreams," sang it to him as surely as she had in her bedroom last spring when the rain blew in her open window. Blake watched him start in surprise, and his eyes bounced between

Michael and Amy as he tried to determine what was transpiring before him. Michael Page sat on the edge of his chair not knowing whether he was going to fall on his face, stand and shout, or faint. The exhilaration lifted him up and for a moment he thought he was surely levitating. His skin was alive with sensation and his being was focused on one thing—Amy, and she was singing to him. He stopped breathing until he grew dizzy.

When the band took a break, he pulled the frizzy-haired singer to a table and opened his mouth but no words came forth. He wanted to profess his eternal love and propose that they marry that very night, but he didn't know how. He couldn't say, "I love you," or "Let's get married," any more than she had been able to tell him in simple words that she was glad to see him. Dear Lord, he prayed silently, give me the gift of tongues. He needed a new language. The language used on earth was stupid and mundane; it was used to describe dead cats and dreaded relatives.

He sat across the little round table from Amy and held both her hands. "I don't know what to say. I know what I want to say, but not how to say it. Amy. . . ."

"I'm right here."

"Amy. . . ."

"You need to hurry because I've got to go make sure Rusty doesn't get distracted like he did the other night. Some girl had her hand down his pants."

Oh, the pressure, the desire, the longing. Well, he thought, he'd just come right out and say it.

Amy's mouth flew open and she looked instantly angry, noticing Rusty talking to a girl. "That little—I've got to go talk to him now, Michael. Don't run off."

He moved through the remainder of the night in a dream-like state, trying to find a car so he and Amy could go get married. He asked Blake if he could borrow his and Blake refused. He offered him ten thousand dollars, even wrote out a promissory note on a napkin and had it witnessed, but Blake was mad. He offered to rent the bartender's car for whatever amount was fair, but the bartender refused also.

When the band finished and all the lights came back up and the drunks started looking for their legs and coordination, he told Amy he was close to finding a car so he could take her home. She laughed. What a fantastic laugh she had, not one of those phony titters the Stanton girls tried to pass off.

"We have a rule, Michael. We all come together and leave together. We made the rule because of problems." They were standing outside by the van. "But you can come see me." She opened the front door of the van and got a slip of paper, writing on it two phone numbers and an address. She pointed at the first number. "This is my day gig." The laugh again. "I work for my uncle."

"I'm going to come see you."

"I hope you do."

He stood watching the band load equipment, listening to Rusty complain because Amy wasn't helping. Blake had already left by himself. He had watched him drive off, thinking a six-mile walk back to school was preferable to riding with Blake on this particular night.

And then the van was gone, Amy with it, and he stood in an empty parking lot, feeling very much as if he were on the vacated set of a movie. He was in a movie, a love story, the best ever made. It would be so well received that at Academy Award time, Johnny Carson would say, "Ladies and gentlemen, in the Best Romance category, we have had a nomination by acclamation."

He walked back to school with music in his soul, praying all the way. Thank you, God, for leading me back to Amy. Thank you because I don't deserve her. You have taken a faithless worm and turned him into a grateful Christian boy who will never again doubt or question or wonder. You are indeed wonderful and I will be thankful from now throughout all eternity.

Ron woke him the next morning and said he'd never seen anyone smile while sleeping. He'd been watching him for a few minutes and thought he was awake, but Ron had pulled his eyelids up and he hadn't reacted.

Michael came awake realizing his visit with Amy hadn't been a dream. He relived the experience of the previous night, giving Ron all the details, luxuriating in them, stretching and soaking in them.

Ron, already dressed, shook his finger and said seriously, "Page, you've got the worst case of PEA rush I've ever seen. You're close to an overdose and we've got to find an antidote."

"What's PEA?"

"Phenylethylamine. Some people confuse it with a healthy emotion, but it's no different from dropping acid to find God. I can see you're in big trouble."

"She wants me to come see her, Ron."

"Under no circumstances should you go."

"I've got to. She invited me. Besides, it's God's will. I've been called, just like a preacher or a missionary. And you can't fight providence. You can run but you can't hide. Ask Jonah."

Ron paced the room, pulling on his bottom lip. "We've got to find an antidote, some reverse aphrodisiac. Maybe a really ugly girl would work, maybe a deformed hundred-year-old midget."

As Ron rambled, Michael dressed. When God was flashing the green light, one didn't wait to see if the color was going to change. Besides, God probably wanted Amy out of rock music, wanted him to guide her into the area of evangelism and to serve as her manager, lining up revivals for her. He was of course the logical person for such a position because he already had numerous contacts in the religious arena.

"Don't do it, Page," Ron shouted as he walked from the room.

"Don't mess with God, Ron. Read your Old Testament and see what happened to those who tried."

"He's crazy," Ron said, "He's really crazy."

The bus ride was only two hours, but it seemed much longer because the bus stopped at every gas station, café, and post office along the way, picking up an old codger here, a black lady with a shopping bag there. He didn't want to wait on these people. He was in a hurry.

As they rolled into Halton, he began to understand God's plan. This was a nice little town with quiet streets and lots of trees and well-kept older homes. In short, it was the perfect place for a young married couple to live. God didn't want Amy in religious music; He wanted her to marry him and live the simple life, the life she'd been deprived of by her mother. Amy didn't know it, but God had a wonderful treat in store for her. She'd be the wife who finally had a home she loved, and he would work in the hardware store selling fishhooks and hinges and nails. In the evenings, they'd sit out in front of their little bungalow and talk to the neighbors, then go inside and make love on a throw rug beneath an air-conditioning unit in the window.

He called Amy from the bus station, wondering where the day had gone. He'd slept late but didn't understand how it could already be 4 P.M.

"Where are you, Michael?"

Such a harsh voice. She sounded like a mother who'd spent the last three hours looking for her child. He answered very nicely, knowing she'd mixed him up with another Michael, some customer of her uncle's who really irritated her, and told her he was at the bus station.

"Here in town?" she asked, unbelieving.

"Yes," he said, about to get mad.

"Well, what're you doing there?"

"I came to see *you*."

"Oh, shit."

Well, thank you, God, he thought. Just thank you a whole lot. What was he doing at the bus station? What was he doing chasing a girl who probably carried cue cards to help her with his name, who had once tried to emasculate him, who had tried to trick him out of sex on his graduation night? What was he doing? How had he become a masochistic fool without knowing it?

"What is it this time, Amy? What's the problem now? Tell me because I love the frustration. I love it. I thrive on it. It makes me feel like a child abuse case."

She was silent for a moment and then said calmly, but formally as well, that the band was scheduled to play that night and the keyboard player and drummer had gone to Mexico. She was sorry if she sounded rude and unfeeling, but she had a splitting headache and he had come for a visit on the worst day of her life.

"Well, forgive me and see you later."

"Don't leave," she said. "And please don't yell."

He could almost see her sitting with the heel of her hand pressed against her forehead and he was sorry for his anger. But he was sorrier for his stupidity. He tried to remember his conversation earlier in the day with Ron and hoped he hadn't said anything about God's will. But of course he had.

"Listen," Amy said. "I'm leaving work in about five minutes and I'll pick you up. Just stay at the bus station."

Stay at the bus station? What did she think he was going to do in the big city of Halton? Take advantage of the afternoon special at Eve's House of Pleasure?

*   *   *

Amy sat looking at a business card for the Allan Parker Band based in Stanton, thinking she was going to have to give serious consideration to moving.

One night she'd been singing in Waco and a guy had come up during the break to introduce himself. At first, Amy hadn't paid much attention. Someone was invariably flirting with her, and she'd become adept at giving glib answers that made the point without offending anyone. But Allan had given her this card and suggested that if she ever wanted to join a new band, she should let him know.

Amy had gone to hear his band play at a nice club on the river in Stanton. The four musicians were creative and cared about their music, and they'd lost their vocalist. Amy had almost signed on that night. But the thought of Andy's recent desertion to Houston, and her resulting anger, took her back to Halton without having made a commitment.

At the next rehearsal, while the keyboard player was making a sound like a helicopter and Rusty was saying, "That woman too bad, wanna make me a dad," Amy announced her intention of moving to Stanton. She was hit was a loud chorus of "What? What'd you say? You can't do that. Please don't. Please don't go." Amy had agreed to stay as long as they were all serious.

They were serious three weeks. Now the two worst offenders were in Mexico getting a disease that, Amy hoped, would rot the appropriate body parts.

When she picked him up at the bus station, he was leaning against the wall. He wasn't in the car completely before Amy said, "Listen, you're here on the worst day of my life and you were the last person I wanted to see, even though this hasn't got a thing to do with you personally. But if you'll help me get rid of this headache by rubbing my neck, I'll . . . I'll feel better about your visit."

"I don't have anything else to do."

They rode in silence to Amy's apartment and clattered up the outside stairs to the second story entrance of an old white frame house. Inside, Amy called the brother of the drummer, then the girlfriend of the keyboard player. "I hope you're not allergic to penicillin." Once she had verified the continued absence of the two delinquents, Amy cancelled the gig.

While she made her calls, he looked around the apartment, wondering if Amy actually lived there. He couldn't see a sign that a nineteen-year-old girl inhabited the place. The furniture was old, castoffs from a funeral home, and only two pictures hung on the walls, dusty prints of a field of bluebonnets and one of a man praying over a loaf of bread. The apartment was really the second story of the house and was built around the landing of the inside stairs. When he went from the living room to see the bathroom, across the landing, he found the landlady standing halfway up the stairs, obviously attempting to eavesdrop.

She was about seventy and matronly looking with breasts like artillery shells. Overall, she reminded him of that great snoop, Ima Inez. He immediately disliked her.

"Friend of Amy's?" she asked.

"I'm her brother, James Ray. Daddy sent me over to check on her."

The landlady sniffed and pursed her lips. "Her brother? You don't look a thing like her."

"Well, we had different mothers. You know how that is."

She shifted her feet, exchanging stairs with them, and leaned against the bannister, giving him a long look. "Mozelle Lara says Amy sings with one of those rock and roll bands."

The distaste with which the woman had spoken "rock and roll" guided him in the right direction. "No, that's her sister, Emmy. Emmy Lou Harris. Maybe you've heard of her. And

Daddy hates that girl so much for singing in one of those bands that he's done disowned her. She won't ever get a piece of the farm. No, Amy works right in Halton for our uncle so she couldn't be one of those dope addict rock stars."

The landlady gave a victorious little snort. "Well, Mozelle's half Messican and she never got anything straight in her life. But you tell Amy if she ever takes up with any of that rock and roll stuff that she'll have to move. I know what happens at those concerts. Heard about it at church. Drugs and Satan worship and lying with beasts. I heard it all. One boy even eats bats." She stood nodding her head in confidence, making her armament bounce.

He walked back to the living room. Amy stood just inside the door, letting her head roll on her shoulders, and before he could relate the conversation, Amy said. "I know. I heard."

She walked into the bedroom and fell face down on the bed. "Will you rub my neck? Please."

"For ten minutes."

Amy sighed as he pushed his fingers up into her hair, following the groove up the back of her neck.

"When my headache goes away, we can go eat or something."

"Then don't go to sleep."

He massaged, thinking about how small Amy's neck was. Perfect choking size.

Looking around the room, he found a mess. The bed was unmade, the covers simply thrown upward toward the pillows, and a pile of clothes lay in one corner. In another corner rested several open boxes of shoes; the lids lay in a pile next to the boxes.

He watched Amy fall asleep but didn't discontinue his efforts. He was, after all, touching her, which was more than he'd done in months, and at the moment Amy's face looked gentle and soft and loving, a countenance that filled him with a newfound

183

confidence in their relationship. At least she'd been glad to see him last night.

After a while, he realized the time—after 5 P.M.—and he hadn't eaten all day. So he carefully arose from the bed and tiptoed into the kitchen. In the refrigerator sat a carton of milk, a jar of Miracle Whip, and a bowl of soggy Cheerios that Amy was saving for some strange reason. The Cheerios box, however, was empty, sticking from the top of a yellow plastic trash can. The cabinets were all but bare except for a small collection of plates and glasses. Amy seemed to be eating nothing at all, at least not in the apartment.

He spied an appointment book on the scarred pecan table and sat to snoop. The first page, under the heading, "Important Phone Numbers," contained several names and numbers, including the infamous Andy, now with a 713 area code, but not that of Michael Page. Throughout the book Amy had noted the dates and places the band was to play or had played, but she'd made no comments, no ratings, otherwise. On the very last page were notes, apparently from a phone conversation.

"Bruce at Summit. On 59. Tickets. Inside loop. No no no."

Bruce Springsteen had recently played the Summit in Houston, and Andy must have invited Amy down. He knew the Summit was on Highway 59, inside the loop, because he'd once gone to see the Rockets play. But what was "No no no"? Andy had probably asked, "Let's go see Bruce at the Summit and then go to prayer meeting," and Amy had replied, "No, no, no, Andy, not prayer meeting. Let's screw till we can't stand up."

Shit. When was he going to learn that he meant nothing to the girl? And that he couldn't change that very basic fact? He wanted to ball up his fists and scream in frustration, but he knew a tantrum would only wake Amy and give her additional reasons to omit him from her life.

He gave God ten minutes to act, to cause Amy to awaken and

profess her undying love for him. And when ten minutes had passed and Amy had crawled beneath the covers, grinding her teeth and practicing her emasculating techniques on wayward musicians, obviously not receiving any messages from God, he walked downtown and caught the next bus back to Stanton.

He prayed as he bounced back. Dear God, I most humbly thank you for this opportunity to demean myself. Obviously you are getting great fun out of this soap opera of my life, and I can assure you that when I die, I want to go straight to hell because I'd rather burn than spend a second with you. Thank you and amen.

20

Back at school, he sat in his room with the trash can between his legs and shredded the three pictures he had of Amy, gleefully disfiguring her. Good-bye, chin. So long, eyeball. Oops, he gouged her tit. He had tried everything and nothing had worked. If he'd stood on his head and recited original sonnets, she would have complained about his rhythm or rhyme scheme. "No, no, no, Michael, a sonnet is never *a b c a b c a b c.*" Well, he was through. She could go see Bruce at the Summit and wear out the 713 area code, but she wouldn't have Michael Page to kick around. He hoped she found her robot boyfriend and her robot band because no human was sinful enough to deserve her.

He stood and mixed bits of pictures by shaking the trash can in a circular motion and said, "Congratulations, Page. You are finished with frustration forever. You're a new man."

Ron looked thirsty so he took him out for a beer to celebrate his new life. Now he was going to focus all his love on Donna.

She was a wonderful, almost perfect person, and the fact that she wasn't sinful enough to deserve him was a thought he didn't consider at length. Instead he was so excited about his future that he called Donna from the bar.

Her mother answered and said Donna wasn't there.

Hot dang, Michael thought, feeling a surge of excitement. Donna was dating another guy and Michael was going to have to fight for her. He'd have to pull out all the stops, use every trick, every ounce of charm he possessed, to win her handsome heart.

But then he discovered the truth—Donna had taken her brother to play miniature golf; she'd call when they returned.

Well, he thought, returning to the table where Ron sat and ordering two beers, you couldn't judge a person by one minor incident. So what if Donna had taken her brother to joust with miniature windmills and leap over dangerous water traps? So what if her brother didn't merit his Ted Nugent T-shirt?

But wait. Wait. There was something he wasn't seeing. There was a challenge, and he'd missed it. The challenge was this: unless he rescued Donna from Goofy Golf, she was sure to end up in a museum stuffed in a glass exhibit labeled, "Vanished American. Last of the Bored Tribe. Now extinct." That was it. He had to teach the girl how to raise hell. And she'd love him for it.

Donna didn't return his call until Saturday morning. The reason she hadn't called Friday night, she said, was because she hadn't got home until ten o'clock and knew it was too late to call. He wiped his eyes but still couldn't see the clock.

"What time is it?" he asked.

"Oh. Did I wake you up?"

No problem, Michael thought. He'd indoctrinate her on schedules for hell-raisers. She'd learn. "What time is it?"

"A little after eight."

First she sounded as though she'd been pitching hay and milking cows and singing praises to the morning; then she turned apologetic. This girl required so much work he didn't know where to start. Her edge of niceness didn't have even a tiny chip in it. Well, a little sandpaper would cure that condition.

"Why don't we go drink some beer and listen to music later?"

"Drink some beer?" she asked.

"Sure, why not. Let's raise a little hell."

"Raise a little hell?"

"It'll be good for you. You'll love it."

"I'll love it," she said in that same uncertain voice.

He was afraid she'd need some remedial work before stepping right into hell-raising—she'd probably never even liberated all the dogs from the local pound—so he amended his invitation to eating lunch, a suggestion to which she readily agreed, however ignorantly. He would take her to the pregame watering hole where football fans prepared for Stanton's upcoming loss with a few drinks. The place was always crowded and festive, and Donna would have numerous examples of falling and fallen Baptists to follow.

When she picked him up wearing blue jeans and a white blouse, he thought she looked like the kind of girl he wanted to taken on a hayride. She had the taste and potential of apple cider. And his plans for them seemed not only appropriate but possibly divinely inspired. He'd give a little too and become as healthy and happy and content as Donna, and they'd be the perfect match. Wonderfully nice and slightly rebellious. What on earth had he ever seen in Amy?

At the restaurant-bar, the crowd was boisterous, working on riotous. A few patrons forgot they were only preparing for the game and got sloppy drunk; they began visiting at tables where they didn't know anyone but wished to get acquainted. One young man demonstrating the fumble feet of a Stanton receiver ran smack into a waiter carrying a tray of hamburgers and sent buns and patties and tomatoes flipping through the air. One onion ring, like a perfectly thrown horseshoe, landed on a candle. The crowd cheered.

He guided Donna through the maze of bodies to a booth and sat across from her. He wanted to look into her golden eyes as he fell irretrievably in love with her. He was already on his way because he'd lost most of his inhibitions with three of Ron's canned martinis, and he could very plainly see Donna's big white bra through her blouse. Yes indeedy, everything was jelly but the jar.

A waitress appeared with menus, but he waved her away and ordered two beers. Donna gave him a look of concern, as if he were her doctor and had just prescribed a lower GI. But he had to get the girl started on becoming a minor league sinner.

Once the mugs of beer were sitting before them, Donna started to examine her nails. Bright red, they needed no attention, so she folded and refolded her napkin. She did almost everything she could think of with the exception of looking at him or drinking the beer. She even read the sugar packets.

He raised his glass. "Well, bottoms up."

"I don't like beer."

"You think it's sinful?"

"No, I think it tastes awful. But you go ahead." She pushed her mug across the table.

When he accepted her offering, she smiled. Her lips were wet and her teeth shined and he could just see the tip of her tongue. He reached over to lovingly pat her hand, and she held his fingertips. It was impossible to fall in love from so far away, so he moved to her side of the booth. Once he was beside her, she gave him a shoulder-curling giggle and he had to kiss her. His hand crept between her legs and marveled at the firmness, the warmth.

He kissed her several more times and said, "I hope nobody minds."

"Listen, I think you could get butt-naked in here and nobody would even know."

They kissed again and Donna slipped her hand inside his shirt, engaging in a two-finger massage of his nipple. Everything was just right—everything—so he couldn't figure out why he was staring over Donna's shoulder, looking out the window at a sparrow with a long piece of dead grass in his mouth. His circuits were shorting out again, just as they had at the stock tank after dinner at her house.

The problem, he decided, was obvious—they were acting too much like parties involved in a one-night stand. He needed to know much more about her, needed to hear her recount the many conversations she'd had with her mother on the necessity of remaining pure and virginal. He needed to know about her struggles with the flesh and spirit, about the times she had dedicated her body to God. Then once she'd talked herself back into purity, he would bang her box.

He suggested they order lunch, and Donna was agreeable. She sat with her arm wrapped around his, her head on his shoulder, and they remained in that position for a few minutes.

Then he sat her up because he wanted to look at her eyes when she answered a question. "What do you want more than anything else? If you had one wish, what would it be?"

Without hesitation, Donna said, "A good home."

"That's it?"

She shrugged. "What else is there?"

"Well," he said, trying to think of something more important than a good home. There were money and sex, both licit and illicit, and hell-raising, major and minor, and fast cars and good music and travel, but none of those was more important than a good home. The conversation was having a strange effect on him. He was sobering up. He wasn't getting excited; he was getting serious.

Donna was an elementary education major, and he asked if she was going to teach school in Stanton when she graduated.

She shook her head and brushed his leg with her fingers. "No, my uncle's the director of a rehabilitation center in Dallas, and I'm going to teach there."

A revelation. The light of knowledge beamed down upon him. No wonder he couldn't get excited—he was trying to make out with his mother. He had planned on taking this sweet wholesome girl and initiating her into the ranks of the rabble, leading her into temptation, suggesting she yield her body to the world. Oh, Lord, he thought. Oh, Lord. What would the children think, the disabled children who loved her? How could they ever respect her, trust her enough to help them walk again? What if she came in hung over from a night with him and let one fall? What if he made her as moody as Amy, as unhappy? He didn't want to ruin her; he wanted to enlist in the army and protect her, make the country safe for Donna and her disabled children. God, he'd be proud lying in his foxhole.

Then he sobered up so much he saw the future. He saw the real plan of God. He had sent Donna, not himself, on a missionary expedition to change him. He would marry her and before he knew it, he'd be twenty-five, an expert in TV listings. During the day he'd sort mail at the post office, looking forward to getting home and watching "Love Boat" reruns with the little woman. Donna would sit at his feet waiting for him to order another chocolate cake and six pack of Bud. He'd weigh three hundred pounds.

He could picture this life very clearly, and the surprising part was, he wished he could want it. He wished he could give all his frustrated love to Donna, but he couldn't. Beside, she didn't need it. She was as pure as cream and wanted only an all-American family. He had to dissuade her before things went too far.

"How do you see me?" he asked.

She squinted and said, "With both eyes."

"Be serious."

She raised her hand, then brought it down in front of her face, turning comically solemn.

Damn, he'd already made her crazy. A little amputee at the Rehab Center would ask, "Donna, do you love me?" and she'd mug and say, "There ain't much of you to love, boy. Hellfire, you only got one leg." The child would drop his crutches and hop off, sobbing, and Donna would yell, "Just kidding, Hopalong."

"Listen," he said. "We aren't compatible. I wish we were but we aren't. I like change and get bored easy, and I like to get drunk and raise hell every once in a while. And see old girlfriends. I don't ever want you to think I'm something I'm not."

Donna smiled, unwilling to believe a word of it because she knew Michael Page was clay in her hands, placed there by the master potter himself. Her eyes were bright and hopeful and confident and she radiated absolute assurance that she could transform him into a Sunday school teacher who went to bed each night at nine o'clock. She'd feed him chocolate cake, but no Bud. No way. He tried to think of discouraging items.

"I hate going to church. My father's a preacher and I don't ever plan to step foot in a church again. The next time I'm in church, I'll ride in a pine box on a dolly."

Donna very calmly took his hand and quietly told him of a childhood friend who had been raised a Pentecostal and who, like him, had vowed never to step foot in a church again. But her husband had introduced her to the Presbyterian church and now she was very happy and was taking courses part-time at a seminary.

His mouth dropped open. Good God Almighty, Donna already knew about the Presbyterian lawyer business. God must have told her. How else could she have known? In his drunken stupor, he had come up against God and Absolute Innocence, and he was already roped and tied. This girl heard God's voice. He was so tired and confused that he decided to submit himself unto them. They'd know what to do.

"Listen," he said, taking her hand. "Sometimes I get a little crazy. I don't know why, but I do. No matter what I say, ignore me."

"Okay," she said.

They left the restaurant and went to the zoo.

In the mail, he received a card, on the front of which were two silhouettes on a beach. Inside was written, "Don't be mad at me. Amy."

He threw the card at the trash can so hard he was afraid he'd dislocated his shoulder. Amy was a huckster in a game booth at the fair and thought he was going to keep throwing quarters at the dishes. She thought he was a sucker. And she probably thought he'd pick up the card from the floor and see if the silhouettes were holding hands—they weren't—and then examine it for secret messages, something Amy was embarrassed to say outright.

He scrutinized the entire card and found *nothing*.

She probably even thought he'd retrieve the envelope and check to see if she'd gotten his address correct and wonder whether she'd had it handy or had to get it from his mother.

He fell onto the bed face down in total fatigue.

How had he arrived at the point where he couldn't want a normal life, a normal girl like Donna? It had to be his father's fault. His father had made him believe that Almighty God, creator and ruler of the universe, a universe that couldn't be fathomed by the human mind and a being that had no beginning and no end, this God was going to direct his life, his life, one among untold billions, maybe even trillions, and he would know this God personally. Well, if you could deal direct with a cosmic force like that, why would you want to bother with dominoes on Saturday night?

But this time, he was determined to forget about Amy. She was going to have to make a much bigger stroke than sending a silly little card to get his attention.

He started talking more and more about Donna to Ron. If he convinced himself that she was the perfect girl—and who could deny that she was?—then he wouldn't be tempted by Amy. But every time he mentioned Donna, his mind answered like a perverse echo. Donna, he said. No, Amy.

"Donna is the nicest, sweetest girl in the entire civilized world."

"Try listening to 'Dreams' with her. You'll never know sexual ecstasy or spiritual accord."

"I don't care. I want a level life. I don't like all these ups and downs. I've spent half my life depressed."

"You're not suited to life with Donna. You couldn't stand living in Mayberry. Amy will give you one to a hundred; with Donna you'll get a level twelve."

He really didn't want to go home, but he was glad when his mother called and wanted to know if he was ever coming for a visit. She didn't want to forget his face. He told her he'd come because he wanted to forget about Amy.

Five minutes after his arrival, he knew he'd chosen the wrong change in routine to provide relief from thoughts of the singer. He was glad to see his parents but he walked right back into the old life he'd wanted so badly to escape. At supper on Friday night, he felt beneath the table and his initials, constructed with chewing gum, were still there from the sixties. The holders for corn on the cob, those little yellow plastic ears of corn with two silver prongs, were still in use.

He heard gossip with the same characters playing major roles. Lottie Swenson had heard the Methodist minister watched dirty movies every Saturday night on "this newfangled movie tape recording whatchamacallit" and had decided to investigate. She'd parked her '58 Imperial in the street and trained her binoculars on the minister's window, trying to see through the cracks in the venetian blinds, and she was hanging halfway out the window of the car when Shortstop Peterson, the city marshall, rearended her. Lottie swore she was parked at the curb, the old Imperial broken down, and Shortstop knocked her into the street. She couldn't explain why her binoculars had gone flying through the air and cracked the windshield of the squad car, however.

After supper he drove around town in his mother's car, trying to find something changed. He wanted to see a new shopping center under construction, an office park, some sign that things could and would change, but all he saw were the green grocery store, the orange pharmacy, and the hot pink bank. The fertilizer sacks out front of the grocery retained the same indentations where the old men sat during the day talking about the exact meaning of "twenty percent chance of rain." The litter bucket in Mrs. Page's car probably contained the same Kleenexes with which she had blotted her lipstick when he had been at home.

He was stuck; things would always be the same.

He had taken his one suit, a gray pinstripe, to Stanton, and then brought it back home without having worn it. He put it on Sunday morning, and once he was at church, he felt terrible over his desire to escape his own upbringing. Everyone welcomed him back and asked how he was doing and whether he was learning anything. He loved the women of the church with their massive bosoms and comforting hugs, and he knew that his thoughts on God and the world would not only disappoint his father but those wonderful women as well. Deep down, they weren't much different from Amy's suspicious landlady; they didn't understand the allure of rock and roll or problems with fundamentalist theology or anyone slightly different from themselves.

Brother Page's sermon was one of those that always drove him nuts—how one could know he had been saved. Brother Page said he was always puzzled by those who wondered about the state of their salvation, but he was constantly asked to preach on the matter, so he would. He went through the steps of salvation, and Michael knew exactly what was going on in the congregation. Everyone sitting there projected outward calm while his mind caromed off his skull. They had mental checklists and were ticking off mentally. Yep, got that. And that. Oh, got that one too. Whew, looks like I'm okay. They all wanted a ticket with every block checked, validated for a one-way trip to heaven.

But then Brother Page fixed on a requirement he had never heard.

"If you didn't feel sorrow for sin, if the state of mankind didn't bring you to your knees, if the necessity of Jesus' death didn't bend your head in real sorrow, why then, you have reason to question your experience—you weren't saved."

Son of a gun, he thought. That's it! That was his problem. His motivation in being saved at the age of ten had been a vision of hell and not sorrow for sin. He hadn't cared much about sin one way or the other. He'd just wanted to avoid the fire. And he hadn't shed one lonely tear over Jesus' pain and agony on the cross or the sin that had taken him to that terrible sacrifice. He had never heard God's voice because he'd never been saved. God didn't speak to those merely masquerading.

But God was giving him another chance. All he had to do was walk forward during the invitation and meet his father before the pulpit and tell him he'd never been saved. Nothing could be easier. Just a few steps down the aisle and a simple admission were required. And when Brother Page stood before the congregation after the invitation had ended and said, "Michael comes to us today because he realizes he's never been saved and wants to accept Jesus as his personal Lord and savior," all those people who loved him would cry right along with him. After the benediction, they'd walk by and hug him until he couldn't breathe and whisper in his ear that they loved him and would be praying for him. "I'm so happy for you, Michael."

He had to hold on to the pew in front of him through the invitation, his hands finally aching from the strain, because the magnetic pull was almost too strong to ignore. And when he left church an unredeemed infidel, he went looking for the cowardly Presbyterian lawyer who had left him in the lurch. Where was he? Why hadn't he stuck around to point out that the preacher had added a brand new wrinkle to the steps of salvation, one that wasn't even mentioned in the Bible? Why hadn't he pointed out that the very man who had led him to Jesus nine years ago had at the time omitted sorrow for sin in general as a prerequisite?

He returned to Stanton hoping the bus ride would transform him back into Ron's junior scientific assistant, if not a wholly Presbyterian lawyer, but he left the Stanton bus station feeling more emotionally stunted than he had upon his arrival two months ago. He hadn't walked a block toward the campus before he reversed his course and returned to the bus station so he could call Donna. She'd be leaving for Sunday evening services at the church within an hour, and he wanted to catch her before she left.

She was at home and he asked if she was going to church.

"I'd planned to. Unless you have something else in mind."

He didn't quite know what to tell her. He wanted to see her because she had no neurosis to exercise at his expense. He wanted to be sucked into her inner whirlpool, her aura of utter pleasance. But he simply said, "I don't have anything in mind really. I just wanted to see you."

She picked him up at the bus station, and he threw his suitcase into the rear seat of the Malibu and asked her to drive. She had been dressed and ready for church when he called and she was wearing a navy blue dress with white stripes. With her autumn hair and skin that was as remarkable as spring water, she looked beautiful. He slid across the seat and sat as close as he could, stroking her arm and marveling at the texture of her skin. Since Donna didn't understand his problem, he didn't try to explain. He just smelled her hair and kissed her neck and tried to lose himself in her goodness.

He lost control and stuck his hand in her dress, in her bra, kneading a breast as large as a grapefruit. Donna placed her hand on his and helped him fondle, emitting purrs of satisfaction. They stopped at a red light and Donna, after checking to make sure no cars were closing in, unbuttoned her dress, unhooked her bra, and pulled it up over her breasts so Michael's enjoyment would be unhampered.

He was so happy riding through the middle of Stanton with several pounds of raw femininity in his hands that he wanted to shout with joy. He kept peeking into her dress and pulling the top of her slip forward so he could see ungirded there the swelling stuff of dreams. He lay with his head in her lap, his hand traveling from left breast to right, again and again.

Donna stopped the car and cut the engine, and since all he could see was sky through the windshield, he asked where they were.

"My house," she said. "Be thankful for good Baptists.

Otherwise my folks would be here and we couldn't use my bed."

Before she had unlocked the front door, he had undone the remainder of the buttons on her dress, and they entered the house with the dress hanging open like a robe. After Donna had relocked the door, they stood in the entryway and kissed as if they had to cram a lifetime of sex into twenty minutes. Donna's hands were as busy as his; they tried undressing each other without breaking their kiss, without falling over furniture as they moved toward the bedroom.

"I've been thinking about this since the first time I saw you," Donna said, breathing hard. "I've never dated a boy just because I wanted to make love. Never. But you're the sexiest thing I've ever seen in my whole blooming life."

They reached the bedroom at the head of a trail of discarded clothes, and while he tried to comprehend what Donna had just said, she sat him on the bed, shoved him backward, and started licking at his throat and didn't stop until she reached his feet.

Then she stopped, on hands and knees hovering over him, her hair brushing his stomach as she viewed the appendage straining upward toward her face.

"Looks just like a popsicle," she said.

In the next few minutes, the term good fortune acquired a world of new meaning.

Afterwards, Donna wanted to talk. They picked up their clothes and locked themselves into her bedroom, lying naked face to face on the bed. She told him she had been trying to think of a way to get him in her bed since their first history class together. "I don't know why because I never dated anybody just for sex. Maybe it was because I'd been thinking about marriage, and I'd never be unfaithful, so maybe I just wanted to do this while I could."

She smiled and touched his mouth. "The day you said we weren't compatible—the day you wanted me to drink beer—I knew what you were thinking. You thought I was looking for a husband, didn't you? I started to tell you I wasn't, but you were so funny that day, I decided not to. That's mean, isn't it? I wanted to be sexy and mean, just to see if I could.

"You were right, there's no way we're compatible. You were right about that. You can't sit still in class, how could you ever sit still at home? But we're compatible in my bed, aren't we? That was great, just great. You want to try it again?"

Later he reviewed the conversation they'd had at lunch when he'd decided she had husbandly designs on him. He was guilty of gross assumptions, assumptions about what she wanted, about who she was, about her view of him. He had followed the highway signs to Okahoma City and ended up in Baton Rouge. Very perceptive.

He decided to apply this lesson in wrongful assumptions to Ron. Ron had been extremely demonstrative, had questioned his desire for Amy, and had so little interest in his intrigue with Donna that they hadn't discussed her. And he had again begun to suspect his roommate of homosexuality when the guy was nothing but a nice guy. Confused and brilliant but nice. And since he wanted Ron to know he thought Ron was a nice guy, he started patting him on the back occasionally.

"I'm working on male intimacy, Ron. How's that?"

"Progress, Page. You're making real progress. You should be proud."

Ron tried to reciprocate every gesture and once pulled him into his marshmallow side, hugging him.

He wished he wouldn't reciprocate.

2 1

Amy wanted a cigarette and didn't even smoke.

She stood in a phone booth in the middle of Stanton, the receiver in her hand, the sounds of a riot rolling over the phone line like a scream.

"Is Michael there?" she asked.

"I'm already in. Leave my money alone. Who do you want?"

"Michael Page."

Amy listened to the person who had answered the phone advise Michael he had a call and she wondered, while she waited, about the number of boys occupying a dorm room. What on earth were they doing at nine in the morning that caused so much noise? Everyone was either protesting or shouting with glee.

"Hello?" Michael said.

Amy identified herself and asked if she was interrupting anything. No, no, Michael said. They were involved in a poker game that had started at a friend's apartment the previous evening and had moved to the dorm when the friend's wife threw them out.

As he talked, the sounds of the game receded as though Michael were shutting himself into a closet and now Amy wondered if she had made the correct decision. She was certain about the decision to join the Allan Parker Band, and resigning from Heat Lightning had been a definite analgesic relief. But calling Michael for his "help" in finding an apartment? She wasn't sure. When he saw her moving toward him so openly, he'd forego all niceties, grab her ankles and split her open like a wishbone, then rape her on the sidewalk in front of the dorm. His friends would pass by and say, "Oh, I guess Michael found a new girlfriend."

Looking at the phone numbers and obscenities etched into the side of the phone booth, she asked, "Willyouhelpmefind-anapartment?"

"Help you bombard what?"

"Help me find an apartment."

There was a pause. "Over here? In Stanton?"

Amy briefly explained that she was joining a new band and needed his knowledge of the city in her search for suitable living quarters.

"Of course, I'll help you. When are you coming?"

"Well, I'm here right now. But if you've been up all night...."

"Hey, don't worry about that. You're going to pick me up?"

Amy said she would and made arrangements; then she hung up and emitted a sound not much different from a bird call in a jungle movie. What was she doing?

Of course, he didn't act a bit like she expected. Instead he was the gentleman tour guide, escorting her through apartments and rendering judgments. "This one's too close to the freeway; you'd be better off just putting your bed on the median. At least you'd catch the breezes from passing trucks." And, "The parking lot's too close to that convenience store. You'll have kids slashing your tires."

The most personal thing he'd said was "Good morning." Why was he being so nice? Amy couldn't concentrate on apartments because she was watching Michael, waiting on him to touch her. But after several apartments, she was as pure and untouched as brand new snow. And instead of telling her he was glad to see her, he said instead, "Yuk. The carpet's filthy."

Michael, armed with the want ads, was apparently prepared to spend days looking at apartments, so Amy decided on one. She couldn't remember exactly where they were or what the complex looked like from the street, but she saw a beautiful green and white striped mattress in the bedroom, and the sunlight fell very softly through the trees outside, and right there in the shadows of the branches was where she wanted Michael to remove her clothes and hold her, to make her warm and wanted and thoroughly used.

"You wait here," she said. "I'm going to pay the deposit. Don't move. Okay?"

He waited, looking over the dingy white walls and badly matted shag carpet, knowing his resolution to treat Amy in the manner of an old buddy, as she wanted, was crumbling before the looks Amy had been giving him. They were level looks from deep in her mind, offered as she squeezed her hands together. Knowing Amy was much like taking a carnival ride, one of those where you got strapped into a circular cage and then rotated while spinning. You never knew exactly where you were or when the thing was going to stop or how sick you'd get in the process.

Amy returned with the key, and he watched her enter the room, viewing her from behind, trying not to look at the tight Levis, the well-endowed blue sweater, the wild brown hair that he wanted to smell, the contours of the shoulders he wanted to explore. They stood in a silence broken only by his slapping the folded want ad section of the newspaper against his leg.

"Well?" Amy asked, walking to the bed. She sat on the bare mattress, then bounced on it lightly as if testing its firmness. She looked at the walls on either side of her, then at her knees.

"Well, what?" he asked, sliding to the floor, back against the wall, thinking he knew where they were headed, but he wasn't making any assumptions. A naked Amy, with her untamed hair, was an image too erotic to consider standing. A jungle girl.

Amy said, "Michael, you know I'm sorry about your last visit, don't you? But you made my headache go away, and then when I woke up, you were gone. I was feeling better and you weren't there. It was nine o'clock and I didn't have anything to do."

He was silent for a minute and then said, "Amy, I never can figure out exactly where I fit in when you're around. I can't ever figure it out."

Amy leaned forward and shouted, "Michael, why do you always have to figure things out?" She was so shocked by her outburst, she lay backward so she wouldn't have to look at him. She knew, of course, why he had to figure things out—so he could find your weak spots and exploit them. She wanted him to kiss her, not query her as though she were the first volume of his set of encyclopedias.

"I don't know," he said, "but I have to. My mother told me that when I was little, she'd tell me something and then I'd repeat it fifty times with slight variations until I thought I understood what she'd said. Anyway, just forget I said anything."

On her back, Amy stared at the ceiling and watched a small wisp of spiderweb hanging from the ceiling sway in an unfelt breeze. She sighed, then moved from the bed to the floor, sitting in front of him. She slid her feet between his drawn-up legs, then drew up as close as she could, close enough so she could put her hands on his near-vertical thighs. Her hands, like tiny sliding saddles, moved up, then down. She watched his face, seeing it fill with frustration as well as excitement, and she wished they could find some balance, something that worked for both of them.

"Dang, Amy, you just change things whenever you want and I go along. I used to think you never played games, but you do. Yours are just more complicated than most girls'."

Her thumbs met at his crotch. "I'm not playing games."

"Maybe you don't think you are, but if I ask in five years if you were playing games today, what'll you say?"

"I'll say I probably was."

He laughed, his face softening, and Amy knew she could then stand and offer her hand. He took it and they walked to the bed.

"Haven't you learned anything in college?" she asked. "When a girl wants to make love, you're supposed to make love."

"Maybe I ought to start reading *Cosmopolitan*."

Everything was out of whack, he thought. He and Amy lay on a bare mattress in an apartment devoid of other furniture in the middle of the day, sun shining on their feet. Amy wasn't supposed to be in Stanton, and, according to their history, they certainly shouldn't have been in bed together. Nothing made sense.

He shouldn't have cared, because Amy lay sleeping beside him, now dressed because she'd gotten cold. Everything about the day seemed miraculous, especially her, her slow respiration, her relaxed face. His eyes followed the streak of almost invisible fuzz down her head, just in front of her ear, where a man's sideburn was. He wanted to kiss her there but was afraid he'd wake her up.

There was a gremlin in his head, however, and its job was to shovel doubts into consideration. Swish, scoop: here's a question for you, Page. How long do you think she'll stay? Swish, scoop: why do you think she called you in the first place? And with one little swish and scoop, the gremlin gave him the solution to his problem. If Amy truly wanted him back in her life, if she had a spot for him, then she'd let him live with her. They could live in outrageous sin. And if Amy was agreeable, then he would know everything he needed to know. And he'd never again have to wonder about their relationship.

He placed his hand on her shoulder, wishing the sweater were again removed, and gently shook her. "Amy. Amy. I've got a great idea. Wake up. You'll love this."

He watched her blink as if trying to throw her eyes open, looking as though she couldn't quite place his face, looking, in fact, for a moment horrified to find herself in bed with a large naked boy.

"I've got a great idea. Why don't we go get my stuff too and I can stay with you a while. See how it works."

Amy said nothing. She'd expected the suggestion but not so quickly, thinking he would at least wait until she'd moved in, but he wasn't even waiting until she woke up. She knew the answer because she'd already decided, but now she had to warn him. She had to tell him she'd never tried doing two things at once, two things that required emotional involvement, and she honestly didn't know if she was capable of such simple juggling. She wanted to explain how much thought her singing required, how much time, but now she couldn't. He thought she was confident and emotionally ambidextrous, and she didn't want him to know she wasn't, didn't want him to know that deep down she was nothing more than a little girl consumed with doubts and fears. Then he wouldn't want to live with her at all. Besides, how was she to tell him anything when he was rubbing her breasts?

She sat up and moved to the edge of the bed, feet on the floor.

"Michael."

He maneuvered into position behind her, fitting against her like a spoon, and wrapped his arms around her upper body.

"I've never lived with anybody, not like that, so. . . ."

"It's going to be *great*. Perfect." Perfect failed to characterize his vision. Michael Page's finest hour was at hand. He was going to bathe her and wash her hair and apply her deodorant and paint her fingernails. He was going to shave her legs and help her dress and fall asleep smelling her. Perfect was an inadequate word.

"But, Michael."

"But, Michael, what?"

"What if you learned something about me and decided that. . . ." She shrugged. "What if you just decided. . . ."

"I'd never decide anything but that I just loved you more and more."

"Not if it's not like what you're thinking. Then you might not like me at all."

She was about to be absorbed into his body and she couldn't think clearly. She watched her leg bounce, knowing she needed to say something specific to warn him, but she looked at her hand and all she could think about was that fingers were funny looking with the wrinkles and nails and tiny hairs. So she didn't say anything specific. Besides, she had called him for a reason, and if she thought about how miserable she'd been living by herself, if she remembered the paralysis of the apartment in Halton, then she would also remember why she had called him.

"It won't be like you think, Michael. I want you to remember that."

"You're right there. It's going to be so much better even Ripley wouldn't believe it."

She shook her head and unwound his limbs so she could stand. Then she turned and looked at him, sitting on the bed naked and smiling, so joyous that Amy's heart hurt for him. She had never once wanted to steal his smile, but knew she had, and knew she would again. But on this day she wouldn't.

"We're not in any hurry, are we?" she asked.

He shook his head. "No hurry at all. I've already cut all my classes."

Amy pulled her sweater up, then over her head. Seeing him through the blue fabric mashed against her face, she said, "Then move over. You're on my side of the bed."

22

He had never seen a wish granted, but in the course of one day, he'd learned exactly what the granting of a wish felt like. (His first wish would have been spiritually based: to know why the world worked as it did. At least he thought it would have been spiritually based. Since his second would have been physical—to find himself in the precise situation with Amy that he suddenly, without warning or lengthy prayer, found himself in—and didn't need to be granted, he was fairly sure his first would have been spiritual.) He had awakened that morning in a desolate dorm room, staring at a great white walrus, never even vaguely suspecting that the day would find him helping Amy move to "their" apartment, would find him sitting in Halton with a dresser drawer on his lap, sifting through her lingerie. Beige bras, lacy panties. Nighties that were lemon yellow, cherry red, midnight black. Lime green slips, icy blue ones.

"Amy," he said, feeling his heart flutter and his voice get sticky. "Would you model this stuff?"

Packing a box with bottles of makeup in the bathroom, she said, "Why don't you get out of all that?"

He picked up a black nightie that was bordered with pink ribbon and carried it into the bathroom. "Amy, I know this'll sound trite, but I want you to know that you have the power to make my dreams come true. In fact, you already have. But this day could be totally perfect if you'd put this on."

She seemed to consider the request, then went back to her

packing, making room in the box for a bottle of bath oil. "Let's finish packing."

"If I begged, if I got down on my knees and actually begged, would you?"

He thought she was about to agree and he changed his mind. "No, wait a minute. Put on the green slip with no underwear. I want to see—" He stopped, thinking the red nightgown would be much sexier. He'd never seen a girl in a red nightgown. But actually, the image of her in bra and panties would be much more intimate. And even more intimate would be Amy in powder blue panties *without* a bra. The montage of images was driving him crazy. What if they had a wreck going back to Stanton and he never got to see her in all those items? What if he never got to take a bath with her? Oh, Lord. A bath. What could be finer than taking a bath with her? "Could we take a bath together? Right now?"

Amy laughed and picked up her box, moving it to the kitchen table. "Michael, we'll do all that in Stanton. Tonight, we can play all you want. But first let's get out of this place."

The landlady stood in the front yard as they packed Amy's car and offered advice as Amy passed each time. Once it was, "Now you make sure you get a good lock on your front door. And I'm not talking about those kinds you can open with a credit card. I saw that on TV the other night. I'm talking about one of those bolt things." The next time she mentioned the hazards of parking lots. Never park next to a van because you could get out of your car and be jerked into a van and nobody, not even God, would know Amy was gone.

Amy, who was rarely known to joke, said, "James Ray's going to take care of me. That's why Daddy sent him over here."

The landlady shook her finger. "James Ray, you better take care of this little girl."

And then they were driving to the promised land, with plans

to stop by the dorm so he could pick up a few items. Michael rode, experiencing difficulty with reality. He knew bad things could happen, but something like this? This good? Riding with Amy as though they were married? On their way to live in a bathtub? This was a dream. Michael Page was going to live in sin. Going to shack up. He was going to have an old lady. Oh, how weird, how downright weird. What else could he do? Could he become a biker? A gypsy? A con man?

Danged if it wasn't possible to free yourself. He could become a Presybterian lawyer. He could.

At the dorm, Amy waited in the car while he went up to quickly pack. He walked without feeling the ground beneath his feet, walked as though he were a projected image of himself.

Ron lay on his bed, hands clasped behind his head, watching a news show. Assuming Michael was going to join him, he gave a briefing on what had preceded this movie star's collapse and subsequent commitment.

"I haven't got time to watch, Ron. I'm moving out. I'm going to live in sin."

He opened the drawer of the dresser. Oh, what about a few socks, a few underpanties, a few T-shirts, which he hoped would seem much whiter in Amy's presence. Maybe one Baptist handkerchief to go live without the benefit of holy matrimony.

Ron sat up. "You're moving out?"

He nodded, filling a suitcase. He would go over to the registrar's office tomorrow and change his religious preference on his records to Presbyterian just to get matters straight. Then he'd call his parents and explain his problems with faith. He never had done such a thing, but the time had drawn nigh. For some reason, he'd always avoided problems, and at the moment he couldn't imagine why. You couldn't live without problems, he thought, but when they came your way, you had to look them in the eye. And if you didn't weaken when the bull offered his horns, then life was a simple process of twisting the head off one problem, then moving on to the next. Why had he always felt so intimidated?

"Why're you moving out?" Ron asked. He rarely sounded mystified but now he did. He got up and lowered the volume on the TV.

"Because a little genie must've appeared in my sleep and offered to grant me a wish. I don't know how it happened."

"Michael."

Although his back was to Ron, Ron's voice was like a glass of ice water poured over his neck. The tone was different, utterly different, from any Ron had ever used. And he got a nauseated feeling because he recognized the tone. It was that of unfulfilled desire, and never in his life had he heard one boy use it with another.

He turned, thinking he might vomit right in the room, but he had to look at Ron's face to verify his belief. And Ron's face told him what he didn't want to know—that the reason he had thought Ron was a homosexual was because Ron *was* a homosexual. He had been living with one, dressing and undressing in front of one, had even patted him on the back.

He closed his eyes and thought, *holy shit.*

He slammed the suitcase shut and without taking the time to engage the latches picked it up, holding it to his chest. He carried it to the door, stooped to grasp the handle, and let himself out.

"Can we talk before you go?" Ron asked.

"I don't have time. See you."

He ran, bouncing off two guys and one fire extinguisher, turning two circles, thinking that if there was anyone more ignorant in the world than he was, that person deserved the best in full-time protection. Life was like a surprise birthday party, except when he walked into the room and the lights were turned on, the crowd didn't shout, "Happy birthday!" They shouted, "Surprise! You were all wrong, you idiot!"

How was one person capable of such extensive stupidity?

Amy made him forget Ron and she curtailed his self-flagellation. Luckily for him, his intelligence hadn't put him in Amy's good graces, so his stupidity couldn't take him out. Over the next few days, he found concentration difficult, classes impossible, but touring the countryside in Amy's black Firebird very easy. She found a job working as a receptionist in a bank immediately, and he took her to work, then, at her suggestion, kept her car. With ZZ Top rumbling from the stereo, a cold six-pack beside him, he explored the small towns and surrounding area.

He called home several times, hoping his parents would feel any calls to Stanton were unnecessary, and he planned to leave Ron a note, asking him not to divulge his whereabouts and to let him know if his parents called. He wasn't yet ready to talk to his former roommate, not face to face. He feared homosexual dreams and so ordered himself not to engage in any before falling asleep, and so far he had heeded the order except for one dream in which he was squashed by a giant marshmallow.

Even the weather cooperated with his joyous mood. The heat of the summer was fading with the first cold fronts, and although the temperature hadn't dropped below forty, the evenings were pleasant and cool. He prepared simple meals for them, hamburgers and French fries or fancy omelets, and they ate outside on the balcony.

He knew Amy wasn't going to have much free time, not between working all day and rehearsing with the new band at night, and he tried hard to enjoy whatever time they had together. What he wasn't prepared for was waking up in the middle of the night and finding himself in bed alone. Every night he'd get up and stumble through the dark and locate her on the couch, sitting with her legs drawn up before her, chin resting on her knees. On the first two occasions, he thought she'd experienced a nightmare or was just unable to sleep, but on the third night she said, "I'm working on a song."

"In the dark?"

"Umm hmm."

"How can you be working on a song in the dark with no pen or paper?"

"I'm trying to work it out. I don't need any paper yet."

"You mean right now you're—what're you doing?"

She sighed. "I can't explain it. I hear it."

"Amazing. That's amazing. How do you hear it?"

She laughed quietly, although the sound was more that of crying than laughter. "Michael, there are some things I can't do. I can't explain what you want to know, and I can't get this song worked out when I'm talking."

"Do you mean I should shut up and go back to bed?"

She crossed the room and sat in his lap, curling up as a child would. "I don't want you to shut up. I just don't want you to say anything."

He moved the strap of her gown off her shoulder and let his finger follow the ridge of her collarbone. "I was thinking this afternoon I was a character in my own dream, but nothing this good happens in my dreams. Usually in my dreams I see an angel with a flaming sword who's really pissed off at the way I'm living. All he says is, 'Michael Page, your time is at hand.' And I wake up scared shitless. And now I wake up in your apartment. Now I'm holding you. Amy, nothing this good has ever happened to me before. Not ever. And I never thought it would."

"Do you really mean that?" she asked.

"Every word of it. Every word."

23

He was growing increasingly worried because *something* was going to happen. He was aware that a Southern Baptist was scripturally prohibited from experiencing continued happiness while living in sin, and he would have felt much more secure had he not been so happy. Unhappiness and misery were the only keys to avoiding divine punishment, and everyone from theologians to titmice knew that God would intervene to extract you from happiness and sin, but would practice benign neglect should you wish to rise above pain and squalor. Daily he began entertaining a sense of impending doom. Either the apartment was going to blow up (the newspaper would attribute the disaster to a gas leak, not knowing Jonah was a resident) or Jesus was going to return that evening just as he and Amy were getting into the bathtub.

The telephone, that hateful instrument that connected him to the rest of the world, from whence doom originated, rang one afternoon, and the voice of doom sounded just like Ron's. Which, once he thought about it, seemed appropriate. They hadn't talked since the night of his departure; their only communication had been a written request he left in the dorm room regarding phone calls from his parents.

They exchanged greetings, and he was surprised that Ron sounded as though nothing had ever happened.

"Your father called," Ron said. "He invited us to attend a revival. What's a revival? Is that where everybody gets up and marches around the church and screams?"

"You're thinking of the Pentecostals."

"What about speaking in tongues?" Ron asked, uttering a long chant he'd borrowed from an Indian in a John Wayne movie.

"That's the charismatics."

"Hmm. Then it must be pretty dull. What *is* a revival?"

"It's just your normal church service except longer."

He found himself reluctant to end his conversation with Ron, happy to know that they could talk without Ron requesting a date or an hour in bed. (Did a girl feel this way every time she talked to a boy who failed to attract her?) Still, he needed to notify his father immediately that neither he nor Ron possessed the slightest interest in attending a revival service.

"Where'd you say I was when my father called?"

"In the library researching the Visigoths."

He thanked Ron for calling, hung up, then dialed his home phone number. When his mother answered, he told her that he couldn't possibly come to a revival service because he had tests and papers and book reports and lab experiments and research projects and grant applications and government questionnaires to complete.

"I understand," Mrs. Page said.

"He doesn't understand college isn't like it used to be. They want us working on thirty-hour days over here."

"I know."

He had always disliked lying to his mother, but in this case, he was really only asking her to pass along the lie to his father. Neither did he want to make an overly abrupt call to her, but he couldn't very well sit and gab for an hour when he had just briefed her on his murderous schedule. Besides, he'd already missed the first few minutes of "The Andy Griffith Show" rerun, so he told his mother good-bye, popped a cold beer, lit a cigar, and made himself comfortable on the couch, hoping the rerun was one of those with Don Knotts in the cast.

He sighed, waiting for the picture on the television. Doom, as an event, was highly overrated. All you had to do was say, "Get thee hence." And it was gone.

Brother Page was enthusiastic, already thinking about letting the revival run indefinitely. The evangelist was a friend of his, a dynamic speaker, and the church was experiencing real revival for the first time in years. The most telling sign so far had been the transformation of Peggy Alford, a thin lady with orange hair whose husband had died of cancer several years ago, leaving his wife alone and bitter. She had been working out her meanness on the church as effectively as any tool that Satan had ever possessed in Ashworth, Texas, with the possible exception of Kraut Brunner, who pushed each year for a liquor election.

Over the years, Peggy had engaged in any number of clandestine operations, the worst being the letter she'd mailed to all the members, over the signature of Brother Page, threatening to publish the names of nontithers. Brother Page, these three years later, was still mystified by the instantaneous ire brought by a letter written on plain paper, without the church letterhead, with a signature forged by an obviously feminine hand, that contained at least ten grammatical errors, including, "I tired of you tightwads." Half the members had planned on deserting the church without even talking to the pastor.

But last night Peggy had come foward during the invitation, hugged the preacher, and asked for his forgiveness while sobbing in real sorrow. Her appeal to the congregation afterwards for their prayers and forgiveness had moved everyone present, and Brother Page hadn't seen a dry eye in the building. She had also apologized specifically to several of the members, including Big Bill Watson, who, Peggy had once reported, had made passes at her in the church kitchen.

Brother Page had stood beside Peggy during her public confession, wishing devoutly that Michael had been in attendance. He had called the dorm that afternoon, getting Ron, the egghead intellectual, who also needed to be in church, and invited them both. Michael, of course, declined the invitation. Disappointed, Brother Page had entered the empty sanctuary and sat on the podium, looking at the stained glass window of Jesus holding the lamb—Brother Page's favorite piece of art—and wondered what he could do to convince Michael to come to this most wondrous of revivals.

In the silence of the church, the answer came easily, so easily Brother Page was embarrassed. The preacher sought Jesus because their relationship was of the utmost importance. And Michael didn't seek his earthly father because the relationship lay in ruins, may not have even existed except in a legal way. And looking at the sorrowful, loving eyes of Jesus in the stained glass, Brother Page felt a heavy sadness descend upon him. He and Michael had experienced some truly pleasant times when the boy had been small. They'd sat arm in arm in the living room, watching spring storms through the picture window, the disturbed sky illuminated by lightning. Michael had made numerous trips with him when he'd visited members in the hospitals of Dallas and Waco and Tyler. Brother Page could almost see a seven-year-old Michael riding beside him, notepad on his knee, keeping track of the number of cars, pickups, and trucks he saw. Occasionally the child would sit in his father's lap and drive, demanding that they turn as often as possible. There was no challenge to driving a straight line. Which should have given the father a clue to his personality.

Trying to maintain a good relationship with Michael, as he got older, had been like trying to drive two cars at once, jumping from one to the other while both continued moving. While trying hard to keep the car of faith on the road, Brother Page had watched the car of relationships keep running into the ditch. And once Michael had learned how to drive, he kept veering off into the bushes and onto side roads, reappearing a few miles distant to ram the car of faith. There had been wrecks all along the line.

Shamed by the number of church members who had been overcoming grudges and setting matters right among themselves during the revival, Brother Page set out to Stanton the next morning to visit with Michael. He left early so he could return for the noon service. He arrived at the dorm, he supposed, in time to eat breakfast with Michael and called the room from the lobby.

When Brother Page asked Ron if he could speak to Michael, Ron seemed confused. "Oh, he's at the . . . he went to . . . oh, I know where he is. He went to eat breakfast. But off-campus. He went to eat breakfast off-campus. At a little café where he goes sometimes. I can't think of the name of it. But he may be back to get his books before class. Maybe. Probably maybe."

Brother Page, who had waited on his son before, sat to wait again, wondering as he did if Ron had said, "Holy hatband," before hanging up.

Ron called Michael, who was shaving when the phone rang. His razor stopped in midstroke and he froze. The phone had never rung at seven in the morning. Never. It's all over now, he thought. Everything but the crying. Someone was calling to tell him to look at the sky so he could see Jesus and his angels descending. Within a few seconds, the entire world would hear the trumpet of the Lord. And Michael Page, only eighteen years old with his entire life ahead of him, saw not his life but his unfulfilled future flash before his eyes.

"Page," Ron said. "Get over here quick. Your father's downstairs. I told him you'd gone to eat off-campus but would be back to get your books."

"I've got my books. How can I get them from the room?"

"Get mine."

"Right."

"And don't forget to act surprised when you see him."

"Right. Thanks for reminding me."

"And if he invites us to the revival again, tell him we'll go. That's my price for cooperating."

He thanked Ron without agreeing to accept such an invitation, and washed the shaving cream from his face, now too nervous to take a chance on holding a razor blade close to his face. He went running to the bedroom, thinking if he wasn't safe from a parental visit during a revival, he never would be.

Amy watched him with barely opened eyes, thinking that when a day began with a boy caroming off the walls of the apartment, flapping his arms because he couldn't get them into the sleeves of his shirt, and screaming when he gouged his gum with the toothbrush, then that day was probably going to suck all day long. How she was going to get ready for work and take him to school as well was a puzzle she couldn't immediately solve.

She delivered him to the campus, a few blocks from the dorm, and he hurried without running, mentally working out a checklist. Let's see, I have to be surprised when I see him. I just ate breakfast so I don't know why my stomach is rumbling with hunger pangs. And I have to get my books from the dorm. Lying was getting difficult; he was out of practice. Besides, he felt half-dressed and unprepared for the day, much less for a performance.

Brother Page, on a couch in the lobby, was about to go off in search of a pen and paper, having just experienced one of those head-slapping reminders that a task was undone. Last week he had been staying in a motel in Dallas and had turned on the television to watch the ten o'clock news. The set flashed on, but instead of a local newscaster, Brother Page's eyes had fixed on the images of a boy and girl walking through a meadow. The girl had said, "I want you to fill my mouth with your cock." Thinking he had surely misunderstood—maybe she had wanted him to bill her spouse for a lock—the preacher had made a grave error in judgment. He'd sat and watched. And even though cable television and porno were always in the news, Brother Page had difficulty in believing he was actually seeing such things on TV. Within a few minutes, the boy had stuffed every opening the girl possessed, and the girl had used language that would have singed the ears of Satan himself.

The preacher couldn't very well preach a sermon on what he'd seen, and he had got on his knees and asked for God's forgiveness over his painful curiosity. He'd vowed that he would write a letter to the owner of the motel chain and tell the president that one of his guests felt as though raw garbage had been shoveled into his room. And what if an ignorant litle child had turned on the TV? The letter, however, remained unwritten.

When Brother Page saw Michael approaching across the lobby, he had just scheduled another stop on his trip to Stanton. He needed to find the name and address of the president of the motel chain in the library.

"Hey," Michael said, shaking his father's hand. "What're you doing here?"

Brother Page invited Michael to sit, but Michael suggested they go outside. The father followed, thinking that on his hour-and-a-half drive to Stanton, he had known exactly what he wanted to tell Michael—that he wished he'd been a better father and wanted Michael's forgiveness for his failings, but now all he could think about was the unwritten letter. Maybe they could walk over to the library and talk along the way.

Michael guided Brother Page to a rather out-of-the-way bench that sat within some hedges. Brother Page tried to switch gears, trying to remember the specific ways he had failed Michael, trying to dredge up just one of the examples he'd thought out on the way over, but he couldn't decide whether "raw garbage" was an appropriate term for a letter. He sat beside his son, rubbed his eyebrows, and thought.

Oh, yes. The bicycle.

He explained the purpose of his visit, his desire that Michael forgive him for his failings. "One thing that comes to mind is that bicycle you wanted when you were thirteen. I agreed that if you saved enough money, you could buy it, and then when you did save enough, I changed my mind because there wasn't anything wrong with the bicycle you already had. One of these days you'll be a father, and you'll look back and wonder why you did the things you did, and you'll wish you could undo them, but. . . ."

He wondered about his father's motives in mentioning the bicycle, which had only been a very small part of the problem. "If you remember, when you told me I couldn't get the bicycle, I got mad and bought a registered cocker spaniel without asking you or Mom. And the dog barked through the night and you got rid of him." That dog disposal had led to a further problem—his periodic raids on the local pound to free the dogs—but he decided against mentioning those operations.

Brother Page shook his head. "No, no, I didn't get rid of a registered cocker spaniel. You're thinking of the beagle. I wouldn't have done that with a registered dog."

"You not only would have, you did. I remember because I paid a hundred and twenty-five dollars for the dog."

Brother Page pivoted on the bench, his mouth open. "You paid *what* for that dog?"

"One hundred and twenty-five hard-earned dollars. I mowed a bunch of yards for that money."

Brother Page sat for a moment in mild shock. "I've never

heard this story. How'd you manage to spend that much money without me knowing it?"

He shrugged. "I put the money in my pocket and walked to Tubby Malone's and I gave him a hundred and twenty-five dollars and left with a registered cocker spaniel."

"Well, I'll be."

The father sat in an exceptionally clear fall morning, listening to the sounds of a calm college campus, amazed by what he'd just learned. He'd never known the dog was registered or that Michael had spent that much money on it. How did a father so quickly and eagerly transport a dog to the pound without the facts? The relationship with his son needed much more than a father blithely asking for his son's forgiveness. The undisputed fact was that Brother Page had a son whose entire life, almost, was a mystery.

"What're you majoring in?" he asked.

"Business, but I want to go to law school."

"And be a . . . trial lawyer?"

He nodded.

"Well, you'll be a good one." He added, "Have you prayed about it?"

He hesitated before answering. "I think I'm doing what I'm meant to do."

Brother Page nodded and didn't speak until the chimes from the administration building had stopped. "Well, I'm sorry about that dog. I wish I'd known he was registered, but I don't suppose that really makes any difference. If it's the dog I'm thinking of, he was the one who used to wake up Mrs. Washburn. We couldn't very well have a dog waking up the neighbors every night. You know, being a preacher is probably like being a politician. You can't do things the way other people do them."

He started nodding before his father was finished with his

statement. "I know, I know. If you recall, I lived with you for eighteen years."

Brother Page laughed and they sat for a few minutes without talking.

"Ron wants to come to the revival, although not for the reasons you want him to."

"Well," Brother Page said, pleasantly surprised by this revelation. "I don't think his reasons matter as long as he's there. Why don't I come over tomorrow about four or so and pick you up."

Not quite believing the words that were leaving his mouth, wondering what force had seized control of his brain, he nodded and said, "That's a lot of driving for you."

"It's nothing if you'll come."

"Okay. We'll see you about four."

24

He was sure that Ron would be disappointed in a simple revival service because he was expecting something as outlandish as snake-handling or as esoteric as peyote-popping, and all he'd witness would be a mild display of old-time religion. Revivals were usually enthusiastic affairs, designed to renew the members' spirits, but they were nothing extraordinary.

Before the appointed hour, he walked the two miles from Amy's apartment to the dorm, thinking about his father's visit. Every time they seemed headed in the same direction, he always had a brake applied to his expectations. Although the visit had been a good one, he had been thinking the entire time, if he knew where I was living, he'd hate my guts for the rest of his life, and if he even suspected my infidelity, he'd murder me in a second. Any peace they had seemed phony, based on ignorance.

Ron was ready out front when Michael arrived, and greeted his former roommate with words on a subject Michael hadn't expected to discuss. Ron stood with his hair freshly combed, a drop of water hanging beneath the right lens of his glasses, and he said he hoped Michael hadn't been embarrassed by Ron's behavior the night he had moved out.

"You'll have to admit, Page, that what most people call love —just your basic PEA rush—is nothing but a chemical reaction. Now I analyzed this experience, and here's what happened. We're opposites, Page, you won't have any trouble admitting that, and we epitomize each other's alienated characteristics. See, you've retained that essential male, action-oriented, girl-chasing, two-fisted, football-playing part of me that I suppressed ten or fifteen years ago, and when you walked out, I felt as though I was losing it all over again. I felt a longing for my alienated characteristics. And I got the traditional PEA rush most people call love. I know this has happened to you at one time or another, with a male Amy, as it were, some boy who represents your own alienated characteristics."

Michael was glad to have the matter out in the open, right on the sidewalk in front of the dorm, because he liked Ron but wanted to squelch forever the possibility of any relationship besides simple friendship. And then a funny thing happened. He said, "Ron, there's no such thing as a male Amy," and with the speaking of the words, an image blinked into his mind— old Andy, the charming bass player in Amy's old band.

He was glad to see his father's car pulling up at the curb because he didn't want to consider the significance of that image.

He suggested Ron ride in the front seat with Brother Page, and Ron climbed in without hesitation, greeting the preacher as though they were old friends. Ron's suggestion that they attend the church service took some of the pressure off him because Brother Page considered Ron more spiritually retarded than his son.

Brother Page explained along the way the purpose of a revival and the magnificent heights to which this one had risen. He hoped Ron would listen carefully to the gospel as it was presented that night, especially by a guest speaker who was a former hit man with a miraculous story to tell. Elmer Fish.

"A hit man named Elmer Fish?" Michael asked.

Brother Page nodded, either failing to see or failing to acknowledge the humor.

Something besides the incongruity of Elmer's name bothered him. He'd never understood why all the guest speakers at revivals were former criminals or heroin addicts. At times revivals seemed to derive the same benefits from sensationalism as television or the less reputable tabloids. He hadn't shared his father's theology for a long time, but he had always admired his father's dedication, and he could never understand why his own father would stoop to the sensational. Why didn't he invite some meek little woman who simply loved God and had never experienced "the monkey on my back"?

He tapped Ron on the shoulder and said, "I bet you a hundred bucks old Elmer was saved right before his parole hearing. That's when all these guys are saved. It hasn't got anything to do with trying to influence the parole board, though. It's just coincidence."

Ron glanced back at him, then at Brother Page, unsure how he should respond. Brother Page's face discouraged him from responding at all.

They finished the ride to Ashworth in silence.

For the first time, he approached church feeling like the Presbyterian lawyer he wanted to be. The church sat in the small-

224

town quietness attracting residents in a steady manner. They parked their cars and walked through the afternoon shadows, greeting one another as though they hadn't seen each other the previous night and the night before that. Possibly he felt like the Presbyterian lawyer because he was viewing the proceedings through Ron's eyes.

Before they got to their seats inside, he had introduced Ron to a hundred people, been hugged by half that many women, and had his shoulder squeezed by an equal number of men. And even after they were seated, they were still greeted by a large number of people, from five-year-old boys, who wanted to know if he was playing football at Stanton, to the old and decrepit who had to hook up the hearing aids placed on the back of the third pew so they could hear the sermon.

"All these people know you," Ron whispered.

"That's what happens when you live in a church for eighteen years."

He tried to maintain his different point of view, noticing the energy released in the singing. The church always had a guest music director during a revival, someone who specialized in pumping new life into the old songs. He waved his arms in godly vigor and had one side of the congregation compete against the other on alternating verses, to see "who can let 'em hear us in heaven." They engaged in men-women competition, and when they sang "Amazing Grace," he had the congregation substitute "ten million" for "ten thousand" when they sang, "When we've been there"—that was, in heaven—"ten thousand years. . . ." A number of members liked the thought behind that substitution and expressed their approval with hearty amens. All in all, the music director did his job and gave Machine-Gun Fish, who was introduced by the evangelist, a warmly enthusiastic crowd.

Elmer looked much more like the brick salesman he was than

a former button man. He wore bright red pants and a plaid coat. He told a joke he probably told his customers and then gave his life story. He'd been born the son of a prostitute ("a bastard," he said proudly, giving every kid in church permission to use the word and causing several parents to look disapprovingly at their spouses) and was neglected to the point that he'd been completely unsupervised, having to pitch pennies so he could buy food. By the age of eleven, he was making money running errands for his mother's friends, who happened to be some of the town's outstanding citizens, and by twelve he'd discovered even more profitable errands, those involving the movement and sale of drugs. He was hooked on the big H by sixteen and fell in with criminal elements because of his need for drugs and the ever-increasing amounts of money required to support his habit. He started boosting cars, a financially welcome branch of his growing business but also the crime that put him in the joint at eighteen.

It was in the joint that he learned the art of contract killing, sitting at the feet of professionals. "I'm talking about men who'd slit your throat for twenty dollars. I'm talking about men who'd killed prominent lawyers and bankers and businessmen for much bigger payoffs. I learned from them all, from the Mafia to the gutter rats."

Since Elmer's sentence was relatively short, he was offered and he accepted a contract to kill the wife of a businessman who wanted to collect on life insurance. "He was into the sharks, the loan sharks, and he was scared, he was running scared."

But God intervened. He provided Elmer with a vision. Elmer saw this lady as she sat before her Sunday school class of junior high girls, and Elmer began having second thoughts. And about the time he began having second thoughts, the prison chaplain began working on him as well. And soon enough, God had convicted Elmer of his worthless life, of his previous sins and the sin he was about to commit. A month before his parole hearing, he was gloriously saved.

"You owe me a hundred bucks," Michael said to Ron.

"Don't be such a cynic."

The prison chaplain helped Elmer obtain employment at a brick factory upon his release, and today Elmer worked for that same company, setting sales records and then breaking them. "Right now I've sold more bricks than all the other salesmen combined who ever worked for that company."

This admission drew a renewed chorus of amens.

Following Elmer, the evangelist preached for forty-five minutes, shaking the ceiling tiles with stories that could have had different endings. The man who had sat through a church service wrestling with a decision to accept Christ, failing to make it, and getting killed in a car wreck on his way home. "Now, my Bible tells me that today, today and forever, that man is burning in the pits of hell. He *could* have gone to heaven. He *could* be singing praises to our Lord. He *could* be walking the streets of gold. He *could* have had a mansion reserved for him in that heavenly city. He *could* have. Instead, he's weeping and wailing and gnashing his teeth in a fire that will never be quenched. Never."

He told of the deacon whose clandestine life as a transvestite prevented him from ever fully yielding his life to God and who one day took a chain from his daughter's swing set and hanged himself in the garage. "This deacon, who claimed to be a child of God, was hanging in the garage when his precious seven-year-old daughter got home from school. She went into the house and got her Strawberry Shortcake doll, because that doll always rode the bicycle with her; she got Strawberry Shortcake and went to the garage to get her bicycle and there she saw her deacon-Christian-father hanging there with his eyes bugging out and his tongue sticking out of the side of his mouth. That little girl screamed for two days; she cried for months. She won't ever be the same, she won't ever recover, because her father couldn't turn his life over to God. His perversions were too important."

The evangelist wound down his sermon with a plea for those who needed to make decisions to come forward during the invitation. Brother Page stood before the pulpit as the congregation stood to sing.

Michael had always disliked the invitation. The hymns were mournful dirges that slowly encouraged you to come to Jesus because he was calling softly and tenderly, because you had wandered far away and needed to come home, because you could come just as you were, without one plea. The congregation sang "Just As I Am" and it had the normal sobering effect on him.

He stood thinking about a little girl with her Strawberry Shortcake doll happily running to the garage and finding there a sight more horrible than any she would ever again see. A seven-year-old girl initiated into the real horrors of life by a father who couldn't get himself under control.

They had sung the invitation hymn through a number of times, but few had gone forward, none of those for momentous decisions because they had all returned to their seats after speaking briefly with Brother Page. And after a few more moments, Brother Page conferred briefly with the evangelist, who took Brother Page's place before the pulpit, and his father headed up the aisle. Toward Michael.

He edged in front of his son and put his hand on Ron's shoulder, pulling him into a seated position on the pew. The preacher in his dark blue suit and the visitor who looked like the personification of all fleshly sins made a picture that could have been used in a church ad. Michael reverently bowed his head so he could better hear what was said.

"God never ceases to amaze me, Ron," Brother Page said, seated beside Ron. "He's brought you here tonight to hear his word preached. Ron, God loves you. Praise his holy name, he loves you more dearly than any father loves a son. And he's given you the means through which you can truly become a child of his." His hand on Ron's shoulder, Brother Page said a short prayer of thanksgiving for the sacrifice of Jesus on the cross and for the delivery of Ron to the revival service. "Ron, I want you to think about what you've heard here tonight. Jesus wants to become your Lord and savior. He wants to enter into a personal relationship with you and change your life. He wants to, but the decision is yours. You have to take the first step. Ron, will you accept Jesus as your Lord and savior?"

Michael could only see the top of Ron's head because Ron was sitting forward, looking at the floor, but he could tell that his friend had swallowed. His manner indicated that he was listening and not out of mere curiosity as Brother Page kneaded his shoulder as if trying to imbue it with spiritual salt. And as Michael watched, he thought about the chain of events that had brought Ron and him together, and he couldn't help but wonder if God hadn't actually brought Ron to this church. Neither could he help but wonder if Ron didn't need to be saved, to turn away from his gluttony and homosexuality and find some principles, render some judgments.

The music director brought the congregation to a halt on "Just As I Am" and switched to "Almost Persuaded," the chorus of which had this haunting line: "Sad, sad that bitter wail, 'Almost,' but lost!" His father sat waiting on Ron, and Michael didn't know if Ron was listening to the music, but he was. And he knew without a doubt that Ron needed Jesus, needed what the hanging deacon hadn't possessed. And suddenly Michael wished he wasn't the perfect practicing infidel he was because he should have been praying for Ron.

Brother Page said, "Ron, you're here and Jesus is there. 'Behold, I stand at the door and knock,' he said. Consider what he's saying to you, Ron. Consider this the only night of your life, the only decision you'll ever make that matters. Your eternity hangs in the balance right now, and only you can decide your fate." Brother Page paused, giving Ron time to respond, but Ron said nothing, still staring at the floor. "If it wasn't for our sinful nature, we wouldn't need to be reconciled to God. If it wasn't for our sinful nature, Jesus wouldn't have had to die on the cross. We wouldn't be faced with such a monumental decision. But, Ron, there's no middle ground. Either you accept Jesus or you reject him. Either you live or you perish."

In a mechanical voice, Ron said, "I'll have to get back with you re: the matter of salvation."

Brother Page nodded, but barely, and then looked at the back of the pew for a minute to see if God was going to work a last-minute miracle and Ron was going to change his mind. And after waiting a minute, Brother Page stood and walked back to the front of the church.

Standing with the evangelist before the pulpit, Brother Page called for a second love offering of the night, this one for Elmer Fish, and then pronounced the benediction, asking God to continue blessing the services, asking also that any person who needed to make a decision and hadn't, be deprived of any and all peace of mind until he had arrived at the right decision.

Ron didn't stand through the prayer as the rest of the congregation did, and after the final amen, when he finally looked up at Michael, his round face was drained and confused. Michael couldn't decide if he hated his roommate for rejecting Jesus or admired him for resisting Brother Page. At the moment, he didn't know anything. He just wanted to go somewhere and forget the entire service.

He and Ron left the building, listening to the many members who wanted to assure Ron they would be praying for him. He was now a designated sinner, and those people would be praying for him for months to come. Outside, the two gravitated toward the shadows of the building to wait on Brother Page and the trip back to Stanton. It was going to be a quiet trip, Michael knew, because his father wasn't going to talk; he was going to let Ron stew in his indecision.

Finally Ron spoke. "Page, it was everything I hoped for. And more. I never understood religion before. I never in my life thought about being saved, and then, within an hour, I couldn't think about anything else. I almost couldn't say no. I almost became a Jimmy, just like Jimmy Swaggart and Jimmy Carter. It was the most amazing thing that ever happened to me."

Michael wanted Ron to keep talking. He wanted his different point of view back, and the only way he could reclaim it was through listening to Ron's scientific voice.

"When we get back to Stanton, let's go get a drink. I've got a million questions to ask you. At least a million."

They walked to the car, but once there, Michael continued walking across the parking lot. He moved away from the voices and lights, wanting to feel the sky above and the air around him. He wanted to look at the stars and think.

All he knew was this—he understood something of what had transpired in church, and he knew nothing about the stars or sky. And although he couldn't account for his father's faith, the change in Elmer Fish, or the death of the transvestite deacon, he didn't think those things had much to do with the rings around Saturn or the position of Betelgeuse.

There were some things he just couldn't believe, and he was sorry, but there was nothing he could do about it.

25

Success made balancing two emotional tasks more difficult than ever for Amy. The band had engagements scheduled into a surprising future, and Allan had crossed paths with a former record producer in Austin who had retired there but who still maintained a small recording studio. He said he might be interested in helping the band produce a demo tape. Visions of a recording contract fluttered before Amy's eyes day and night. So Amy succeeded and Michael suffered.

She wanted him to feel good as well, and he couldn't when Amy was ignoring him, as she had been. He undoubtedly thought she spent all her hours merely vegetating in a chair, but she had to think. Poor Michael. He was sweet and easily pleased. At times he seemed completely satisfied if Amy agreed to go eat pizza and drink a few beers, or to pass an hour sitting on the bank of the river.

One afternoon she walked in from work and found him cooking an omelet. She had planned a night in which she intended to pursue the pleasing of Michael. As she walked behind him, she lifted his shirt and kissed him on the back, her hand in front of him, her fingers trickling over his stomach. She walked silently to the bedroom.

He forgot about the pan on the stove until he smelled butter burning, and then he noticed the fried brown bubbles. He moved the pan to a cold burner, trying to figure out what was going on. With Amy, he never knew. He stood indecisively for a few minutes, until he heard her call from the bedroom.

He went. The room looked like a den of iniquity with a candle burning on each side. Shadows that overlapped jumped across the walls. Amy had pulled all the covers from the bed, thrown off the pillows, and lay naked, rubbing the soles of her feet over the one blue sheet stretched across the mattress. He thought she should have been a porno film producer because the effect of the darkened room with its flickering shadows and fleshly centerpiece was stunning. Amy said nothing, just beckoned him with a finger.

For an hour, they played with each other and made love.

Later, still in bed, he propped his head on his hand and admired the small body of the girl next to him. He patted her stomach and said, "Sounds just like a thumped watermelon."

Amy trapped his hand against her stomach and held it there.

"Finish your song?" he asked.

She shook her head. She had enough on paper to release her mind from worrying about its escape, enough to know it wasn't the big song. But it wasn't bad, and when she finished, it would exist whereas it hadn't a week ago. It would be one of her creations.

"Sing what you've got."

"I'm not going to sing it until it's finished."

"Sing it. You sing it to yourself. Sing it to me."

"Michael."

He sighed and lay back down. Last night she hadn't said a thing to him other than, "What I want is for you to leave me alone." He had made a diligent effort to avoid imposing when she was working on a song, but that side of Amy was one that made her see him as a hindrance, in the same class with the mumps or a bad cold. It made her fall in love with the negative, transformed her to Miss Black Hole, the Coal Queen.

"I want to hear the song."

Amy raised up on her elbow. "Michael. Why're you doing this?"

"You know what I've been thinking? I've been thinking about why you called me when you moved over here. You called me for the same reason you came looking for me when you agreed to sing at Beth's, even though you supposedly hated me at the time. You remember that? There are times when you need me and there are times when you could care less if I'm dead or alive. You needed me when you came over here, so you called. Last night you didn't need me and if you'd had the power, you would have put me on Mars."

Amy sat up. "That's not true and you know it."

"If it's not, then do something for me when things are going right for you. Sing me the song. I want to know for three minutes you remember who I am when you feel good."

The monster was coming out of the closet, just as it had on the day of the church's anniversary. "It won't work, Michael. I know what you're doing and it won't work."

"Begging won't work? Pleading won't work?"

In two hops, Amy was off the bed and on her way to the bathroom. Inside, she locked the door behind her, then shook the handle to make sure the door had locked securely, and sat on the edge of the bathtub. Uncomfortable with her nudity, she searched through the dirty clothes hamper for clothes, finding Levis and a blouse, which she put on.

She listened to him as he stood at the door. "You're the only person I know who could turn me into an inanimate object, Amy. You've made me into a rabbit's foot. You know I love you, you know I love your voice, you know that I'm intrigued and mystified and completely hung up on you. So you know you can use me and get away with it. And when I make a simple request, you also know you can tell me to shove it and nothing will happen."

Amy was glad to know that she had told him to shove it and nothing had happened. That was why she was locked in the bathroom, frightened he would get mad and walk out on her.

She listened to him leave the apartment, glad he hadn't taken the time to pack, glad also he hadn't pushed her to the point of giving in because she didn't want to feed his monster. The only way she knew to discourage it was to starve it to death.

They were both so much alike, both insecure, both afraid they didn't matter. But she had come home with the specific intention of demonstrating that he did matter, and the monster had ruined the night.

He sat in a Steak and Egg drinking coffee, watching the traffic, cars carrying husbands home to loving wives, wives off to meet caring husbands. While sixty percent of all marriages were ending in divorce, the principals involved in the other forty percent were parading back and forth in front of Steak and Egg. They may as well have been shouting, "Hey, lookee here, boy. Look at how happy we are. Why, we all found people who love us, every one."

He shook his head until his neck got tired, unsure anymore of what he wanted. He'd had what he wanted, had been lying in bed with the girl of his dreams, had been in paradise when the gremlin in his head had shaken his juju and he had attacked. What kind of sense did that make? He didn't know how many songs Amy had written, but he knew of several that, once she'd finished them, she had sung for him first, not to anyone in her band, but to him, Michael Page.

What did he want? And why did he listen to the gremlin? Dang, but he was tired of being stupid. He was acting just like a fascist, just like his father, just like little Benito. Amy was Amy, and if he changed her in any way—not that he could—she wouldn't be Amy anymore.

Then he thought, son of a bitch. I *am* acting like my father. And he realized that he had apparently planned, without consciously thinking about it, to take Amy, short a few circuits, and maker her into a modified little woman. Not a true little woman, but a singer who'd still respond to, "Beg, Lucille, beg."

Who the hell is in charge here? he wondered. How had he acted in such a way and been ignorant of his own motives?

He left his coffee and went running back to the apartment.

Amy was in the shower when he got there, panting from the exertion, and he stood by the bathroom door listening to his breathing, listening also to Amy as she turned off the shower and slid the curtain back. He had intended to tell her he was there so he wouldn't frighten her when she opened the door, but she surprised him.

Her hair was a mass of towel-dried thatches and she wore a blue terry cloth wrap from breast to thigh. On her way out the door, she stopped when she saw him.

"I'm sorry," he said. "You knew what I was doing but I didn't."

She led him to the bedroom and guided him onto the bed, then lay beside him. She pulled his face toward hers and whispered so quietly in his ear that she almost didn't hear herself say, "I love you." She'd never said anything that made her so nervous and didn't know why, other than this: she'd never spoken the words to any person, not even her father. Ever.

He didn't move for such a long time that Amy began to wonder if the surprise of hearing such a sentiment come from her had given him a stroke. But then she saw a tiny tear trickle from the corner of his eye toward his ear.

And since she really did love him, she told him again.

26

Brother Page had celebrated on September 30 because he had gone one entire month free of rumors concerning Michael. It had been years, possibly eighteen of them, since he'd spent such a relaxing month, and he was prepared for many more. He even thought about erecting a sign in the church study as many companies did to encourage safety: "30! days without a rumor. Help eliminate gossip." Before he had the chance, however, October had already been blemished by the story that Michael had been arrested in Stanton for solicitation of a police-woman who had not been posing as a prostitute. And midway through the month Brother Page had heard Michael had mooned his religion teacher.

November was proving disastrous, though. Ima Inez had walked into his study, dropped her suitcaselike purse onto the desk, causing a noise that made Brother Page think she was carrying a carton of soft drink bottles in it. She launched into her usual prescription of remedies for the world's ills, while Brother Page noticed she had added a bumper sticker to the side of her purse that said, "Where the hell is Ashworth, Texas?"

In the middle of her discourse, the phone rang, and the preacher excused himself to answer it, suspecting, and rightly so, that the caller was Lottie Swenson. She and Ima Inez were less-than-friendly rivals, competing to see who could claim first knowledge of any particular rumor. Brother Page made the mistake of saying, "Hello, Mrs. Swenson," a greeting which caused Ima Inez to reveal prematurely, before she was ready, that she already knew Michael was living with Amy. She did, however, want to beat Lottie to the punch.

Lottie, as garrulous as usual, didn't know she'd been beaten and took her time. "Preacher, you know Jolene Destry's girl Linda, don't you? I'm sure you remember that girl because she walks real pigeon-toed and had to get false teeth when she was just sixteen years old. Had to. Her mouth looked like it was full of coal, her teeth was so rotten. Pitiful. Came from eating candy all day long. But Linda lives over there in Stanton and one day she goes into the grocery store—H.E.B., a real nice store, I wish we had one—and she sees your boy buying groceries with that little Hardin girl. Well, Linda don't pay a lot of attention till she hears 'em talking like they was married or something. You know how people do. 'I don't like those Tater Tots as much as you and I want some frozen French fries.' Linda says they look real cute together and wants to know if they're married. And I say, 'No, Linda, I don't believe they are because you'd think if the preacher's boy got married, I'd know it, and I don't know it and I know just about everything else.' So Linda says, 'You know, Lottie, I think I'll do some checking because if that boy's living with the Hardin girl, I know the preacher'd like to know.' So she called the Hardin girl's apartment one morning pretty early and says, 'Can I speak to the man of the house?' And just as nice as you can imagine, the Hardin girl says, 'Just a minute.' And she put your boy on the line. Linda knew it was him 'cause she's real good at voices. Her first husband's been gone going on twelve years—they married right after she got her false teeth—and he don't even know how to disguise his voice so's he can fool Linda. She's that good with voices. But when your boy answered the phone, Linda says, 'I'm sorry, I got the wrong number,' and hangs up so she won't give anything away, see?"

Brother Page, faced with both Ima Inez and Lottie simultaneously, wanted to close his eyes and sleep. For at least the remainder of his life. He knew that Amy Hardin was in Stanton and he suspected there was a strong possibility that Michael had taken up with the girl again, but he couldn't quite believe Michael had *moved in* with her. Surely Michael hadn't sunk that low. It was true that when he or his wife called Michael, he was never in the dorm room, but he'd rarely been at home when he'd lived there. And Brother Page, still standing on the mountaintop of the recent revival, decided the rumors this time were wrong, just as they usually were.

But there was more at stake here than Brother Page's ability to relax. He saw the world as composed of three levels. On top were the godly, the followers of Jesus, the lights of the world. On bottom crawled the devil's own, the porno stars and rock singers and purveyors of sin. In between were all others, the vast majority of the world's population, and that middle level was the battlefield, the place where good fought evil for the control of a person's mind and behavior. And if Michael floundered there, as he could be doing, then Brother Page owed it to God and Michael both to investigate his present circumstances.

Brother Page knocked on the door of the apartment, looking over the battered metallic numerals on the door. Someone with a bad aim had hammered them into position, missing the small nails more often than hitting them. Humming his favorite hymn, "Amazing Grace," he decided to run by Michael's room at the dorm as soon as he verified that Linda Destry was a malicious rumormonger and nothing more.

The door opened and Michael appeared.

The two looked at each other with matching opened mouths.

Michael was dressed in a white T-shirt and Levis, wasn't wearing shoes, but was holding a King Edward Tiparillo. He hadn't experienced the sensation that settled on him in fourteen years, not since he'd been standing just inside the garage of the parsonage with his pants down around his ankles, exposing himself. He was feeling the breeze and sunlight on his tiny erection for the first time when his father had rounded the corner of the parsonage and found him.

He searched his mind for an explanation. He wasn't living with Amy; he'd only stopped by to clean up and it was a very good thing because Amy had left this little cigar burning, and, unaccustomed as he was to handling tobacco products, he had almost thrown it into the trash, which could have set fire to the entire complex, and that thought had made him so hot he'd removed his shirt and shoes. He couldn't think of a coherent explanation.

Brother Page felt the last note of "Amazing Grace" die in his throat, realizing he hadn't expected to see Michael at this apartment. In fact, the sight of his son half-dressed and obviously quite at home caused such a constriction in his throat that he closed his eyes. He gave serious consideration to simply turning, eyes still shut, and wandering off. For the first time in his life, Brother Page hoped Michael lied, hoped he acted as though he were only visiting, because there was nothing the father could do. He had tried. For eighteen years, he had tried. He had attempted to name the boy Samuel, he had punished and admonished and prayed and demanded, and to what avail? Through the cigar smoke wafting out the door, Brother Page could also see a green jug of wine on the kitchen counter and an empty Coors can on the coffee table.

"So what's going on?" Michael asked, flipping the cigar over the railing of the balcony, hoping belatedly no one was standing below.

"Well," Brother Page said, discovering no other words would follow. He didn't know what was expected of him anymore.

240

"How's Mom these days?"

Brother Page nodded an affirmation of her good health, which was due to last until her husband returned from Stanton with the news of her son's living arrangement.

"And I guess the house is okay, and the driveway and all that."

Undoubtedly God knew that the preacher had a streak of pride that would rise in sinful demonstration if he wasn't kept humble. He wanted the strength of Job, who, after all, had lost property and family and friends and health. All Brother Page had lost was his chance to stand before God and hear, "Well done, thou good and faithful servant." He turned to the wrought iron railing and quoted Job: "'Oh, that I knew where I might find him! that I might come even to his seat! I would order my cause before him, fill my mouth with arguments. . . .'"

Michael was unfamiliar with Job's longing, his desire to plead his case directly before God, but he stood listening to his father speak in an eerie tone of voice, swallowing suddenly with fear, fear that his father had been pushed beyond his ability to cope, that he would collapse on the balcony and go comatose.

"'Behold, I go forward, but he is not there; and backward, but I cannot perceive him: On the left hand, where he doth work, but I cannot behold him: he hidest himself on the right hand, that I cannot see him. . . .'"

Whatever had happened to his father, the fault lay with him. How could a son torture his father? He had never been the son the father deserved, yet all the father had wanted was a God-fearing son. Not a nuclear physicist, not a professional football player, not even a good student. Just a simple God-fearing son. It was now Michael's punishment to see the result of his failure—a man so broken that his ministry was probably at an end. What would his father do now? Work in the funeral home or sack groceries or patch roads for the city?

"You want a drink? Of water?" Michael asked.

His father stood, stoop-shouldered and sagging, at the rail, looking over the lawn toward the street, and said nothing.

Michael was assaulted with images—his father holding Michael's head as he vomited his guts up once when he'd had the flu; the father's patience and consistent attempt to comfort him night after night when the son was frightened, convinced that a witch had taken up residence beneath his bed; the father's smiling offer to let him sit in his lap and drive when he was only ten years old. He could still hear his father's comment from their last visit when he said he wanted to be a trial lawyer: "Well, you'll be a good one." They had never been a loving father-son combination, and the fault lay primarily with himself. And now, at this late date, he couldn't figure out why he had never even tried. How low can you go? he wondered.

"You want to go get a cup of coffee or something?" he asked.

Brother Page hadn't moved or spoken, and the longer his father stood in his distressed silence, the more he felt as though he were suffocating. He'd taken in an immense breath and couldn't expel it. Something was required of the son, even though he was too late in acting. But something.

"I'll move back into the dorm," he said. "I'll move back in tonight." He tried to say the words in a manner that promised more than he was giving, hoping his father would hear them as, "I'm starting back to church Sunday, and I'll be surrendering myself to the ministry. I'm a deacon now, and a tither as well, and I pray for the missionaries each and every day."

After a silence that seemed to stretch into another century, Brother Page sighed—it almost leaped into a sob beyond his control—and said, "Well, I guess I'll go on home now. Mama's probably wondering where I am."

"I'm moving back into the dorm tonight."

"Your mother's a fine woman. I don't know what I would have done without her. She's just really a fine, fine woman."

"I know. Maybe you won't have to tell her you found me over here. I mean, I'll be back in the dorm in a little while."

Brother Page looked at the sky and blinked as though the light hurt his eyes, absently reaching for the railing and missing, almost falling. For a moment, in his stumbling attempt to steady himself, Michael thought he looked very old.

"She named you Michael. I was going to call you Samuel. I don't know if you knew that or not, but she wouldn't even talk about Samuel. For eighteen years now I've wondered why she did that, why she didn't want you named Samuel, and I think she knew something I didn't. I don't know how she could have, but I think she did.

"Your mother's a smart woman. She never went to college or studied anything, but she knew what I didn't, and I think she was trying to help both of us. The only bad thing is, it didn't work out. I was eighteen years too late figuring out what she knew all along."

For the first time since Brother Page had turned toward the railing, he faced Michael. "I sure don't understand much of what happens in this world," he said and walked off toward the stairs.

He stood near the open door of the apartment, watching his father walk slowly. Samuel. He'd never heard that story but he had to agree with his father—his mother had known what she was doing when she'd refused to go along. Had the father expected a son who heard the voice of God, who became a prophet . . . well, he was disappointed enough as it was.

On the way from his promise that he'd return to the dorm, to the reality of moving out of Amy's apartment, he located a spot called depression. For three hours he sat on the couch, as still as Amy when she was working on a song, so still he wouldn't upset the equation he was working out. If you took a son who'd been consistently inadequate in that capacity, added to him a desire to improve his ways, then how did you arrive at an answer that was farther than ever from the truth? How could an act of propitiation carry a relationship backward?

He hadn't considered telling his father the truth, hadn't been able to say, "Listen, Pop, here's the deal. I'm sorry but kids grow up and live their own lives. Don't blame me; blame God. He started it." Why hadn't he said that? Because if he'd known his father was standing at the door of the apartment, he would have hidden between the bed and wall and covered his ears so he couldn't have heard Brother Page's knocking. That was the way of fathers and sons. Amen.

When Amy came in from work, she found him still sitting on the couch and knew from his churchlike look that something bad had happened. And Amy, who hated the surprise of bad news, thought of the worst development possible and told herself, "I knew it. He's leaving. I knew from the beginning it'd never work."

Unknowingly he committed a grave error by patting the couch and asking her to sit beside him, a gesture that her father had always used when he'd been forced to divulge the latest report of her mother's departure, and a very old and familiar sensation settled over her, causing her chest to somehow tighten and her neck to ache. Amy said, "Hello," and walked into the short hall, turning into the bathroom. She needed a bath. Right now. She needed to pour two capfuls of oil into the running water so she could sit and rub her legs, down and back, down and back.

"Amy."

"I have rehearsal in thirty minutes, Michael. I've got to hurry."

Why had she said that? She wanted to sit in the tub for hours, maybe indefinitely, because if she didn't she'd start crying. Staring at her face in the mirror on the medicine cabinet, she said

244

to herself, "If you start crying, you're a bow-legged whore. You knew it wouldn't last."

He appeared at the bathroom door and leaned against the jamb, hands stuck in the pockets of his Levis. "I don't know how he found out, but my father came by this afternoon."

Amy moved closer to the mirror; her noses almost touched. She needed to think about her breathing.

"I don't know how to explain what happened. I think he'd heard I'd moved in with you, but he really didn't believe—"

"Excuse me," Amy said, edging past him, her eyes carefully fixed on her feet. She walked back toward the front door, picking up her purse from the kitchen counter as she passed. She was going to get in her car and drive around until time for rehearsal. This weekend the band was playing the nicest club in Waco—Friday, Saturday, and Sunday nights—and she needed to think about that. Her career was moving forward, and she was going to sing this weekend. That was what she wanted to do, sing, not get involved with someone.

"Amy."

She opened the front door. "I have to go, Michael."

"What's wrong with you?"

She'd waited too long because now she was crying. Her eyes were hot and her nose was running already. "I have to go." She turned and walked out the door.

He caught her arm before she got to the kitchen window, pulling her to a stop. She wrenched it free.

"Do whatever you have to do, Michael. Good-bye."

Someday, she thought as she walked toward the stairs, I'm going to find someone who loves me so much he won't leave me. Someday I will. I really will.

He watched her go, just as he had watched his father go, stunned and puzzled by Amy's reaction. She hadn't even allowed an explanation. But maybe her peculiar behavior was for the best; she was making it easy for him to leave.

The day had been the most stupefying of his life. In the morning, he'd left the bed of the only girl who had ever completely captured his imagination, had drunk orange juice and coffee with her while they were half-naked, had kissed her good-bye and known when she walked off that she took part of him with her. He couldn't have felt better, nor could he have possibly predicted the turn of events. Consider the dogs of the street, he thought. They neither smile nor weep. They have very even lives.

27

The thought of sitting around the dorm, comparing his present situation with that of a few hours' past, was more than he could tolerate. So he invited Ron to go get drunk.

"I don't drink to excess, Page, but I'll keep you company."

They walked to Candy's Bar and Grilled Cheese, a nearby dive that provided temporary lodging for the homeless and lonely. It gave them a place to shoot pool and watch TV and pass part of their long nights. It was small and filled with smoke that undoubtedly had been hanging in the air since Candy lit her first cigarette thirty years ago. The TV contributed to the feeling of inebriation because the vertical hold rarely held and the sound was partly obscured by a buzz. It was a no-frills bar decorated with neon beer signs. Ron drank beer and ate a microwaved pizza on a paper plate while Michael kept the waitress busy transporting Seven and waters. He was serious about getting drunk.

He hadn't told Ron why he had moved back into the dorm, so Ron speculated between bites of pizza.

"Your mother's sick. Your father's giving up religion. No, I know. Amy fell in love with a female country singer with a blonde beehive hairdo and they've run off to audition for 'Hee Haw.' Come on, Page, tell me what's wrong."

"I'm just depressed."

"Well, listen to this and you'll feel better. I got an F on my psychology report. 'The Manipulative Effect of a Minister. Or, How I Almost Became a Jimmy.' I got an F. Can you believe it? The teacher wrote, 'Blasphemous!' across the top. And I thought this was a real school, Page, I really did. He marked out, *marked out*, my conclusion. 'A wholly distorted response to cosmic loneliness.' Can you believe a teacher who edits a student's thoughts? What kind of a place is this, Page? And you think you have trouble."

Michael finished one drink and started another. "That's not depressing at all. You could've made an A if you'd wanted to, if you'd written, 'How I Came To a Saving Knowledge of Jesus.' I, on the other hand, didn't choose the girl I love or the father I have. Besides, I don't have anyone to talk to."

Ron emitted a loud burp and waved his empty mug at the waitress. "What do you mean, you don't have anyone to talk to? Who am I?"

"You're an analyst, Ron. I don't want to talk to an analyst."

He didn't want to talk at all. His eyes were closing and he was having trouble maintaining thoughts. The waitress, a huge woman wearing a full skirt, delivered Ron's beer and walked off. He watched her tremendous hips working like pistons, shaking her skirt, and his eyes, which had adjusted to the rolling picture on the TV, closed.

They were joined by Rob, their next-door neighbor in the dorm, except tonight he was Robert. Sometimes he was a preppie, wearing his sweater over his shoulders, arms tied around the neck, but tonight he was wearing his Robert T-shirt, the one he had specially made that said in crimson letters across the front, "Stanton Sucks." He sat and joined the conversation.

"You guys don't know what depressed is," Rob said. "Depressed is wanting to major in premed and flunking chemistry. Then realizing you're going to end up selling life insurance. Then realizing you can't even do that because you can't get a date. I just called a girl to ask her out, and you know what she said? She said, 'I can't talk right now. I'm waiting on a call.' The best I can even hope for is door-to-door. I'm talking encyclopedias and vacuum cleaners. Somebody'll ask me, 'Hey, Rob, you making big bucks?' and I'll have to say, 'No, I'm selling big books.'

"And if that's not bad enough, I have a toothache." He pushed with one finger on his cheek.

Ron shook his head. "That's nothing. I'm out of pizza."

Michael raised his hand. "I'm unclop—unclop—uncloplomising sad. I have been dummed by everbody I know. I am also shit-faced."

With that admission, he fell into a deep hole and let Rob and Ron continue the competition for saddest story. He may have slept for a while, he wasn't sure, but when he next opened his eyes, the waitress was delivering Ron another pepperoni pizza, the crust of which was something of a burnt golden color, just like Donna's hair. And on the spot, he had a revelation: God spoke through pizza.

God couldn't go around using a voice because he'd scare the crap out of twentieth-century man. He spoke through the insignificant and less-than-obvious. He probably had said a million things to him from street curbs and shoe soles. And Michael would bet any amount of money that on the bottom of a plate somewhere in Amy's apartment was the message, "Go thou and takest Donna as thy wife." He just hadn't seen it.

He pulled himself up into a standing position and pointed

at the crust of the pizza, waiting to speak until he had the attention of both boys at the table.

Michael pointed at the pizza and said, "You see that?"

"Is it a roach?" Ron asked, looking. "I told them not to bring me any more microwaved roaches."

"No, it's a message. It says, 'Marry Donna.'"

Ron spun the paper plate around so he could see the spot that Michael had pointed out. "Let me see that. I bet it's ants. Probably lined up like a band at half-time."

"I am going to that phone over there and call my beloved," Michael said, "so I can—" He started to add "propose" but instead passed out, falling across the table and smothering the pizza with his chest.

"I'll lift him up and you get the pizza," Ron said.

Rob nodded. "Right."

He spent the next day hung over and grateful he hadn't called Donna to propose. He'd never been a predictable drunk, not like those who grew invariably mean or teary or happy. Once he'd grown immeasurably sad, gone home, and thrown his arms around his father's neck. "You're a good old father, you know that?" Out of deep gratitude over this expression of affection, Brother Page had grounded him for a month. Another time he had called a cousin serving time in a federal detention center and told her that if she could just hold on, he would get her out upon his graduation from law school. At the time, he was fifteen and the girl was serving a one-year sentence.

He did feel the need to talk to Donna, however. They had seen each other a number of times since the passionate Sunday afternoon at her house, and at the core of every conversation was the unanswered question—why had Michael grown distant since that Sunday? To explain, he asked her out for a Coke after history the next day.

The weather was cool, and Donna wore a green suit, beneath which was a green crepe blouse with a big bow at the neck. He took her hand as they walked, not because he wanted to initiate anything but because she was such a pleasant person.

"You remember that old girlfriend I mentioned?" he asked.

"She's back?"

He nodded and a strange thing happened. Donna thought he was going to tell her he couldn't see her anymore, and a look of relief passed over her face.

"Whew," she said. "I've been in a fix. You know Danny Meaders, don't you?"

He knew Danny, a Huckleberry Finn type, freckle-faced with sandy-colored hair and a great big country grin. If Danny had ever taken offense with anyone or anything, he would have been surprised. Like Donna, Danny flowed unbothered, a slow river with smooth banks.

"We've had a few dates," Donna said. "And I wouldn't tell you this because it's personal, for Danny anyway, but he's afraid to kiss me. And I couldn't figure out how to handle the both of you. It just didn't seem—I don't know—right or something. Does that make sense?"

He laughed, feeling less amusement than he exhibited. He understood Donna's problem, her difficulty in dealing with two extremes in her love life, and he also understood the kiss-off when he got it. Michael Page was on his way to becoming a celibate again. He looked at the sky, made pure blue by the filter of winter air, and thought, winter, spring, summer, fall. Everything worked on a cycle, and he did too. Welcome back to Step One.

"Well," he said. "The next time Danny walks you to your door, kiss him."

"Maybe I will. I'll probably give him a few more dates to work up his nerve though." Donna stopped and smiled, squeezing his hand and then letting it go. "I hope everything works out with your old girlfriend. I bet she's a lot like you."

He nodded, unsure of Donna's exact meaning but thinking, yeah, she's a lot like me—frustrated and confused.

Brother Page showed up in the afternoon at the dorm room, bearing a gift. He said he was visiting the local hospital and since he was coming, Mrs. Page had sent a cake tin filled with chocolate chip cookies. Michael looked the gift-horse in the mouth and saw inside the face of a detective attempting to verify that his son had returned to the dorm as promised.

The three of them—Ron appeared when the scent of cookies wafted through the air, and he commandeered the tin, placing it in his lap—sat in the room and talked about football. Brother Page was probably sorry he had introduced the subject because Ron had a theory that encompassed everything from primitive urges and modern martial attitudes to social group identification. Brother Page, attempting to steer the conversation away from the theoretical, said he wished the Dallas Cowboys didn't play on Sunday so he could go see a game. He thought Tom Landry was a great coach and fine Christian man.

Michael tried to be pleased with the visit but couldn't muster any emotion other than suspicion. Now that the old man had verified his son's presence, obviously he planned another go at converting Ron to Southern Baptist Christianity, and he was leading into it naturally by narrowing the conversation to acceptable Christians, specifically Tom Landry. His father was as predictable as a life insurance salesman.

But before beginning a sermon, Brother Page stood and said he had to be moving on. "Can we have a word of prayer before I go?"

Here it comes, he thought. One of those vicious but godly prayers that Ron's life be made miserable until he saw the light.

Ron hadn't heard the mention of prayer; he was sitting on his bed examing the cookies as a jeweler would fine diamonds. Brother Page walked over and patted Ron on the shoulder, bringing him out of his Tollhouse trance.

"Oh, yeah," Ron said. "Good to see you again. And thanks for the cookies."

Without making a second request for permission, Brother Page bowed his head and prayed, and he surprised his son by skipping right over the matter of Ron's unsaved soul. His father's prayers were, as often as not, mini-sermons, and his prayer today was a short exposition on love. If they looked to Jesus as teacher, they had to see the vastness of God's grace and his unconditional love. And as Christians, they weren't to restrict their love any more than God did.

On his way from the room, Brother Page kissed him on the forehead.

His mouth fell open. The gesture both touched and disturbed him. He was certain that his father had kissed him during his childhood, but he couldn't remember a kiss in the last ten years. His forehead felt branded. He was afraid to place his fingers on the spot for fear he'd find a damp residue.

"You said your father's not affectionate," Ron said.

"He's not," he said, shaking his head. "I don't know what's going on."

He left the room to go wander the campus, knowing his confusion was out of proportion to his father's very simple act. But he passed students knowing they were staring at the hot spot on his forehead. "Look at that. Somebody kissed that guy right over his left eye."

The only way out of the labyrinthine mysteries of ministerial behavior was through his mother, so he called her.

She didn't look sympathetically upon Michael's suspicion.

"You're right," she said. "His *real* purpose in coming over wasn't to see anybody in the hospital; he came to see you. And you're *wrong* about the reason. You're wrong because you think you're smarter than you are. Every night for the past week, I've listened to him talk about love and how he's failed you as a father. He's doing what you've always wanted him to do—treat you like a son rather than a church member—and I don't think you can handle it. I don't think you can even give him credit for trying."

Unbelievable, he thought, remembering his father's prayer. Unconditional love. A concept almost too profound to fathom. The man had driven to Stanton to tell his son that God loved him without reservation and so did his father.

Now there was only one thing he couldn't figure out—life.

28

He had been contemplating a good drunk when Ron saved him from the subsequent hangover by announcing that he'd got twenty bucks from home and they ought to go eat a steak. He agreed immediately and they ended up at an inexpensive steakhouse sitting next to a family with a little blonde girl, who was about four and wore lace stockings and a frilly pink dress. While the rest of the family ate meat and potatoes, Blondie frittered away with a piece of cherry pie. After every infrequent bite, she left the spoon clamped in her mouth and turned to mug at him.

Then she offered him a spoonful of cherry goo laced with mashed-up crust. "Wanna bite?" she asked, making the question one word.

"No, thanks."

"It's good," she assured him. "It tastes like . . . do do." She said "do do" very sweetly, her lips pursed, and wiggled her entire body.

Concerned with his refusal to share her pie, she tried to think of another way to entertain him. Slyly, she reached over to her father's salad bowl, removed a crouton soaked with French dressing, and placed it in her spoon. Then, holding the spoon handle in her fist, she placed the index finger of her other hand farther up the handle, and flipped the crouton into the air, following its arc with her eyes until it disappeared on the other side of the restaurant.

"Bombs away," she said gaily.

Her father, alerted by her declaration, prevented any further acts of war by confiscating her spoon.

He watched her, reminded of Amy's childhood pictures. Somewhere in the world was a little boy getting ready for bed, putting on his Doctor Dentons and promising he'd be good if only he could watch one more program on TV. And one of these days he'd spot Blondie and get a dart of feeling so deep in his chest, he'd never get it out. And for the first time, the world would make good and perfect sense. And that same world would do its damnedest to destroy their relationship. And if the world didn't succeed, the boy and girl would finish it off in their own ignorant ways.

Good luck to both of them, he thought. They'd certainly need it.

The little girl pushed her plate of half-eaten pie away from her and said, "I'm through."

"You didn't eat two bites," her father said.

"It tastes like do do," she said, giving Michael a conspiratorial smile.

The smile gave him such a surge of good will, a feeling of absolute brotherhood, that he decided to call Amy. For the first time since they'd started dating, he was going to deliver a mes-

254

sage of good will to her, untainted by any attempt to persuade or manipulate her. He wanted her to know that he'd always consider her one of a kind, a unique person and a wonderful singer.

Just as the waitress set before him a juicy T-bone with a baked potato, on top of which sat a scoop of butter, he excused himself.

"Where're you going? Your steak's here."

"Be right back."

At the cashier's he got change, deciding then that he wasn't fit to be Amy's friend. Quarter in hand, he walked across the foyer to a wall phone and dialed her number.

Amy was sitting in her apartment in a euphoric mood. Allan had just left after delivering two items of wonderful news and a bottle of celebratory wine. The retired record producer had heard the band play the previous Saturday night and had set a definite day to start working on a demo tape. And through the same producer, Allan had lined up a gig in Austin.

Amy Hardin in Austin. At one time or another, everyone famous had played Austin. Everyone she could think of. And now it was her turn.

She answered the phone and heard Michael say, "Amy, I just wanted to call and tell you I admire you and think you're the finest person I've ever known. You're one of a kind, just like one of the old explorers, setting off on an uncharted course, and I want you to know, I hope you make it. I truly hope you make it."

Amy's response was much different from what she thought would be appropriate. Michael sounded as though he were calling his boss on Christmas Eve to wish him season's greetings; he sounded as though he hadn't been suffering a bit since he'd walked out on her. It was overall the most irritating call she'd ever received.

"Still there?" he asked.

"Michael, why are you calling me?"

He sighed loudly. "What is it this time, Amy? The drummer went to Mexico? The guitar player was a minute and a half late? What is it?"

"It's not any of those things, smart guy. It's a demo tape and a gig in Austin."

He stood looking at the chrome coatrack next to him, wishing he'd been given a guidebook on human relations. Amy had good news so she was mad at him? "You're making a demo tape? When?"

"On December third, the same day we play down there. *I'm singing in Austin, Texas.*"

"When did all this happen?"

Amy recapped her conversation with Allan, walking around the kitchen as far as the cord on the telephone would allow her to go, sipping wine and feeling just as she had always wanted to. Exactly as she had always wanted to. Even if the world ended tomorrow, tonight was a dream fulfilled.

He listened to her news, still confused. "Then why're you being mean to me?"

"Because, Michael. You sounded like some goofy guy on a talk show who just wrote a book called *Feeling Good*. You didn't sound like someone who missed me. You didn't sound like someone who . . . used to pull up my dress to *Hot August Night*."

He switched the phone to his other ear and leaned against the wall, wishing he had a booth. "Keep going."

"You didn't sound like the guy who made beautiful speeches about love . . . or the one who told me if the lemon industry would use me as a model in my yellow nightie, they'd have to rewrite all the cliches about apples. You didn't sound like the reason I've been crying for five days."

"Will you come get me? Please?"

"Where are you?"

He gave her the name of the restaurant, and Amy said she'd pick him up. He returned to the table and explained to Ron his reason for leaving. Ron seemed hardly concerned once he had pushed his plate across the table and suggested Ron eat his steak.

"I wish you'd ordered it rare," Ron said.

Outside in the night, he waited. The parking lot was full of cars glinting beneath streetlights, and the sky was clear. The still air seemed to confirm the prediction of subfreezing temperatures overnight. In the morning he would wake up to see frost on the cars and rooftops and grass, and the sun would seem ineffective as it rose, unable to adequately warm the earth. He loved those mornings and always tried to get out early before the world woke up and the frost melted.

By the time he opened the door of Amy's black Firebird, he was nervous. He kept losing her and didn't know how to prevent it. He didn't want to lose her again, and the only hope he found was in the fact that they kept getting back together.

In the car, he left the door open for a minute so he could look at her in the illumination of the dome light. She wore a pale blue warm-up suit, which provided a rather mundane counterpoint to her wild and wicked hair. She looked like the essence drawn from his dreams, the essence of mystery and delight that was as pure and ephemeral as one snowflake.

He closed his door and held her hand as she maneuvered across the console and into his lap. A hundred pounds covered with the thick cotton of her warm-up, a hundred pounds of assurance that she was real.

"I want to tell you something," she said. "I've only been fishing once in my life, and my father caught this little fish with spiny fins and streaks of yellow and green in his scales. He'd swallowed the hook. And my father solved that problem by grabbing the fish in one hand and wrapping the line around his other hand, and jerking. He jerked the fish's guts right out of the fish."

She paused for a moment as if trying to decide whether she wanted to complete the story, giving him the opportunity to smell her without having to concentrate on her words. She smelled of flowers and wine and love.

"Well, the day you left, I felt like that fish. I swallowed you, Michael. I absorbed you way down here. And when you left, I felt like my guts had been ripped out." She stopped and sucked on her lips, protection against crying. "Can we please decide right now if we're . . . permanent? I don't mean where you live. I mean—" She shrugged, knowing if she said anything else she'd cry.

He didn't speak for a moment. The knowledge that she needed him wasn't nearly as impressive as the fact that she had openly stated it. Such a revelation came easy for some people, but not for Amy. And he was struck with this amazing act of humility and trust.

"When I see you," he said, "I wonder why I ever bothered getting up in the morning before you came along. What a boring life I had." He pulled her against him; she placed her head on his shoulder. "Amy, I wanted this permanent all along. That's all I ever wanted."

"Then that's what you've got."

"Then why don't we go celebrate this state of permanency?"

Amy slid across the console back into the driver's seat, asking as she went, "Are you thinking of the same kind of celebration I'm thinking about?"

"I'm thinking about the one where you join together and kiss and lick and say I love you."

"Yeah. Me, too."

29

Michael didn't move back into Amy's apartment, not because he didn't want to but because the field of vision of certain eyes in Ashworth was exceptionally wide. He didn't know the local spy's identity, and although he disliked building his life around unknown observers, he was feeling pangs of sympathy for his father for the first time in his life. His father shouldn't have to listen to people like Lottie Swenson and Ima Inez Randolph.

Still, he seemed to be spending almost as much time with Amy as he had while residing in her apartment. She picked him up at the dorm on her way home from work almost every day, and they ate and talked or played until Amy returned him to the dorm as she went to rehearsal. Sometimes, however, before they left the apartment, Amy asked, "Michael, will you use your side of the bed tonight?" She sometimes explained the reason for her request—nightmares—and other times didn't. His sense of obligation required him to stay the night regardless of the reason.

He called home to tell his mother that he'd found a job at a grocery store for the semester break and wouldn't be coming home, but he never got the chance. His father got on the line.

"Oh, Michael," he said in a manner that indicated he was about to impart impressive knowledge, "I wish I'd been a better father and example for you. Here I am forty-four years old and I don't seem to know any more than I did the day I was saved. I'm only now figuring out what 'Christlike' means. I'm going to start a series of sermons on this I wish you could hear.

If you're coming home between semesters, then I'll wait to start until you get here. I want us to learn together."

He listened, shaking his head, but he never told his father he wouldn't be home. And he shook his head for more than one reason—they were getting farther and farther apart, but he was the only one aware of the distance. He could either continue a charade or he could tell his father the truth, and both options seemed so reprehensible that he thought surely there existed some third or fourth or fifth option. He tried locating one or two and found only irony. His father was the man responsible for his belief in honesty and dislike of pretense, conditions which seemed to require that he tell his father the truth for the first time ever, but the more he thought about the generally despicable manner in which he had treated his father, the more reluctant he was to tell the old man anything approaching the truth.

What finally made him select a course of action was this—he couldn't mesh fantasy and reality, couldn't live with a fundamentalist's view of life. His concept of God as vengeful and occasionally apathetic, infrequently merciful and concerned —something like a dimwitted, sociopathic Santa Claus—wasn't one he could tolerate. And although he wasn't certain how he had arrived at that concept, and didn't particularly blame his father, he knew that as long as he remained within the Southern Baptist church, he'd retain that destructive image.

And so he had to go home, but only to tell his father the truth. It might kill them both, but he didn't see any alternative.

Brother Page had always doubted his intelligence (unless some fool was questioning it, which gave him total confidence) and he began to doubt it severely one morning when Missy arrived at his office, already crying. Ten minutes ago, her husband had walked out the front door on his way to work, and Missy had attempted to deliver her usual good-bye—have-a-nice-day kiss. Her husband had shielded himself with his forearms as though Missy were assaulting him and said, "My God, woman, you're like a blanket. Why're you always all over me?" Missy had been in such devout and extensive need that Brother Page had recited the first thirteen chapters of John while listening to her and patting her shoulder. Then two items demanded his attenttion: one was that Missy was kissing his neck and murmuring, "Oh, love me, please love me," and the second was that the preacher had never seriously thought about the thirteenth chapter of John.

He sent Missy on her way, thinking that a hug lasting through thirteen chapters of the Bible was surely sufficient, and sat to contemplate Jesus' humility, especially as shown in John chapter thirteen, in which he was described as washing his disciples' feet. For years Brother Page had been holding forth Jesus as the example for all Christians, but he had actually considered the composite figure of Jesus so briefly, he was ashamed. The preacher had always been theoretically humble, but only theoretically. In fact, he'd always deeply desired to be widely recognized as a father in total control of his son, a father whose son *always* had one ear attuned for the sound of his father's fingers snapping, ready to pop to attention. Brother Page wanted to hear, "That preacher has got the best-behaved boy I've ever seen in my whole life." He hadn't wanted to hear, "God gave that preacher a kid to keep him humble." But Michael had taught the father a lesson he should have learned long ago on his own.

And he found that his response to the next call from Lottie was different. She said, "Preacher, you might be real interested to know, that boy of yours done flew the coop again. He's gone back to his little chickie, probably a-cluck-cluck-clucking all the way. See, Linda Destry has to walk ever day 'cause her doctor told her to, but her neighborhood's not pretty at all and there's this one white gal living with a nigger man, and they cuss right loud if you poke into their business. So Linda drives over to where that Hardin girl lives to walk. . . ."

Brother Page started to hang up without ceremony but recognized his past encouragement of Lottie and her sisters throughout town. He had after all used them to keep up with Michael and now had no grounds to complain when they wanted to continue their services.

"And she seen your boy over at that Hardin girl's apartment and she said they reminded her of a couple of kittens. You know how kittens are; they kinda climb all over each other—"

"Mrs. Swenson, if you don't mind, will you please do me a favor. Ask Linda Destry to stop by the Hardin girl's apartment the next time she's walking in that neighborhood and see if Michael has my blue tie. He borrowed it and I don't think I ever got it back."

"Your what?"

"My blue tie. And, Mrs. Swenson, I hope to see you in church this Sunday."

Once home, Michael began to doubt not only the wisdom of his decision but his ability to execute it. In that house, he simply couldn't visualize himself as anything but a preacher's kid, rebellious and irreligious, confused and confusing, a person incapable of conducting any reasonable conversation. So he decided to walk off a little at a time; he'd start by telling his mother that his job was going to prevent him from remaining home during the semester break, and his work schedule would preclude any Sunday visits. He timed the conversation for Saturday afternoon when his father always spent time at church in preparation for Sunday services.

Mrs. Page sat in the living room, her legs covered by an orange afghan, and he stood at the picture window looking at a cold drizzle falling as he began to squeeze out his news in bits. He had a job. In a grocery store. He started Monday. He'd be required to work Sundays. Here he paused, expecting some Baptist antipathy toward toiling on Sunday, something that was acceptable only for restaurant workers where Baptists ate after church, but Mrs. Page sat without speaking, weaving her finger in and out of the afghan.

He finished this recent update on his life and asked, "So why don't you tell Dad because I've got to go back to Stanton now."

"Michael."

"Please?"

She shook her head in a long arc, more definitely than she normally did. He fell into a chair and closed his eyes, thinking he needed a nap.

"A time comes when fathers and sons have to talk," she said.

"Anything worth doing is worth putting off," he said in a tone more lighthearted than he felt. He wanted help. He wanted more than help. He wanted to be relieved of his sonship in the Page family. He'd become a transient with a small amount of luggage who had happened by, boarded a bit, and was now moving on. And while he was waiting to be magically transported out of his legal relationship, his father walked in the front door.

"Wooo," he said. "It's getting cold out there." He removed his overcoat and hung it on a brass coatrack by the door, then looked at Michael, who had stood. "You're not leaving already, are you?"

Michael, simultaneously squeezing and stroking his chin, said, "I was just telling Mom—" He looked at her to plead for assistance but she had picked up a tablet of paper and a pen and was writing. "I was just telling *Mom. . . .*" Still no response. "I've got a job at a grocery store in Stanton and I won't be here between semesters." He watched his father's eye sockets shrink with disappointment and he added, "I need the extra money."

Brother Page moved toward a chair in the far corner of the room. "You can't make extra money if you're having to pay room and board somewhere. Why don't you talk to the store here? If they could put you on, you could stay here. We don't charge much." He smiled. The small joke was an indication of how much he wanted him to stay.

"I've already told the guy I'd start Monday."

Brother Page looked at the floor, then back at him. "That really sets me back, Michael. I was really hoping you'd be here. I know it's important to follow through on your commitments, but. . . ." He frowned and shook his head over the gravity of his thoughts.

"Michael, I don't think we've ever done anything at church that'd give you a greater blessing."

He stood and looked out the picture window, wanting to tell his father, fine, yes, he'd be there. He knew how much this meant to his father, so he would sit on the front row and ask questions. He'd become a faithful child of God because he knew how much his father wanted him to become one. He talked because he didn't know what else to do. "I don't know. I really feel obligated about this job. The guy who hired me made a point of telling me he'd hired students before and they'd always been unreliable. He was willing to take one more chance. Now if I don't show up, he won't ever hire another student again." He was making it up as he went. He didn't start Monday, and the old man who had interviewed him had been looking for an employee who would sit and drink a beer with him after work. "I'd sure hate to be one who eliminated employment opportunities for students in Stanton. Not many people are on scholarships like I am."

His father sat silently, giving him the stare that he'd seen a million times, the stare that guided you in the right direction. He looked back out the window at a bleak winter afternoon. The yellow grass, as brittle as straw, was wet from the light rain. His father was forcing him into doing what he had always studiously avoided—coming clean. The father was going to make the son deny him. He thought about an alternative —coming home on weekends and sitting through, but not listening to, the new sermons. But he wasn't going to do that.

He turned and said, "Listen, I know I haven't been a good son. We both know it and we're both sorry about it for different reasons. I wish you had a son who was everything you wanted him to be. I wish you had a son who wanted to preach and who'd take notes on every sermon you preached so he could preach them again someday. I really do wish that. But what you've got is a son who—who—what you've got is a son who isn't anything like that. Not a thing. I don't know how it happened and I wish it hadn't happened, but that's the truth."

If Brother Page was truly humble, he wouldn't have felt as though he were the only person on earth who knew what Michael needed to know. Humility didn't come easily. If only John thirteen had mentioned the difficulty with which Jesus had knelt to wash his followers' feet, Brother Page would have felt better. "Michael, if you'll come hear these sermons, if you'll come so we can learn together . . . I don't want you to take twenty-five years to learn something so basic. I want you to be smarter than I am."

Michael stood at the window rubbing his forehead, and the father watched, fighting down the urge to guide his son, forcibly if necessary, to the correct decision. He mentally eliminated the unimportant and extraneous. What the open eyes of the town saw or thought wasn't important, nor was the father's image as an effective preacher or father. But his son was important, and his son's eternal home was of paramount importance.

"Michael, I'm afraid for you."

Michael turned from the window and flopped into the chair in exasperation. "I don't know how to tell you, but I just don't believe like you do. I can't tolerate the Baptist line. I can't live with it. It's driven me crazy for years because what I see out there doesn't match what I read in the Bible. I can't take the Bible as my guide to what's real and what isn't."

"What *do* you believe, Michael?"

Michael was getting a preview of the Last Judgment. God was asking him that question, and he was about to feel the divine foot unceremoniously boot him into the lake of fire, where lost sinners of all time were burning and screaming forever. He tried to swallow but may as well have been trying to swallow a baseball. He told himself he no longer believed in that vision, but he wasn't so sure. Still, there was a point beyond which he wasn't going to pass because he and his father could and would argue different points of view for the next forty years without settling any differences.

"I don't know what I believe when I'm around you. I believe what you want me to believe."

Brother Page shook his head. "Michael, your entire life is a miracle. A miracle. You wouldn't even be here except for the grace of God and the faith of your mother. If you don't believe that, ask her. She's sitting right there."

He was so afraid his mother was going to look up from her tablet and speak, afraid that if she did he'd fall immediately to his knees and remain there, a permanent Baptist, that he said, "I don't care if my life is a miracle. I don't care. I didn't ask and I just don't care. It isn't a miracle when I look at the paper in the morning and see that some woman's boyfriend has killed her baby by dunking it in boiling water. Or a seventy-year-old woman was stabbed by a guy who broke into her house. I always wonder if she prayed when she saw the knife raised, if she cried out for God to save her when she saw it fall. I wonder what God thinks about that, about people who think he'll help. I wonder what he thinks about doing a real rush job on creating this place. It took him six days and if he'd spent a little more time, maybe there wouldn't be so much suffering. I think he botched the job. I think the only miracle is that we've managed to overcome all the obstacles he gave us."

Brother Page listened to this emotional response, amazed not only because he was, and had been, personally ignorant of his own son's pain, but because he suddenly wondered if Michael, whose misbehavior had always seemed random and undirected, may have had a much larger problem than simple rebellion. Whatever the son's problem, the father hadn't cured it in eighteen years and he wouldn't in one conversation or eight sermons. The only comfort Brother Page could find was in Jesus— of his twelve disciples, one had betrayed him and another had denied him. And Brother Page didn't have the ability to perform miracles, the authority of the Son of God, or the charisma to influence his followers, all of which Jesus had possessed and which had still failed to impress two disciples.

He stood and walked across the room, stopping in front of Michael, and pulling him from the chair. Once the son was standing, Brother Page hugged him. Always, during those few times the son had been in his embrace, he thought about how big the kid had gotten, how tiny he had been for so many years. And then he was taller and broader than the father. Oh, for the ability to return to the days of a small son and start over. How many opportunities had the father missed to assure the son of his love? Far, far too many. There wasn't much that could be undone, but there was much to make up for.

"Michael," he said. "I always thought I was too busy to stop and say, 'I love you.' I wish I could have back every night you'd gone to bed in this house. When you were little, I used to come sit on your bed and you'd tell me knock-knock jokes before you went to sleep. The last one was always, 'Thistle. Thistle be the end of the knock-knock jokes.' And then I got so caught up with everything else that I stopped sitting on your bed at night, and I wish I could have every one of those nights back." He started crying and stopped talking, and somehow things had changed slightly. The father wasn't hugging the son; the son was hugging the father.

"I love you, Pop," Michael said, the words coming out with a poor audio quality because they were mixed with a groan.

Outside the rain continued to fall and a car passed before the house, emitting vapor into the cold air. But inside it was warm, and Michael, smelling the familiar and old comforting smells of his father's hair and suit coat, thought about Christmas, about the tree that would stand in the corner with its multicolored lights and thin coat of icicles. He'd almost decided to stay in Stanton Christmas but now changed his mind. He didn't want Christmas to become another missed opportunity, like the knock-knock jokes of the past. He'd already missed too many opportunities.

Epilogue

Michael Page stands at the window of the parsonage, watching his father. Dressed in a dark blue suit, the father is looking for beans in a garden that occupies what was once the backyard. It's quite a garden—okra plants as big as trees, several rows of corn that run the length of the yard, peas, squash, tomatoes, peppers, and plants that his son cannot identify. The father has given up every kind of food bought in a store and now eats only what God allows him to grow. This is a demonstration of faith. The father hasn't revealed this to the son; the mother has. All the father says about his garden is, "It's coming along pretty well." And it is.

He walks out the back door, remembering a question he wants to ask his father, and walks between two rows of pepper plants in the freshly tilled black earth.

"Did I borrow a blue tie of yours one time?" he asks.

Brother Page, stooped over, snaps off a bean and then stands up, a slight smile on his face. "No."

He nods, puzzled by the fact that Amy believes he did.

"Regardless," Brother Page says, spying another bean ready to be plucked. "Don't worry about it. I've got plenty of them."

Michael wanders the garden, looking at tomatoes turning various shades of pink from green, and okra pods sprouting hundreds of tiny hairs. He stops at a yellow squash that is beautiful enough to be artificial.

He thinks, my father's faith will keep him healthy.

Michael Page will return to the Bible, but not for several years. He'll find himself drawn back by the insight he sees displayed in those old pages, especially in the story of the creation and the fall of man. Thousands of years ago some unknown men understood that life's greatest problem came when man acquired the ability to distinguish right from wrong. By knowing evil, man would acquire a capacity for regularly practicing it, and it would naturally emerge in his dreams and imagination. It would emerge in insidious ways in his dealings with those he loves.

And although he will never tell his father, he'll return to Jesus for salvation, salvation from the creation of hell on earth. He won't come as his father would want him to, walking the aisle to profess a belief, but slowly, recognizing that those who love their neighbors as themselves are already creating heaven.

But his favorite answer will come from the most famous of

all father-son stories, that of Abraham and Isaac. The answer won't be the faith of Abraham or the voice of God or the miraculous nature of Isaac's birth. It will be something entirely different, something human and natural, and it came from Sarah, the mother of Isaac.

Laughter. That's what Isaac's name meant.